WHITE FLAG OF THE DEAD BOOK III

AMERICA THE DEAD

JOSEPH TALLUTO

1

I used to enjoy spring. The warm days, the cool nights; it was a great time to think about all the things you wanted to do outside, and all the things you should have gotten done over the winter but didn't want to because it was too cold.

That was the spring of the past. Spring these days meant the dead were shaking off the rigidity of the cold weather and headed out hungrier than ever. Being dead, they were not bound by the same rules regarding the human body. They never tired, didn't feel pain, and existed to feed and spread the infection that caused them to exist in the first place.

Such was my world, two years after the Upheaval, the name we called the end of our world when the dead rose and devoured the living. Some of us managed to survive the overturning of society and in the following years established places of relative safety—places where we could live, places where we could strike back at the undead hordes that still roamed the land. By my estimation, there were probably one or two hundred million zombies out there in our country alone. We couldn't kill them all, but we sure could try to outlive them and take the ones who threatened our new way of life.

We had managed to save a number of communities and we had set up trade routes and lines of communication among the communities. Each community was responsible for itself in terms of basic needs, but we all relied on each other when the zombies came calling. I had just returned from a brief jaunt to

Morris where a large crowd of roving zombies had attacked the town's defenses.

I stood at the stone wall that surrounded my patio, overlooking the river and forest I now called my home. When I had come to this place originally, I was looking for my brother. But I came back, realizing it was the best place for me. I had been part of a community, but the isolation of this resort appealed to me on a deeper sense than I had thought and I found myself back here, claiming it as my own. To me, it was perfect. We had water, we had a forest for game, we had isolated land for livestock and crops, and we had peace of mind. I had no fear when I was here and I allowed myself to live, not just be alive.

A touch on my leg caused me to break out of my reverie and smile down at my son Jake. He had managed to sneak up on me and was now asking to be picked up in the timeless "hands up" fashion of three-year olds.

"Hey, Buddy," I said as I swung him up to my left hip. My right side still carried my battle-proven SIG P226 in its scratched and dinged holster. I put that gun on before I headed to the bathroom in the morning and took it off at night only just before I hit the sheets.

"Hey da," Jake said in his limited vocabulary. Jake turned his head and looked out over the forest we called home. In another world it was a state park, covering two thousand, six hundred acres. We had eighteen waterfalls and canyons, giving us water and shelter if need be.

Jake pointed to the north. "Pretty reevah."

"River," I corrected automatically. I looked out at the Illinois River which formed our northern border and once again was amazed at how we managed to get to this place.

"Kitty," Jake said and this time I looked hard. Sure enough, a large tawny paw was hanging down from a branch near the Visitor Center. Looking closely, I could see a large tail twitching slightly as flies irritated its owner.

Welcome back, old son, I thought as I watched the cougar who shared our forest lounge in the morning breeze. We discovered the cougar on our first trip out here and the best I could figure was it had escaped from a zoo or private pen. Either way, it had killed several zombies in the area and as long as it left me and mine alone, I was okay with it.

As Jake looked out over the land, I studied him. He was getting to be such a big boy, but he still retained those adorable big cheeks and little pug nose. His eyes were what got me, they were big liquid pools of chocolate that were used to good effect in getting what he wanted. I didn't know how I managed to be so lucky and get us both to survive the Upheaval, but I promised to keep doing whatever it was I was doing. Jake was my world and without him I wouldn't have much left to go on living for.

He grinned as I gave him a hug and kiss, then kicked his legs, signaling to me he wanted to get down. I put him on the ground and watched as he ran over to his toy chest. I smiled and waved at Sarah, who was walking out onto the patio.

"Hey you," I said, shifting to the wall again. "What's up?" Sarah and I had married in the middle of this mess after what had to be the strangest courtship ever. We both had lost our spouses to the disease and managed to survive numerous encounters with the dead. We realized we needed each other on several levels after Sarah had been kidnapped and subsequently rescued by yours truly.

"Not much," Sarah said, sidling up and giving me a quick kiss. "Charlie radioed in and wants you out on the farm. He says he thinks someone is out there"

"Zombie?"

"Nope. Alive."

That made it news. We didn't get many visitors by land and ninety-nine percent of the time they were roaming ghouls looking for a meal. We had built up an earthen wall to keep out the odd zombie from the forest, using a borrowed back hoe from a local farm. We had a hell of a time finding gas for it, but eventually we did manage to dig a trench and use the dirt to create a five foot wall around the park. We piled the dirt up on the inside of the trench, making the actual height ten feet. Unless we got swarmed by thousands of zombies which filled the trench, we were pretty good to go.

I gave Sarah a hug and kiss of her own and went inside to put my gear on. Experience had taught me some hard lessons about the world I now lived in. Passing by the huge fireplace of the main hall of the lodge, I threw a wave to Rebecca, Charlie's wife and Julia, their adopted daughter. Julia was tottering around and getting herself into all kinds of trouble, typical of a two-year-old.

I stopped in the gear room and put on my vest, weighted with AR-15 mags and SIG reloads. I belted on my field knife and tucked my balaclava into my pocket. Last, I shrugged on my backpack which contained non-perishable food, bottled water, a first aid kit, and an extra box of ammo.

I shouldered my rifle, a standard AR-15. I had decided a while ago to forgo my trusted M1 Carbine, given that ammo for it was hard to find. I could reload, since I had the components, but I figured I would do that once I ran out of the factory stuff. Besides, Charlie carried an AR exclusively and being able to share ammo was a plus in the field. More to the point, Sarah had taken a shine to the M1 and since she was better with it than I was, I let her have it.

I climbed the stairs to the second floor and walked through a hotel room to the balcony. From there I climbed down the detachable stairs to the ground outside the lodge. We had long ago sealed up the first floor of the lodge, except the area in the back, walling that part off with brick, rock and mortar. All in all, we could withstand a siege if we had to and we had a fast escape route to the river if the walls were ever breached. In a way, I felt like a feudal lord in his castle. All I needed were a few willing serfs and the world was golden.

I went over to the shed and unlocked the door, pulling a mountain bike out of storage. We tried to save as much gas as possible for emergencies and since Charlie was only a mile or so away, it wasn't worth driving.

"Charlie, you there? Over," I called on the radio, a little walkie-talkie that had surprisingly good range.

"I'm here." Charlie's voice crackled out of the radio and I quickly tamped down the volume.

"What's up?" I asked, swinging my leg over the bike and heading down the driveway. I had two choices for exit. Down to the river road or out back to the farm road. Both were going to require some pedaling.

"Need you to see something. I think we have a camper. Over."

"Roger that. Where are you?" I asked.

"Out on farm two, near the entrance to Matthiessen."

"Roger. See you in about fifteen minutes. Out." I had about four miles to go, so it shouldn't take me too long. I rode up the driveway and headed south, riding up to the south entrance. I saw a lot of new life in the woods and I was glad on a certain level that the earth was taking back what it could, given this limited opportunity. I couldn't say for certain if humans were going to make a comeback, but for the immediate future, I think we reached an acceptable compromise.

After a mile I cleared the trees and saw our barricade. The grass hadn't completely covered it yet, but I could see the weeds were making plenty of headway. We made no attempt to fortify the hill. I figured in time it would become brush covered and zombies never fared well in the brush. To my left and right was farmland and we used what we could take care of, growing vegetables and what not. We had planted some apple and pear trees, but they would take a while before they bore fruit. Right now we foraged for our fruits, getting what we could from salvaged cans. There was supposed to be an apple orchard around here somewhere, but I never did find it.

I rode up to our gate and stopped, taking a moment to pass through and re-lock it on my way out. Not that I was worried about anyone coming to steal something. We didn't have that kind of problem these days. But occasionally a lone ghoul or three wandered around and they needed to be kept out.

I rode west on Route 71, taking in the cool morning air and the quiet countryside. The open fields to my left contrasted nicely with the forested lands to my right and the morning dew was not quite gone, so the world had a pleasant washed look to it. I turned south onto State Road 178 and pedaled quietly for another two miles.

I was nearly at the entrance when a little zombie came tearing out of the roadside ditch, right in front of me. I swerved sharply to avoid it, then looked back as it struggled to chase me down. It was a young boy, probably no older than ten, although it was hard to tell. His skin was badly decayed and great rents in his clothing and tissue told of a tragic, painful end. His face was twisted in a snarl as he pursued me and I had to give him credit, he was far faster than his older contemporaries. The skin around his mouth was torn away, usually an indication that he had been dead for a while and had feasted often.

I pedaled to the entrance to Matthiesson and stopped the bike, hopping off and heading back to the road where the little zombie was slavering away and closing in fast. I stepped onto the road and unslung my rifle. Ordinarily, I would take a lone zombie out with my pickaxe or knife, but I never took chances with the faster ones. Get them down, then finish them off any way you could.

I aimed my rifle at his stomach as he moved towards me, then waited until his head filled my sights. The gun barked once, sending a .223 caliber bullet through the young boy's face, blasting his head apart and sending him sprawling backwards. I had a brief thought about this boy's parents, but pushed it away as I thought about Jake.

I walked over to the body and made sure it was dead. Dragging it over to the ditch, I unceremoniously tossed the small body in, squirted it with kerosene from a small squeeze bottle, then lit it up. I watched the body catch fire and when I was satisfied it would be fully consumed I walked back over to where I had left my bike. I was just in time to see Charlie step from the trees that lined the small road to the park.

"Did you get him?" he called over to me.

"Little runner? Yeah, I got him," I called back as I headed over to Charlie.

"Runner? I'm looking for a crawler. There was a runner?" he asked.

I stopped dead in my tracks. "Where'd you see a crawler?"

"Around here somewhere. It's like he fell in a hole or something."

"Did you stand?" I asked, referring to a zombie hunting method of standing still on a small rise and making noise to attract the crawlers. Once they revealed their position, you put them out of their misery. Or yours.

"Look around. Where could I stand?" Charlie sounded agitated.

"How about the road? There's ditches on both sides," I pointed out.

"Didn't think of that," Charlie mumbled, chastened. He headed over to the road and crossed to where I was standing.

"Runner, hey?" he asked. Charlie was a big guy, nearly as tall as I was but broader. He had lost his family to the Upheaval, but managed to rebuild much of his life by marrying again and adopting a little girl we had rescued. He and I had been through as much as anyone could have expected and by God's grace and a load of luck, we were still around to battle the bad guys. If a better man existed to watch my back, I had yet to meet him. I trusted Charlie with my life, and the lives of my loved ones. If something ever happened to me, I knew Charlie would gladly raise Jake and do a damn fine job of it.

"Yeah, the little wiener came out like a yapping dog and I needed to take him down. Why the kids are fast is still a mystery to me," I replied.

"It's creepy," Charlie said. "I get the slow ones, the virus trying to keep things going and not really doing so well, but the fast ones don't make sense. And why just the kids? It's messed up."

"Yeah, I know, but if we wanted to start with the dead coming back to life in the first place..." I trailed off as I saw movement in the tall grass by the trees to my left. I brought my weapon up as Charlie loosed a tomahawk from its holder. We moved silently across the grass and waited. I whistled for a minute and finally grey-black hands slowly emerged from the edge of the small clearing, snaking out as if they were testing the new open space.

The skeletal hands clawed at the earth as they sought purchase to pull the rest of the body along. I say body loosely, since the zombie was nothing more than an upper chest, arms, head, and about a foot of backbone. The rest was simply gone, torn away, probably eaten. I had seen things like this before. Survivors trying to escape zombies by attempting to crawl through an opening too small for them. They get stuck, then they get eaten alive. Once the rest of the body no longer hinders forward progress, the zombie top can roam free. Generally speaking.

This one was very decayed and the dragging had worn away the leftover skin on the chest until white bone gleamed as it pulled itself forward. I had no idea if it was male or female, old or young. It just kept pulling itself slowly forward, locking its dead eyes on us. Its mouth opened to groan, but without lungs, that wasn't going to happen.

Charlie stepped up quickly to it and with a single chop of his 'hawk, turned off this zombie's lights for good. He wiped the blade off in the grass, wiping it again with a small bit of rag we all carried with us for that express purpose. Even after two years, the virus was still deadly and would kill us quickly if we didn't take precautions.

"Any others?" I asked, as Charlie tucked away his weapon.

"Just a couple of loners. Actually, I expected more, since this is the first really warm spring day that we've had," Charlie said.

I nodded as I retrieved my bike and Charlie went to retrieve his. "Every time I start to think maybe they're starting to thin out and decay away, another one shows up to make a liar out of me."

"Sad, but true," Charlie said. "The stuff I found is this way." He rode his bike down the access road to the state park, passing by a small parking lot and picnic area. The place looked a little forlorn, as the weeds and grass hadn't been controlled in a couple years, but in a few more years, unless you looked really hard, you'd never know there was anything here in the first place.

We pedaled into the bigger parking lot that went up to the main visitor area, then circled around to the large wooden fort that had been a visitor favorite for years. It was supposed to represent the exploration of the area, but no real fort had ever been there. It was a big building, nearly two stories tall, with small windows and a narrow stairway leading to the second floor. Properly provisioned, it would make a decent temporary shelter from roving bands of the undead. Long term, though, it was not a good place.

Charlie swung off his bike and took his rifle off his shoulder. His AR was similar to mine, except he had changed out the upper for a flattop version with a bull barrel. He could hit things a little farther out than myself. I preferred closer work with my AR. For long range stuff I used my M1A.

Taking my carbine off my back, I leaned my bike against the building and nodded to Charlie that I was ready. We entered and as my eyes adjusted to the change in lighting, I saw what made Charlie call this one in. There was a backpack in the corner, a small plastic bag of foodstuffs and bottled water, a long pole, and a hatchet. Everything was arranged for quick pickup in case of attack. I climbed the stairs and looked around, seeing a blanket on the floor and a flat rock with charred twigs, the remnants of a tiny fire.

I went back downstairs and nodded again to Charlie. "You're right, someone is using this place."

"How many?" Charlie asked, looking around again.

"If I had to guess, I'd say they were travelling alone. I don't see any signs of another person, although I could be wrong. I have been before," I said, anticipating Charlie's response.

I wasn't disappointed. "Really? You? No, really?" Charlie snorted, shifting his rifle and raising his eyebrows to the point where they threatened his hairline.

"Anyway, where are they now? I would have seen someone on the road and you've been here all morning. Chances are they heard me shoot the runner, so they're probably hiding out right now," I said, looking around.

"Maybe. Maybe not," Charlie said. "You shot that Z on the road and we went a mile and a half into the woods to get here. If they are down in the canyon area, chances are pretty good they didn't hear much. If they're by a waterfall or fast creek, then they might not have heard anything at all."

"Okay, so we have two options. Wait for them to return, or go looking for them," I said.

Charlie shrugged. "I say we go find them. If we're here when they return, things might get weird. If we go to them, at least we can announce we're friendly."

"True. All right, lead the way, Bwana," I said, moving back outside and checking the area for any Z activity.

Charlie stepped out and went past the visitor center. I noted the doors had been broken into and there looked to be things strewn about a bit. I didn't see any blood so I figured someone was just looking for anything of use or value. These days, money was worthless except for lighting fires, and we had developed a decent system of trade. Canned goods were always useful and so was ammo. Tools were good trade items and quality knives were always in demand. Funny thing, how-to books were very valuable as well. Toilet paper was gold.

We went past the center and walked down a dirt path to a small wooden walkway that took us along the edge of the canyon. The trees overhead were budding in the warm weather, and bright flowers dotted the ground. Here and there a squirrel leaped from tree to tree, and the creek noisily flowed on the canyon floor. There was a lot of beauty here and I could see why people came to this spot. But after the Upheaval, I tended to look at things with different eyes and this place offered no real defense if the dead came in force.

We walked down a ramp which took us to the floor of the canyon. Not having any real clue where we were going, we figured one way was as good as the next and headed north. We tried our best to keep out of the creek, but in spots we had to step in once quickly to get around a bend in the rocks. After about ten minutes, both Charlie and I were soaked up to our thighs.

We stepped up onto a flat rock which the creek flowed over and saw some fifty gallon drums in the water. They had been cut in half and filled with concrete, making stepping stones across the busy creek. I looked on both sides and saw evidence of the original trails, with rotting stairways leading to old paths.

At the top of the rocky shelf, we could hear the low roar of a small waterfall and stepping cautiously over the wet rocks, we rounded another bend and could see the spray of the cascading creek. The water fell a good thirty feet before it hit the pool at the bottom and even from where I stood, I could see it was clear and probably cold. I stepped up to the next rock and Charlie held up his hand. Ducking low and bringing up my rifle, I covered the area to the left as Charlie brought up his rifle and aimed at something up ahead.

Charlie tapped me on the shoulder and I swung back to the right, finally seeing what caused him to stop. A man was sitting on a rock on the right side of the waterfall, filling bottles and washing some clothing. He was tall, easily over six feet. His dark hair hung loosely about his shoulders, his thin arms looked wiry, but strong.. He looked competent, as anyone travelling alone would have to be and he had that wary look about him that the Upheaval had given most of us.

On his hip was a pistol, although I couldn't make out what kind from where I was. We were going to have to be cautious, since I really didn't feel like shooting a live person. I waved Charlie back and out of sight. I was going to announce my presence with Charlie covering me, and hope everything turned out all right. Any hostile move would get the man shot, so I wasn't worried too much, but you never knew. He might get lucky.

Leaning my carbine against the rocky sides, I waited until Charlie had climbed into a shooting position. Given the thumbs up, I stood near the rock corner then called out.

"Hello? Hello?" Right after I said it I felt stupid, and I knew Charlie was going to give me hell for sounding like a doofus.

"Who's there?" The man shouted. "Show yourself! I'm armed, so don't be stupid!"

Too late for that. I walked around the corner with my hands held chest high. While it looked like surrender, I knew I could get my SIG out in a hurry if shooting started, provided I hadn't been shot. The man was standing away from the water, pointing a pistol in my direction. I noticed he used two hands and the gun was not shaking. I figured if this went south I would be lucky to only be shot, if not downright killed. What I was not expecting was what happened next.

"I knew it! I don't know how you bastards tracked me this far, but I'll be damned if I'm going back! You tell the Major to go fuck himself!" The man was really worked up and I was getting nervous about his trigger finger.

I kept my hands up. "I think you're confused. Who is this Major? What are you talking about?"

"Don't lie to me! Survivors don't dress like you. You're one of his men! I ought to kill you right now!" He brought up the gun and I ducked as a shot rang out. I pulled my SIG and went around the corner to hear Charlie yell.

"You're covered! Drop the gun *now*, or I *will* kill you.!"

The man screamed. "Damn you! Damn your Major! Fucking kill me, you shit! Do it! I'd *rather* be dead! *Do it!*"

This whole mess was getting out of hand. I stepped back around the corner and covered the enraged man, who still refused to drop his weapon. "All right, hold it! Just hold it!" I stepped out and the man's arm twitched like he desperately wanted to bring up the pistol, but Charlie had stood up and there was no mistaking the intent of the AR now pointed at the man's head. "Just calm down. Nobody wants to hurt you, but if you do something stupid, you're in a world of hurt." I stepped forward and could see the pistol more clearly. It was a standard .45 auto, and had he shot me with it, I probably would have died, even if just wounded.

I stepped closer. "Holster your gun. I don't want it going off accidentally." The man stared at me but complied. I holstered mine as soon as he did and Charlie lowered his rifle. The man's eyes relaxed and his narrow shoulders visibly sagged. "That's better. My name is John Talon," the man's eyes shot towards me when I said that, but I let it pass. "And that gent up there is Charlie James. We're not with any 'Major', we're just survivors in this messed-up world, like you. We don't want to hurt you. We just want to make sure you're okay and to help you if we can. If you don't want our help, we'll leave you to your own devices and wish you luck."

The tall man looked at me and gave me a sly smile. "My name is Simon Crays. John Talon, you say? I think I'm happy to meet you."

2

We retrieved Simon's things and rode slowly back to the lodge. Simon's long legs allowed him to walk at a mile-eating pace, and he had no trouble keeping up with Charlie and myself. I rode on Simon's left while Charlie brought up the rear. We talked briefly of the Upheaval and I learned that Simon was a computer software engineer, working out of Los Angeles. When the Upheaval hit, he managed to escape the carnage of the city and take refuge in the mountains. He had been living off the land and foraging through the ranches when he was 'recruited' by the Major. He didn't elaborate and I figured we would learn more when we returned home. I told him about where we lived and how we came to be there. His eyes got wide when I told him of the towns and communities we had put together and he expressed a sincere interest in seeing those towns. Simon apologized for his behavior, but he thought he had been chased for hundreds of miles, thinking he had given his pursuers the slip when he crossed the Mississippi. When he saw us in all our gear, he immediately thought of the Major and therefore reacted the way he did.

The sun was high when we reached the outer gate and Simon was impressed with our earthen wall. I could see him running an experienced eye on its effectiveness and I saw him nod his head in approval. As we approached the lodge, I could see Simon openly nodding.

"Very nice," he said. "Was this place a tourist spot before the zombies came?"

I gave him a short nod as I put my bike away. "This place has a lot of history, but the short version is we found it empty, realized its potential, and settled in. We could have done worse and nobody has laid a counter claim to it."

"Not yet," Simon mumbled, but quickly smiled to cover it. "Looking forward to seeing the rest," he said amicably

Charlie led the way and we climbed the stairs to the second floor, then worked our way down to the main room. Simon whistled at the size of our common area, then walked over to the window to admire the view. I shrugged off my backpack and took off my vest. Charlie did the same, although he put his used tomahawk near the fireplace in the center to burn off any trace of the virus from the Z he killed. I motioned Simon to settle in at the big round table we used for discussions and he sat down, relaxing into the chair after his long hike. He pulled a bottle of water out of his pack and took a drink, his eyes glancing around at his surroundings.

His pose was casual, but I could see he was tense. It seemed as if he had some knowledge that he wanted to let go of, but didn't know where to start. For my part, I figured I would just wait, seeing where the silence took me. It was an old trick I had used to good effect once upon a time as an administrator. Those with guilty consciences tended to need to release their guilt and the longer I waited without saying something, the harder it was for them to keep it in.

Charlie sat down at the table, pulled his Glock from its holster, and placed it on the table. The move wasn't lost on Simon, and he leaned forward, placing both hands on the table while leaving his firearm holstered. I chose to stand away from the table, leaning on a low wall that separated the main room from a bar area. My casual pose put my hand close to my SIG and on Simon's right. If he tried to get into action, it would be hard for him to bring his gun to bear before I shot him. Ordinarily, I wasn't so cautious, but the man had reacted a couple of times a little out of the ordinary, so I wasn't taking chances.

"Where do I begin?" Simon asked suddenly.

"Your survival story, I will assume, is pretty much standard these days. You figured out what was going wrong, got the hell out of dodge, fought a few zombies, and ended up someplace you didn't like. Along the way, you have heard my name, and you have an interesting story to tell about a certain 'Major'," I said, starting the ball.

Simon blinked, then he fully smiled. "You don't waste time, do you?"

"Not really. Why don't you pick up where you left off on the way here. You said you were taking to the hills when the Upheaval started," I supplied.

"Right. I had spent a bunch of time up in the mountains around the Tahoe area and I figured maybe with the terrain, the plague hadn't hit so hard. Well, I got to Tahoe all right, but one look around had me running for the hills again. Seems like a lot of people had the same idea and one of them was infected. The whole slaughter had started again and I barely managed to escape the zombies by climbing the expert slope on Heavenly. The zombies weren't great climbers and I got ahead of them pretty quickly. Last I looked, there were dozens of people trying to escape the undead by swimming out into the lake. Trouble is, the lake is cold, and I am sure most died of hypothermia while the ghouls waited at the edge.

"On top of Heavenly is a lodge and I stayed there for a time while the world died around me. The place had been abandoned and I was able to break into their food stores and live for nearly six months. By that time, the weather was turning and it was getting pretty cold at night, so I started to venture out. The first person I encountered was a zombie. But it was cold enough that he couldn't chase me and was moving so slow that I was able to take a large branch and knock him down the mountain. By the time he reached the bottom he was in about six pieces."

I smiled at the description and imagined a Z cartwheeling down the mountainside with limbs flying off and leaving a grisly trail of smashed-up zombie chunks.

Simon continued. "About the time my food ran out, winter was starting to hit the mountains pretty hard. I figured I needed to move on and do it quickly before the passes were closed. I took one of the maintenance trucks that had been left up at the resort and started my way down the mountain. I was hoping to get into Carson Valley and maybe find a decent place to hole up for the winter. There wasn't a large population in that area and I thought that I could winter there and then move on. On the way down the mountain I passed several cars that had reanimated people inside them and more than one family car was covered in blood as a sick family member came back and ate his relatives.

"Carson Valley was relatively untouched by the virus and I spent the winter with a couple who had been living there for a while. They had been monitoring the progress of the disease by the internet and we spent countless hours going over plans and preparations. When winter broke I planned on heading north to the rough country, then maybe going to Colorado. I had heard the military had made a stand there and were welcoming survivors. Rumors told me there were almost a hundred thousand people in the mountain and the military was going to start heading back out to take on the threat."

I paid close attention at this point, because it coincided with information I had found at State Center Bravo in what seemed a long time ago.

"I killed my next two zombies that winter. The couple I was rooming with? Yeah, they went out to their neighbors' ranch and came back with the sickness. Virus took them both out in a short time, then they came for me. I killed the woman with a shovel and beat her husband's brains in with a length of fence post. They were good people." Simon drifted off for a second at the memory, but recovered quickly.

"I took what I needed from the house and left that evening. I drove through the night and when I ran out of gas the next morning I figured I was in Colorado. That's when the Major's men caught up to me."

Charlie and I shifted at the mention of the Major. "Who is the Major? Is he the commander of the remainder of the military forces?" Charlie asked.

Simon's eyes got dark. "No, he isn't. I found out later that the military was wiped out completely, that there are a hundred thousand ghouls trapped in a mountain in Wyoming, just waiting for some fool to let them out. No, the Major is just some guy who likes to be called Major and he runs his little operation like a military base, although neither he, nor his men have any military experience. But that doesn't stop him from acting like it or using it to dupe people into believing he's the sole authority left in the United States."

That was interesting. I ruminated on the possibilities and if a group could pull it off, they could effectively take over a good portion of the country.

Simon continued. "From the beginning, I knew something was wrong. Men and women worked the fields and tended to the animals. There was a rough fence to keep the zombies out, but the Major's men managed that pretty well."

"What was wrong then?" Charlie asked. "Seems like you managed to get to a place of safety, regardless of who was in charge."

Simon glared at Charlie. "It wasn't safety, it was slavery. And those bastards used the worst methods to keep people in line. If a family showed up or was brought in, the husband was immediately beaten and the wife raped by the Major's men. That was standard. If there were children, they were used as leverage. Women who resisted found themselves bound and gagged in a room, with their child put in a dark room next to them. They got to hear their children scream for their mothers. No one resisted long after that, especially if it was a baby left alone to cry."

My hands involuntarily clenched into fists as I thought briefly about Jake locked in a room to cry for his daddy who couldn't get to him. I could see Charlie was just as upset.

Simon looked down. "But the older kids, the ones who were between twelve and fifteen, they got separated from their parents and were held in a different part of the camp. The boys were used for labor and the girls..."

Charlie leaned forward, his eyes hard. "What about them?" His voice was flint and I had no doubt he was thinking of his own daughters, living and dead.

Simon looked up and sighed. "They were reserved for the Major. Seems he liked them young and 'unspoiled'." Simon looked out the window. "The girls were brought to the Major and when he was finished with them, they were broken. If they had spirit before, they were broken afterwards. The life was taken from them."

Simon stopped speaking and I had to rein in my emotions. My first impulse was to pack up and head west, not stopping until I had a chance to confront this mess of vipers, but my more rational side realized it was futile. I couldn't go two thousand miles across country to fight a pedophile bastard and his cronies.

My attention was diverted as Tommy and Duncan came spilling into the room, joking like a couple of teenagers. They glanced over to the table and their expressions turned serious as they felt the mood of the room. They came over to the table with curious looks to Simon and sat down with questions in their eyes at me. I shook my head as I motioned for Clays to continue.

"I was there for twenty months and it reached a point where I couldn't stand it any more. There were women's screams every night and children crying for their mothers. In the bunkhouse where I shared sleeping space with the fathers and husbands, there would always be one or two crying rage and shame at their helplessness. More than once rebellion was contemplated, but it was tamped down because of the kids' camp.

"I finally decided to leave on a night I knew the guards would be distracted. One of the scouting and foraging parties had come across a large group of people who had been travelling. There were a lot of women and children and the men were licking their chops at the new flesh. That night, I ducked the fence, smashed a guard across the teeth with a rock, and took off into the night."

Simon shrugged. "I guess I survived because it was winter and the zombies were frozen. I moved as far as I could every day, and slept only a few hours at a time. I stuck to the country as much as I could, figuring the Major's men would be too lazy to search off the roads. Chances are they never missed me or just didn't care."

I nodded, thinking about what I had heard. It was horrible, no doubt, but in all seriousness, none of my business. One thing nagged at me, though. "When I told you my name, you acted like you had heard of me. Why is that?"

Tommy chimed in. "Hell, you're the biggest badass zombie killer in the country, everybody knows you!" He elbowed Duncan and they both chuckled, but silenced when I scowled at them.

Simon chuckled as well, but answered the question. "One of the men in the bunkhouse talked about you. Ever have a neighbor named Todd?"

My heart sank. So Todd survived a cross country trip, only to fall into the hands of a bigger monster than the zombies themselves. I forced myself to ask the next question. "He had a wife and two girls. One his own, the other one picked up after her parents had been killed." That was a long time ago, but I still remembered the deaths at the drugstore clearly.

Simon shook his head. "He only had one daughter and she went to the major. His wife was used badly by the major's men and died. He committed suicide when he attacked the guards. They shot him down without hesitation."

I dropped my head. It was too bad, they were a good family. I said a silent prayer and remembered the other question I wanted to ask. "You said 'Not yet' when I said no one has laid a counter claim to this area. What did you mean?"

Simon looked sideways at me. "You don't miss much, do you? Well before I left, I had overheard the guards talking about the major looking to relocate, finding someplace where he could set himself up as ruler of the country, since he figures he could do it with the men he has. From what I understood, he was looking to come east. Where specifically, I don't know, but definitely closer to the center of the country. If he hears about this place, he might just take a shine to it and decide you need to go."

I thought about all the macho things I could say at that point and settled on, "I think I would object."

Simon shrugged. "The Major has seventy-five men, all of them well armed. You'd get a few for sure, but those kinds of numbers will eventually work against you."

"I'll take my chances. Besides, I have a few surprises of my own." I smiled as a loud growl sounded up from the forest floor almost on cue as the cougar hunted in the growing evening.

Simon's eyes got huge and I nodded. "Good thing you decided to stay at Matthiesson last night. You might have run into the boogeyman over here. And this one is very pointy in certain places."

Charlie spoke up. "Well, it's a hell of a thing, but the chances of this major finding us are pretty slim and if he does, we'll deal with it."

"There's one other thing." Simon said cautiously.

"What would that be?" I asked.

"The Major is not entirely sane. He had been getting a lot of people in camp lately that have been yelling about their rights and he can't do what he's doing. 'This is America' and all that. Usually the voices have been silenced quickly enough, but some managed to get overheard by the Major. In his warped mind, he probably figures if he destroys the Constitution and the Bill of Rights, he will be able to set himself up as ruler, and no one can challenge him."

I looked incredulously at Simon. "What would be the point of that? Pick up any history textbook and you can find a copy of the Constitution."

Duncan chimed in. "Yeah, but the documents themselves are as much a symbol of our country as the flag is. If it were to become known that they had been destroyed, we'd have a harder time coming together as a country again after the zombies were gone. As it is, we're barely holding it together. If the Constitution and Bill of Rights become destroyed, what we believe about our country would be destroyed."

Tommy spoke up. "What have we been fighting for in the end? Sure it's to survive, but do you want to live in a country where only the strong survive? No thanks. The Constitution and Bill of Rights are what made this country great and whether you believe it or not, they're the only hope of rallying everyone who's left to the cause. If they get destroyed, we're finished."

I looked at Charlie. "What say you, old friend?"

Charlie looked at the floor for a long time. When he looked up, his eyes were clear and his voice strong. "My first wife and daughter died from the virus. I buried them both with my bare hands. I got a second chance and a reason to live with Rebecca and Julia. That chance is wasted if I let some lunatic take over the country. I know it may be crazy, but even though we might be wasting our time and very likely manage to get ourselves killed, I couldn't look at my daughter and tell her that I did nothing to stop it."

All four men looked at me and I glanced over at Sarah who was coming in from the back hallway with Jake and Julia. I thought about Todd, Nola, and their daughter and little Ellen, who I had saved from scum so long ago.

I cannot let you die in vain, I thought.

I looked at Simon. "Do you really think he's coming?"

Simon nodded. "From what I saw for the time I was at that camp, I would bet my life on it. When he gets fixated on something, no matter how crazy, he has to have it. I remember the men hunting for gold watches because he wanted to have a different watch for every day of the year. And God help you if you are in his way or he sees you as a threat."

"Why?"

"He isn't content with just removing things that irritate him, he has to completely destroy them, smash them, make them disappear. A man accidentally got dirt on the Major's boots when the Major came to inspect an earthen wall. The man was beaten senseless, then buried alive in the wall. They forced his family to watch him being buried."

I shook my head as Charlie asked my next question. "How does he get men to follow him? I would think that some might actually be decent men who wouldn't stand for such behavior."

Simon shrugged. "He keeps his men happy with women and loot. Most of them are as degenerate as he his. Also, he's huge. He's six foot six if he's and inch and I figure him to be two hundred forty pounds of solid muscle. I saw him beat a man to death with his bare hands. He's a brute and his men respect and fear him with good reason."

I looked around at the men and my wife and son. Charlie had gathered up Julia and was looking at me expectantly.

I asked Simon again. "You're sure he's coming?"

Simon nodded ruefully. "Absolutely."

I looked back out over forest and river. The setting sun was causing long shadows from the trees and the river sparkled as it wound its way around Eagle Island. I took a minute to reflect on all I had done and all we had been through to get where we were. Tommy and Duncan were right. It would all be for nothing if we let it happen.

I let out a breath. "Well, I guess we better figure out how we're going to stop him."

3

(Six months earlier)

Major Ken Thorton liked being big. He enjoyed the looks he received when he addressed other men. Those wishing to be like him or to be liked by him. Some people would have been happy to just be as tall or as broad, but Ken loved being both. He saw his size as a tool to be used on an unwilling world, to shape that world into a place more suited to his needs. At six foot five, with plenty of muscle packed on his arms and chest, he had plenty of tools to work with.

Before the Upheaval, he worked as a security guard for Reno Airport, watching people all day and thinking about what he'd like to do so some of them that looked crossways at him. He had a lot of time to think and spent a good deal of time thinking about what a perfect world he could create for himself if only given the chance. He had often talked about his ideas with select few like-minded individuals, but nothing ever came from the conversations. Ken Thorton was a bully and bruiser, but he was smart enough not to attract the attention of local law enforcement. He often boasted about what he would do to any cop that tried to come for him, but in truth Ken was a coward. He was brave when he held the upper hand and he did everything in his power to make sure he kept that hand. He was openly contemptuous of anyone he perceived as being better than he and anyone he perceived as a threat to his image was utterly destroyed.

So when the Upheaval came, most people thought of it as the end of the world. Ken realized that it was his one chance to create his own. He had often claimed he had been a soldier, but avoided conversations with real military personnel. With most of them dead, Ken found it the perfect opportunity to be that which he had always claimed to be. He chose the rank of Major, figuring that he couldn't claim higher because people wouldn't believe him. He had outfitted himself in military clothing and set out into the undead world.

Thorton managed to recruit a few unsavory individuals into his band. Ted Tamikara, a twenty-five year old former computer programmer, was Thorton's Captain and right hand man. Ken had rescued Ted from his little apartment in Reno, swinging a makeshift club like a lawnmower blade and hurling ghouls left and right with smashed skulls. Thorton quickly realized that Ted was of a like mind when it came to their fellow man and the two set off to remake their world.

Ted didn't mind being second to Thorton. At five foot six, he was no match for Ken physically, but his agile mind more than made up for what he lacked in physical stature. Ted also had a cruel streak which suited Ken's needs as well. Captain Tamikara was not a man to cross, not without rear view mirrors installed in your head. When Thorton and Tamikara were moving from place to place, Thorton got a clear view as to how his new friend operated. The pair had come across a young couple hiding in a small house. Tamikara quietly asked the young man if he was armed. When the man said no, Ted casually shot him dead. Tamikara then assaulted the new widow, taking what he considered as a 'spoil of war'. Ken didn't object in the least, only insisted on having his turn with the woman. After they had finished their fun, Ken stuck his knife in the poor woman's chest. It was the first living person he had killed and he thoroughly enjoyed the look on his victim's face when the knife slid in. Ted watched with approval and from that moment on, the Major and the Captain were on the same page.

They took what they wanted, recruiting more members. Ken established his base of operations in the ghost town of Bodie, California. He had been there once and remembered it was a defensible place, isolated, with a supply of water and land for subsistence. It was close enough to make raids into several neighboring communities and Thorton used the old mining complex as his personal fortress. There were many buildings still standing and it worked well to serve as a place for families to move into for a modicum of relative safety.

That was the lure. Major Thorton would travel with his band of men, offering a place to stay and passing themselves off as the last of the military of the United States. When the people agreed, and many of them readily did, they were brought into the town and given a home. After they had been taken in, the families would realize their mistake. Women disappeared for days on end, returned to their husbands with broken spirits and bruises. Husbands who complained were immediately beaten, some severely. Children, especially young girls between the ages of twelve and sixteen, were taken from their families to the 'fortress'. Young boys were sent to work on another part of the property, making sure their parents stayed in line. The youngest children stayed with their parents, but were used for coercion as needed.

Major Ken Thorton not only was a bully, a brute, and a murderer, but he was also a molester. In his warped mind he believed he was owed the pleasure of the little ones and he preferred the fear he caused in them as to the disdain and contempt of the older women.

Such was the world as Ken saw it as he surveyed his little kingdom. In truth, that was what it was. He ruled over the lives of the three hundred people who were luckless enough to fall into his trap, and he ruled over the lives of the seventy-plus men he had in his little 'army'. Over the course of the next six months of the Upheaval, while the world reeled from the attacks of the undead, Thorton managed to recruit individuals to his cause, each one having the prerequisite of extremely low morals and dubious ethics. Those who showed intelligence or potential were 'promoted' within the ranks.

Thorton was smart enough to realize he would need overwhelming force to ensure there would be no rebellion from his population, so after raiding a military surplus store for uniforms and supplies, Thorton set out arming his men with military weapons. Ft. Laramondo was the nearest source and after leading thirty men to the post, managed to eliminate the zombies and secure the weapons left behind when the fort had been overrun.

With his new found wealth, Thorton had increased his area of operations and brought more people into the fold. He even had criteria for new recruits. Anyone surviving alone was included and anyone willing to kill a survivor, especially an annoying husband complaining about his wife being abused, was a shoe-in.

Dissent among the ranks was dealt with by the captain and complainers never received a warning, just a bullet or knife in the back. Word spread quickly and the complaints fell to zero.

In the general population, complaints were few since they were usually followed by a beating or a killing, but they persisted. Even now, two years after the Upheaval, people, especially new survivors, lured in by the fake military, brought up the fact that their rights were being violated. It was a common complaint and Major Thorton was becoming tired of it. *Rights*, he thought, *what do these idiots care about rights?* The major contemplated this as he stood naked before his window and looked out of his suite. He could see the town from his perch, a ramshackle ghost town re-populated back into existence. Bodie, California had been abandoned in the 1940's, declared a historic site in the 1960's, and served as a tourist attraction until the dead rose. Now it was a town again, tucked away from the world and isolated by geography. Hills surrounded the town, providing a natural defense, and Thorton had enough men to provide reasonable security should the odd zombie make its way to the town.

But security was an illusory thing for the hapless population of Bodie. If the zombies ever discovered the place in force and attacked en masse, the standing plan was to cut and run, not stand and fight. To hell with the helpless citizens. Major Thorton figured when the zombies were busy killing the townsfolk, he and his men could escape.

"Rights." Ken said the word aloud, startling the small form huddled on his bed. A tousled head peeked out from under the covers as Ken continued his reverie. "Rights. How dare they assume they have rights? When the world ended so did any notion of *rights*." Thorton spat the word. "These morons live because it amuses me. They die because they serve no use." *End them, end their rights*, he thought.

End their rights. A seed of thought planted itself in his mind, growing quickly. End their rights, destroy the source. Ken considered this as he stared at his thralls trudging from the work fields or to and from the saw mill and wells. *Destroy the source*, he thought, then he started to chuckle, an ugly sound deep in his chest. Thorton's twisted mind burned with the logic of his reasoning. The logistics of his idea be dammed, Ken realized what he wanted to do. It didn't matter that his thoughts required moving a large number of men across three thousand miles of hostile territory inhabited by rogue bands such as his own, carnivorous zombies, and who knew what else. Ken mulled the thought over again in his head and came to the twisted logic that once he had destroyed the source, he would be in a position to grab ultimate power for himself. Any rational person would think him deluded, but Ken didn't care about that. Like a petulant child, he was striking out at that which annoyed him and to hell with the consequences.

"So has it been considered, so shall it be done." Ken said to himself as he returned to his bed. He smiled as he flipped back the covers, revealing the small naked girl huddled on the bed. She knew better than to resist or cry. She had seen what had happened to her predecessor and wanted no part of it.

Ken had a small group of victims held in a cage near the main mine shaft. If he was particularly displeased with a girl, he would just throw her in, listening to her screams as she fell the quarter mile to her death. If a girl fought him, he would lower her slowly down the mine shaft head first, to be devoured slowly by the zombies waiting at the bottom. No one had a clue as to how they got there, but when one of Ken's men dropped a flare to see how deep the shaft was, they flocked to the light.

He grinned again as he lowered himself on top of the girl, his mind thinking about his task ahead and the glory that was to be his, ignoring her cries as he thrust himself against her battered, eleven year old body.

4

Later in the day, Major Thorton called a meeting of his officers to discuss what it was he wanted. Captain Tamikara was there, seated in the chair on the other side of the long conference table. On one side of the table was Lt. Lon Hansen, a former police officer who had been fired for misconduct right before the Upheaval. Hansen figured his firing had probably saved his life, keeping him home while his colleagues responded to emergencies and died. Sergeant Nick Harris, a former convict whose crimes included rape and assault sat across from Lt. Hansen. Next to him was the other NCO, Sergeant Rod Milovich, a former petty thief rehabilitated into a truck driver.

Major Thorton looked at his subordinates. His eyes rested on Captain Ted's small frame for a second. Tamikara stared back without blinking. Ken gave a small grin at the little man, then spoke to the group.

"Thank you all for coming at such short notice," the Major began, "I have been hearing the complaints again about the abuse of rights of our refugees. I have thought about this, and I have decided to do something about it." Ken paused for effect while Sgt. Nick and Sgt. Rod shared a look of predatory anticipation. They were certain there was going to be some drastic retaliatory measures taken against the complainers. They were not prepared for what Major Thorton said next.

"These complaints have a source and it is my intention to destroy that source. Therefore, we need to plan an expedition to the nation's capital."

"What are we going to do?" Captain Tamikara spoke up, narrowing his eyes at the major as suspicions began to creep into his mind.

"We are going to D.C. to destroy the Constitution and the Bill of Rights," Thorton said. "I figure if we get rid of the source of rights, then these idiots will finally shut up." Ken stood to the stunned silence of the room. "Tell your men. I want a plan in two hours." He strode out, feeling pleased with himself, his bulk filling the small hallway as he went back to his suite.

Captain Tamikara watched the major leave, then spoke quietly to the men at the table. "You heard him. Two hours. Move." Ted looked on as the men filed out, then looked down the hall that Ken had left through as he thought, *You incompetent ape. What stupidity are you up to now?*

Two hours later, the men had returned. They spoke quietly while they waited for the Major to return.

"How many men do you think we'll need?" Lt. Lon asked the captain.

"With likely losses, I figure if we leave with forty, maybe twenty might make it all the way. Don't know for sure how many would be able to make it back here in one piece." Captain Ted replied coldly, accepting fifty percent losses as no big deal. "We couldn't take more without compromising the security of this location."

"Provisions?" Sgt. Nick asked, mentally calculating what supplies he had.

"Two weeks per man, tops. We'll live off the land and the goodwill of fellow survivors." Captain Tamikara smiled thinly at the chuckles this comment drew. They all knew how they would live and force the issue with the barrel of a gun.

"What's our route?" Sgt. Rod asked, pulling open a large road map of the United States.

Tamikara leaned forward. "We'll use secondary roads. The highways will still have numerous cars and obstacles, including a good supply of roaming zombies. We'll be able to see who's still alive and where supplies are. Most towns off the main highways are dead zones anyway. We'll avoid major towns and cities, since we won't have the manpower to deal with large hordes of zombies."

Lt. Lon nodded. "I see your point, but what about the waterways? We could take the rivers or follow the coast and not have to worry about zombies at all. Everybody knows zombies don't swim."

Tamikara shook his head. "I think the land route is the most direct. Besides, I'd rather not be caught on a boat when a storm hit, would you?" Captain Ted spoke casually, but deep inside he was reeling. Just the thought of being on a boat set his stomach to heaving as he had a deathly fear of water.

Lt. Lon shrugged. "Okay, then, that settles the how. What we need to do is decide the who and when."

Captain Ted looked out the window and tilted his head to the side, looking at the overcast skies. "I'd rather leave when the cold hits. Frozen zombies are a whole lot less of a threat and there is less risk. As far as who goes, I'd say we need to leave behind an officer, an NCO, and support staff."

The rest of the men in the room nodded agreement then came to attention as Major Thorton swaggered into the room. He eased his bulk into a protesting chair, then leaned forward, looking at the map on the table.

"Sorry I'm late. My new toy is *such* a distraction." Ken purred as he leered at his men. All of them, save the Captain, leered back. "What have you planned so far?" he asked, leaning back in his chair and folding his massive arms across his chest.

Lt. Lon outlined the general plan and broke down the specifics. Major Thorton nodded his big head. "I like it." He said. "Except for the part about leaving in winter. We'll stay here, then travel when the snows break."

"Why not travel when the zombies are frozen?" Captain Tamikara asked, the only man there who dared question the Major.

Major Thorton would normally bristle at this insolence, but today he was feeling magnanimous. "I agree it would be easier, but we don't know what kind of shelter we might be able to secure for ourselves. Here we're established and are ready for winter." Reluctant nods were seen around the table.

Ken continued with a wicked grin. "Besides, I was looking forward to a winter tucked away warmly with my toys."

The NCOs shared a glance and Lt. Lon smiled openly. Only captain Tamikara kept a straight face, but it was wasted on Major Thorton. The man was a full blown pathological narcissist and would not be distracted. Major Thorton sat back and waved his hand. "Dismissed. You know what we need to do," he said as he turned in his chair and looked out the window.

The men left the room, to reconvene outside the mill compound. Captain Tamikara issued additional orders. "We will need to make sure we have adequate supplies. Raids from the north will focus on gathering materials for the trip. We'll store them there," he pointed to a tall brick building that once was a saloon, but now was unused. "When the snows break, we'll be on the move. I want to be able to just pack in and go. The sooner we get this... *job* finished, the sooner we can look to expanding our operations."

None of the others seemed to notice the pause, but it summed up what a lot of them were thinking at the same time. Their leader may not be completely sane.

The men dispersed to their various duties and to inform the rest of their men what the coming spring held in store for them. The wind over the hills was noticeably colder and everyone knew that winter was close behind. For the poor people of the settlement, it was a small release from the work that was required of them. But winter was long and cold and the people were literally prisoners in their own homes, only allowed to leave when the time came to pick up their foodstuffs or supplies. The animal caretakers were kept busy, making sure the animals were fed and healthy.

The only thing that broke up the monotony was the raids and the materials they brought back. Sometimes they brought back new people for the town. Sometimes they brought back new equipment. Once in a while not all of them came back.

The big excitement happened when someone actually escaped. A soldier came stumbling in from the outer posts, holding a ruined and bloody mouth. Apparently someone had decided they had had enough and disappeared into the wild.

Captain Tamikara was not pleased. He confronted the man in his office who was trying to clean himself up.

"Do you have a weapon?" he asked quietly.

"Yeth," the private said thickly, dripping blood onto the floor.

"Then why did you not kill the man when he approached you?" Tamikara asked.

"He din't loog lige trubble," the private said, gently dabbing his face with is sleeve.

"Really?" Captain Tamikara's voice softened and the private winced visibly, expecting a fatal bullet . Tamikara continued. "Well, I guess he was trouble. You'd better go get him before more of these fools think it is okay to hit their guards with rocks and leave."

"Now?" the man squeaked, looking at the new blanket of snow that was falling from deep grey skies.

"Right now." Tamikara dropped a hand to his sidearm, a nickel-plated Browning Hi-Power, his one vanity.

The man shouldered his rifle and headed out into the gloom, pursuing prey that would not want to be caught and would fight if cornered.

Captain Tamikara watched the man leave, then shook his head. *First this lunatic wild goose chase and now someone escapes*, he thought to himself. *If I believed in omens, I would say we just got handed a big one.*

After three days, neither the escapee or the soldier chasing him had shown up and Captain Tamikara had new things to worry about. A truckload of prisoners had been brought in and after the separation of families and couples, there were the requisite beatings and rapes and children crying for their mothers. It kept the men busy and the Major was pleased with three new additions to his little harem.

But the additions also stirred up the pot again about rights being violated and the Major was determined more than ever to get rid of that which vexed him.

5

Winter was brutal, with long periods of time when no one could go outside for there was too much snow and it was too cold. Three infants died in the camp, adding to the resentment the people felt towards their captors. A work party tried to overpower their guards and Major Thorton chose to hang them all in the center of the town as a lesson to the rest. As the bodies swung in the wind, the looks around the assembled populace were not defeated, but stoic in their resolution. Thorton was unaware of the animosity, but Tamikara and the rest of the men were all too aware. They gripped their weapons nervously and huddled close together, not wanting to be alone near any of the people.

Winter passed slowly, but eventually came the first signs of spring. Warm air blew over the hills and people emerged from their homes, turning their faces to the brighter sun. The thawing snow reawakened the dormant feelings of rebellion and Caption Tamikara was all too eager to get moving on. He pushed the men with intensity, but urged them not to reveal what was happening. He did not want on uprising on his watch. If the people revolted after he and the others left, what did he care?

The trucks were loaded in the beginning of March and by the start of Spring in earnest, the convoy was ready to go. Ken Thorton inspected the vehicles and spoke with his captain and lieutenant.

"Do we have everything we need?" he asked, looking back over the trucks.

"Yes, we've been over everything twice, Major. We have planned for everything we could think of." Tamikara was barely concealing his contempt these days.

"What about the men staying back, who will it be?" Thorton pressed, looking for weakness.

"Lt. Hansen will be staying behind, as well as Sgt. Nick Harris. They have chosen the men to stay behind as well."

"Excellent. We will be leaving thirty-five men. Will that be enough to keep this place until we return?" Thorton asked.

It had better be, thought Tamikara. "We figure they should be sufficient. We chose the men who would be more brutal than the others, keeping the rest in line until we get back with more numbers," he said.

"Good, good." Ken looked at his fortress and turned back to his Captain. "What about my toys, what were we going to do with them?" Ken was concerned. Not for the well being of his victims, but for his own pleasure when he returned.

Tamikara sighed. "We are sending them back to their families to work. We figured they would be better used as incentives to not fight than as a reason to inspire further hatred." Tamikara was deliberately trying to bait Thorton.

Thorton was oblivious. "Pity, it would have been nice to bring one along."

Tamikara shrugged. "A useless mouth to feed."

Major Thorton glanced sideways at his captain. A suspicion formed in his mind, but he realized the futility of pursuing it at the moment. He changed the subject instead.

"Raid should be coming back tonight from over the mountain. We'll leave as soon as they return," he said.

"At night?" Tamikara seemed surprised. Everyone who survived the Upheaval knew not to move about at night.

Ken shook his head. "I figure them back by this evening. We'll get a good start out and rest over at Maudy's. After that, we're on our own."

Ted nodded once and then turned to Lt. Lon. "Let the rest know and we need to make sure it is quiet."

Lt. Lon saluted, then walked off towards his men. Major Thorton watched him leave, then turned to Tamikara.

"Listen carefully." Ken spoke softly. "If you ever speak like that to me again, I will take your pretty pistol and shove it up your ass before I pull the fucking trigger." He stuck his large face into Tamikara's. "Clear?"

Tamikara stared back a full minute before answering. "Crystal. Is that all, sir?"

"That's enough. Go find a weakling to intimidate, Captain."

Tamikara spun on his heel, seething with impotent fury. He knew he couldn't take Thorton in a fight, and if he had tried to pull his weapon, Ken would have easily killed him. This insult was going to be answered, but it would be on Tamikara's terms, not Thorton's.

Later that evening, the raiders returned. They had various foodstuffs and supplies, but picking were getting slimmer and slimmer. It was noticeable that three men who had gone out had not come back. After the supplies had been stored, the big event was the departure of Ken Thorton and his band of renegades. The people watched from their homes, hopeful their ordeal might be coming to an end after all.

In the middle of the night, Private Levi Denton, a nineteen year old from Vegas died in his sleep. He had been feeling a little ill since he had gotten back from the raid, but he had dismissed it as just a case of indigestion. The truth was he had managed to get infected. The raiders had been surprised by a number of zombies in the store they were looting. The fight had been vicious, short, and in close quarters. Zombie fluids had flown nearly everywhere.

Private Denton had been hit with some zombie gunk on his gloves, but he hadn't known it at the time. A chronic nail biter, his fingertips were usually raw from being worked all the time by gnawing teeth. When he took his gloves off, some of the zombie fluid had gotten on his fingers and worked into the raw sores around his nub-like nails.

The virus had taken a while to reach the vital areas and it was well past midnight when Private Zombie, formally Denton, opened his eyes to his new world. It was dark, but that was unimportant. There were sounds from all directions, causing a brief moment of confusion. Private Zombie jerked his head in the direction of a loud snore which suddenly erupted from the right side of the room. Private Zombie was aware of a hunger in his gut and in his mind. *Feed. Eat. Now, now now!* It was a call that would not, could not be denied. Wonderful smells of food permeated the air and the strength of the smells told him that prey was tantalizingly close. Private Zombie pushed himself erect, only to smack his head on the underside of the bunk above him. He fell back and tumbled out of the bed, causing a few of the lighter sleepers to mutter.

Private Zombie pushed to his feet, the motions familiar but only vaguely, like a memory that stayed just out of reach. He turned his head slowly, locating a source of smell and sound. His eyes fell on his neighbor, Private Samwell.

Private Samwell was snoring softly. He had no idea anything was amiss until he felt teeth ripping through his larynx. Arterial blood sprayed the ceiling, and Private Samwell struggled briefly, but rapidly weakened due to blood loss and was unable to push his attacker off. Private Zombie tore great chunks of flesh out of Samwell's throat, then started tearing at the sweet meat around the chest and shoulders, working to get through the clothing to the succulent organs within.

After twenty minutes, Private Zombie stood up, no longer interested in the former Private Samwell. Private Samwell had become infected with the virus and tasted different to Private Zombie, causing him to stop and look for more prey. Private Samwell sat up in his bunk, blood pouring out from numerous wounds. He stood up slowly, opening his mouth and flaring his nostrils as he took in the smells and sounds around him.

Private Zombie moved over to the next bunk and, opening his bloody mouth as wide as it could go, fell on the throat of his next victim. Private Samwell, learning to walk again, fell against the top bunk of his bed and looked at the man sleeping there.

Private Thames hated to be awakened from his sleep. The last time he had been awakened, he gave the unfortunate a severe beating for his trouble. This time, he was awakened rather rudely, as Private Samwell bit off his nose. Pain woke up Private Thames, and he gasped as his hands flew up to his bleeding face to find his nose was gone. He looked at his bloody hands, then shrieked as his bunkmate came in again and bit a huge chunk of his cheek away, exposing the teeth to the molars.

The scream awakened several others and as they struggled to wake up fully, the zombies in their midst were upon them, biting and tearing. One by one, they fell to the disease. One by one, they rose again, seeking out their former comrades, overcome by their hunger for blood and flesh. Uniforms were red-covered as bits of flesh were torn away. The zombies moved quickly from victim to victim, the spreading virus keeping them away from those who would turn.

Three men managed to make it into a closet, their raw fear palpable in the night. Outside the door it was feeding time for several zombies, two of the victims did not turn and they fed the hunger of the rest. Twenty men crossed the dividing line between human and zombie and not a single shot was fired.

The men in the closet huddled down, fearful to make any noise whatsoever. They were all veterans of the Upheaval and knew they were only a short time away from being discovered.

"Jesus, what the hell happened? Where did *they* come from?" one of the men whispered to the other.

"Keep your damn voice down, they'll hear us!" came the reply. "They didn't come from anywhere, it was *us* that turned. Didn't you see your friends eating each other?"

"Get bent. I was trying to get away, same as you. Situation's the same. What the fuck we gonna do?" The question hung in the air like a fart in church.

"Maybe we can get out through the floorboards, hold on." There were sounds of scraping and scrabbling. "No luck, the boards are nailed down good."

"Shit."

Outside the closet, the re-animated corpses of the remainder of Major Thorton's men slowly rose to their feet. The meal was finished, unrecognizable as anything human. Blood was everywhere, drenching the clothing of the ruined men. Private Zombie, the first to turn, heard a sound at the end of the room and slowly, painfully made his way to the other side. He was followed by his brethren, attracted to his movements. He passed a small closet, but didn't smell his prey in there, due to the overwhelming coppery scent of blood in the room. He was focused on the main door to the room, because light was coming from under the door and shadows moved back and forth, drawing his attention. He stepped to the door, turning his head slightly as one of his brothers fell over a small table. Private Zombie did not know what a door was, he just knew there was prey on the other side of this wall. He pounded on the wall in an effort to make it go away, leaving a bloody streak and was rewarded by the voice of what he wanted to eat.

"Who's pounding, what do you need? The women are done for the night, put it back in your pants." The night guard was irritated at the disturbance.

Private Zombie moaned, a deep gurgling sound because of the drying blood in his throat. He raised his hand to hit the barrier again and the voice came back.

"Whoever is on the other side off this door better get back to sleep before they get their ass kicked!" The voice was very angry, agitating the rest of the zombies and causing them to shuffle forward and group near the door.

Private Zombie raised his hand to strike once more and the door flew open right in front of him. The night guard walked three steps into the room, right into the arms of the hungry zombies, who promptly tore him to shreds. He didn't even have a chance to scream.

In the closet, the trio heard the commotion and accurately guessed the fate of the guard, one Corporal Conche.

"Jesus, we are so screwed."

"Stop crying, we're not dead yet."

"No, but we will be. It's only a matter of time."

"God, will you shut up. Can't you be more like Turner here? He hasn't said a word since we got in here. Probably figured out a way out of this mess. Right Turner?"

"Turner's scared like I am. I don't want to die and I don't want to be a zombie!"

"I swear if you don't shut up I will shove your sorry ass out there for dessert for those fuckers! Shut up!"

The whispers were getting louder and some of the zombies turned their heads towards the sounds, but were unable to figure out where it was coming from.

"We have to do something, now!"

"We're safe here, can't you see that? They can't get in and we can wait until they leave. With all the blood they can't smell us, so if you shut up, they won't know we're here. Shh..."

Several minutes passed while the men in the closet listened to the sound of rending meat, the epitaph of Conche. One of the zombies thumped closer to the closet, curious about some sounds it may have heard. The men in the closet listened as the footsteps slowly, slowly moved closer.

"Oh God, oh God, oh God, oh God."

"I'm finished with you. Turner, what you want to do? Turner? Dude, you okay? What's with your eyes? *Oh God!*" the man screamed the last, causing several zombies to turn their heads to the closet.

Turner sank his teeth into the arm of his former friend and the first man in the closet shrieked as he realized Turner was one of them. He fumbled for the doorknob, spilling out into the room, right at the feet of ten of his former mates. The dead hands reached for him and in a very short time, he knew no more. The other man in the closet broke away from Turner, clutching his arm. He barreled through the grasping arms and made it as far as the front door. He threw open the door, but the hesitation allowed the zombies to reach him and he was pulled back screaming by half a dozen hands that drew him to waiting mouths.

In the small town of Bodie, families heard the screams and knew them for what they were. They quietly blocked their doors, blew out their candles, and hid in the dark, waiting for the demons to pass them by.

6

There is snow on the ground, but even though I am sitting in it, I don't feel it. I don't feel the cold, I don't feel the tingling numbness from exposure to the freezing winds. Snow is falling, but I don't even notice the flakes that tumble down in perfect silence. I don't notice anything except what I am holding.

Around me are the signs of battle. Destroyed lives splattered across the pristine landscape, crimson stains slowly turning to brown in the cold. Bodies twisted in pain and death, each one more violent than the last. Weapons are scattered about, useless now to those who had held them, had trusted their lives to them. Friends and enemies, they are all dead now.

I am wounded myself, but it doesn't matter. My blood drips slowly onto the frozen ground, but I don't see it. I don't notice the pain that centers around the wound. It cannot match the pain in my heart. All of my focus, all I can see, is my baby son's lifeless body as I hold him in my arms.

Snowflakes drift around his pale face, but they do not touch him, respecting this young life taken so brutally. I cannot contain myself. I try to hold back, but choking sobs rack my body as I cling desperately to my son, trying through sheer will power to give him my life, to make the tiny heart beat once again, to make the beautiful eyes open one more time.

Unable to save him, I throw my head back to the sky and scream my rage, my pain, my sorrow.

"Aaarrrgh!" I sit bolt upright in bed, unaware of my surroundings as I release the rage of my dream. As I slowly realize where I am, I tumble out of bed and stagger towards the door, ignoring the sleepy stirrings of Sarah. I entered the hallway and barely glanced at Charlie, who was stepping into the hallway with a gun in his hand, a quizzical look on his face at the sight of my sweat-drenched features. I went to the suite next to mine and moved quickly to the bed. I fell to me knees and looked closely at my sleeping son. The steady rise and fall of his little chest showed me he was just fine and the realization washed over me like a shower and I could feel the relief cleansing the horrific feelings my nightmare had created.

I heard movement behind me and turned to see Sarah coming into the room.

"Everything okay?" she whispered, placing a hand on my shoulder.

"Yeah," I said, standing and turning to face her. "We're fine. Just had a bad dream, that's all." I could see Charlie poking his head in the door.

"All good?" he asked.

"Yeah, thanks." I replied.

"Same dream?" Charlie pressed.

"Yeah," I sighed. "Same one as before. No changes."

Sarah looked at me sympathetically. "Come on, let's get back to bed." She took my hand and the three of us went back to our respective bedrooms. I caught a glance of Rebecca in the doorway of her and Charlie's suite. I heard her say, "Dream again?" to Charlie before he shut the door.

Sarah and I dropped onto the bed and I turned the pillow over to lie on the dry side.

"I don't understand where this is coming from," I said to Sarah. "I would have thought that the nightmares would have been earlier, when our survival was in doubt and I was doing everything just to stay alive. Nothing then. But now, when things are relatively secure, I'm dreaming about everyone I care about dying all around me. And Jake, he's dead in my arms. What the hell?" I put my arm over my eyes and tried to get the images out of my head. Lately this dream had been happening more frequently. I wish I knew what it meant.

Sarah put a hand on my chest. "I know I can tell you it's just a dream, but something is eating at you, something you may not even realize. And it's manifesting itself in your dreams as the one thing you're most afraid of."

"What's that?" I looked over at her.

"Failure." She said.

"Failure?" I didn't understand.

"Think about it, John. You've beaten back the zombies. You're taking back what we lost, restoring our world to us, one small region at a time. You may think you're not part of it, but people still look to you to lead them, to bring them out of the dark. You've been successful in nearly everything you've done for this miserable world and I think you're scared of how hard the other shoe is going to drop."

I had to admit she had a point. I had been unbelievably lucky and the fact that I had managed to get this far was stunning in the extreme. I guess I might have been waiting for my luck to run out.

Sarah continued. "Problem is, you get scared, you get killed. If you start thinking too much about what you are doing and how it might affect the future, you're going to hesitate when you shouldn't." Sarah put a hand on my chest. "Maybe it's time you accepted the role you avoided when you left Leport."

I looked over at her in the dark. "What do you mean.?" I asked.

Sarah smiled. "You've created these communities and they are alive, but in order to live, to grow, they need a cohesive leader, someone to step up and say 'Follow me.' Whether you like it or not, John, you and Charlie and the Knucklehead Twins are the best leaders this country can produce right now."

I turned to face her. "Then we're seriously more screwed than I originally thought." I tried to make light of the situation, but it wasn't working.

Sarah smiled at me. "You were the only one in that school that had a vision for the future and you never lost sight of it. You refused to accept living on the fringe, taking what scraps could be had for existence. You carved out a life for people who had no hope, taking from the monsters who were coming to get us. *You* did that, John. You and Charlie and Tommy and Duncan. You did and no matter what happens, people will never forget you for it."

"That's why I came here, I didn't want..." I started but Sarah wouldn't let me finish.

"Dammit, John! Face the truth. You're the leader this country needs to bring it back," her voice softened. "Everyone else knows it. It's time you did too." Sarah snuggled into my arms and murmured into my shoulder. "Now go to sleep. Sunup is coming earlier and earlier."

I wrapped my arm around her and settled back into my pillow. *Like I'm going to sleep now.* I thought to myself. But shortly, I was drifting off, and thankfully, no more nightmares.

7

In the morning, after I had fed Jake and made sure he was happy, I went to the workout room for my daily routines. Charlie and I had spent considerable time finding and bringing home workout equipment. We had decided that a certain level of strength and fitness helped a great deal when it came to combating zombies and we also did it because once the crops were planted and the animals were fed, there wasn't much else to do. After our workouts with free weights, Charlie and I sparred for an hour. We fought for real and a casual observer would have thought we were trying to kill each other. But I had realized that we needed to train like we fought and the only way to do that was to forgo pulling our punches and make it for real. After months of bruises, black eyes and the occasional broken fingers, we got better and were able to protect ourselves more effectively, not allowing strikes to connect, or turning them away without injury. Between the two of us, it would have been hard to determine who was the better fighter. But I felt confident going into combat that I could reasonably account for myself.

We finished our sparring and I was smarting from a hit to my shoulder. Charlie was nursing a forearm, but apart from that we were sweaty, but okay. Every other day was weapons practice and both Charlie and I made sure Jake and Julia watched us. I wanted the kids to get the images into their subconscious on how to protect themselves and when they were old enough, they were going to be trained. Some would argue that I was being paranoid, but I knew full well it was going to be a long time before we could count on others for our security and safety. For now and the immediate future, it was every man for himself.

After I cleaned up I went to the main room where Sarah was reading to Jake and Rebecca was watching Julia play. Warm spring sunshine reflected off the stone patio and a cool morning breeze worked its way through the lodge, promising a very beautiful day.

I sat down in a chair and watched the kids play for a bit. Sarah smiled at me then returned to reading to Jacob. I sat back and let myself relax for a minute, then stood up as Charlie and Simon walked into the room. Simon was wearing his pack and looked like he was ready to keep moving.

"Not staying?" I asked, moving over to the big table.

Simon shook his head. "Just feel the need to keep on the move, you know? Maybe I'll find another place like this for myself. There's a lot of parks and such up north in Wisconsin and Michigan."

I nodded. "Probably. But you're taking a huge risk walking all that way."

Simon laughed. "I figure if I can get here from California, I can pretty much get anywhere."

I smiled. "True. Well, if you need anything or if you find yourself back this way, you're always welcome."

Simon extended his hand. "I appreciate that. I really do. I'm grateful for your hospitality, wish I could return the favor somehow."

Charlie nodded. "We'll think of something. Right now, the best thing you can do for us is to let anyone you meet know about us and if they want to come down to the communities, they're welcome."

Simon looked sober. "I can't begin to tell you how glad I am I met up with you guys. After what I saw in California, I figured it was every man for himself. But you guys really want to get the country back together, don't you?"

I considered my answer. "If we don't do something, then we'll fall apart, into little kingdoms where the only law is violence. We have been cursed with this virus, but in a way it has been a blessing. We've been given a chance to correct the mistakes we made in the past, to build a better, stronger country. We can't let the bastards win."

Simon and Charlie looked at me, then looked at each other. Charlie spoke first. "Now do you understand?"

Simon nodded. "I certainly do."

"What?" I asked, only to be ignored.

Simon headed for the door. "Thanks again. I'll probably be back this way someday, so look for me."

"Will do," I said .

Charlie went over to Julia and scooped her up. He motioned me to take Jake and picking him up, we followed Simon out onto the patio. "You have to see this," he said.

I was vastly curious, so I followed the three of them down to our drawbridge and watched as he lowered a section of the winding staircase down into place. Any zombies chasing us from the river would make it halfway up the stairs, then fall forty feet to a broken existence on the rocks below.

When we reached the bottom, we walked a ways towards the dock where our boat was tied up. When we had gone about halfway, Charlie put Julia on the ground and motioned that I should do the same with Jake. Curious, I put him down and watched him toddle over to Julia. The two of them walked together for a minute before settling down on the ground. Jake squealed as he played with a couple of sticks and Julia rolled a rock around.

A deep growl from the forest ahead caused me to whip out my SIG and train it on the woods. As I stepped forward to get the kids, Charlie held out a hand. "Hold on. Keep your gun out, but wait. You won't believe it."

I was doubtful as I waited and then turned incredulous as a huge cougar stepped from the shadows of the forest. It was ten feet long from nose to tip of tail and looked incredibly fit and healthy. It looked at me with deep green eyes and then looked at the other two men. After that it walked slowly towards the two children. I tensed, but Charlie shook his head. "Wait," he whispered.

The kids saw the big cat and laughed with delight. They walked and stumbled over to it and to my complete amazement, the big cat lay on its side as the kids came within reach of paw and fang.

Simon was just as stunned as I was. Charlie looked at the two of us and grinned as Jake and Julia played with the big cat, crawling on its side and tugging at its ears. The cougar was as gentle as a house cat with the babies. Charlie walked slowly over to the big cat and held out his hand. The cat sniffed him then let him rub its head. The deep grumbling I heard was a cougar equivalent of a purr.

Charlie motioned me over and I walked slowly over to the big cat, its eyes never leaving me as I reached out with my left hand, keeping my SIG in my other. The cat flattened its ears a little at me, but once it smelled me and recognized the scent from Jake, it was fine with me petting it. I shook my head in disbelief as I rubbed the fur of the great cat.

"Amazing, isn't it?" Charlie asked as the kids tumbled over the cougar. It rolled onto its back, stretching its great legs and flexing the hind claws, hooks that could disembowel a human in an instant.

"Yes, she is," I noted, discovering for the first time that our cougar friend was a female. I withdrew my hand from a yawning head, two inch fangs were not my favorite playthings. I was still amazed when the big cat leaned over and licked Jake across the face. He giggled, then buried his head in the cat's shoulder.

Suddenly, the cat rolled to its feet, tumbling the kids to the ground. I picked up Jake and Charlie grabbed Julia. I wasn't sure what was wrong, but the cat suddenly growled and lowered its head, bearing its fangs and growling. I looked back and saw the problem. Simon had come closer and since his was an unknown scent, the cougar had dropped into a defensive pose.

"Just step back slowly, Simon," I said, stepping away myself. Charlie was backing away with Julia, who was struggling to be put down again.

"No shit," said Simon, who stepped back quickly. The cat relaxed a bit, then with a final glance at Charlie and myself, disappeared into the woods.

I looked over at Charlie, who shrugged. I shook my head and said, "Well, its nice to know we have a kick-ass babysitter, although I sure won't leave the kids alone with her."

"No kidding," Charlie said. "But did you see her get protective? It's almost like she was getting ready to attack."

"Yeah, I saw *that*," Simon said shakily.

I laughed and we kept walking, heading down towards the river. When we reached the edge, I pointed to the west. "Follow that trail until you get to the north/south road. Head north across the river and you'll be in Utica. Keep going north and you'll hit I-80. Head west and you'll hit I-39. Take that as far north as you want. If you want to, Galena is a nice place. Head west on 20 until you hit it."

"Is it like this?" Simon asked, looking around again.

I shook my head. "More remote, more hills, lots of valleys and farms."

Simon considered it. "Maybe I'll head there. Look for me if you're up that way."

I nodded. "We'll be on the river if we do. Good luck." I shook his hand and he shook Charlie's. Shrugging his pack into a more comfortable place, Simon headed off down the trail, his long legs eating up the journey. Charlie and I watched until he rounded the bend in the river, then we turned back to the lodge. We had to get ready for a journey of our own.

8

We debated for a couple of days as to what we were going to do. I favored going up to Leport by myself and talking with Nate, while Charlie and Tommy thought it would be a good idea for more of us to go. Eventually it was decided that we all would take a trip to see old friends and acquaintances. Sarah and Rebecca were delighted to be heading back to Leport and I had to admit, I was looking forward to seeing some familiar faces as well. It had been a long winter and we needed to shake off the cabin fever that always came from too much cold weather.

As we carried our belongings down to where the boat was docked, a telltale moan wafted across the parking lot. All of us tensed as we looked for the source and Charlie finally spotted the lone Z working its way through the dense brush at the western edge of the main parking lot.

We waited for a moment and determined that it was alone. I waved on the rest of the crew and put my supplies down. I took off my backpack and rifle and after a moment's consideration, I put down my trusty pickaxe. Drawing just my knife, I walked quickly to the stumbling zombie. It groaned loudly and raised a hand in my direction. It was in better shape than some I had seen, making it a more recent convert to the undead. As I approached, its mouth opened in anticipation of a meal, baring dirty white, chipped teeth.

I dodged its outstretched arm, sweeping it aside with my left hand while bringing my knife hand up to bear. The zombie stumbled and in the second it took for the Z to regain its balance, I slammed the heavy tanto blade into its skull. The ghoul stiffened and I twisted the blade, scrambling its eggs. The corpse dropped and I pulled out my knife as it fell. Walking back to my stuff, I wiped off the blade and set flame to it with a lighter, burning away the virus.

Picking up my things, I noticed my entire crew was watching from the boat dock. Charlie was standing on a small rock, lowering his rifle as I came nearer.

Duncan spoke first. "Nice one. You make it look almost easy."

I nodded ruefully. "I wish I didn't. "

Tommy looked at me. "Why not?"

I tossed my gear into the boat. "Because it means I've been killing them for a long time. Takes something from you, you know?"

Everyone nodded, then boarded the boat, stowing gear below decks and making sure there wasn't anything for the kids to get into.

We pulled away from the dock and pointed the bow north and as we passed Eagles Nest, I was reminded of the note that first brought me here, over a year ago. I was searching for my brother and we managed to figure out he was here, waiting for me. Charlie and I realized what a great home this could become so we packed up our women, our kids, and the few belongings we had and made it our home. I couldn't imagine living anywhere else and as we pulled along the river, I began to think more of why we were making this journey and what the future might bring.

I was frowning into the breeze when Tommy came up and sat down next to me. We were passing the nearby towns and making our way to the big turn which would take us past Joslin.

"Gonna be nice to see some people again," he stated, watching the edge of the water. His blue eyes narrowed slightly and I looked to see what had attracted his attention. We both relaxed when a squirrel leapt from a tree to the water's edge.

I nodded, keeping my eyes to the shore. "Seems like we've been gone a long time, but when you seriously look back on it, it wasn't so much."

"Yeah," Tommy said. "But it's been busy. Listen, can I ask you a question?" he queried.

I turned to look at him. It seemed odd to me that Tommy was hesitant to talk to me. Normally he just shot his mouth off and took the consequences as they came. It was one of the things I liked about my friend. "Sure, fire away."

"What are we going to do after this is over?" Tommy looked intently at me and for once, I didn't think he was goofing around.

"What do you mean?" I asked, not understanding his question.

"I mean, what are we going to do after we travel thousands of miles through zombie infested territory, encountering who knows what kind of survivors, heading off this 'Major', and rescuing the Founding Documents? What then? Assuming we survive, of course."

I had to admit he had me stumped. I hadn't thought that far ahead and told him so.

Tommy shook his head. "Not good enough, brother. You can hold off the rest with answers like that, but you and me have been through too much for me to even *think* you haven't thought ahead."

I smiled and looked back to the passing river shoreline. "All right. You got me on that one. I did think a little about it and I do have something that resembles a plan, but we got a whole lot to do first."

Tommy stood up and clapped me on the shoulder. "I figured. Knowing you, it probably involves some sort of fire."

I laughed. "Ain't tellin'."

9

The rest of the trip was uneventful, save for a lot of zombie activity around Joslin. Dozens lined the shore, moaning and grasping. They looked to be in pretty sorry shape, although I found it grimly amusing that some were wearing what looked like gang banger clothing and jewelry. They weren't moving too well since their pants were around their ankles. Remembering what the family we rescued from the river near here told us about what the gangs had been doing, I found it fitting that the scum had joined ranks with the Z's.

Passing Joslin and the groaning groupies, we made our way upriver to the dead town of Romeoville. The zombies had been cleaned out of here last winter and the streets were silent. No one had wanted to try to set up another town here, so it just sat, content in its slow walk to decay and ruin. Many towns were in the same position, I would bet.

We moved past Freeport, throwing waves at the people who were out taking in the spring air. There were shouts of recognition and by the time we had passed, at least a hundred people had come down to wave hello. I had to admit, it felt good to be back in this area.

Rounding the bend, I got my first look at the improvements made by Nate in the community of Leport. The hills to the north were covered in small farm plots and there was ample grazing for the herds of animals found on the slopes just slightly to the south. I could see many people working their small plots of land, turning over the soil with hand tools, getting it ready for planting. I noticed two small buildings near the animal pens that hadn't been there before. I also noticed several guard towers on the tops of the highest hills, manned with two people each.

Pulling up slowly through the canal, Charlie eased the boat along the waterfront. I had picked up Jake and was standing with him on the front of the boat. I saw several people stop what they were doing to stare at the unusual visitors. I waved at one of them and he waved back, not really sure of who we were.

There was a shout and from a lookout tower I saw a figure running like hell towards a house. There was a small commotion, then I saw the huge form of my old friend Nate come outside, look in our direction, and even from this distance I could see him smile. He shouted back into the house, then began heading to the pier, yelling as he went. A small crowd was forming and working their way down to the docks.

Charlie pulled the boat up alongside the dock and a group of about forty people was waiting for us. I saw many familiar faces and I couldn't help but smile at them all. The boat was secured and we disembarked carefully one at a time.

I gave Jake to Sarah, who handed him back to me after I had left the boat. I was immediately swamped with greetings and spent several minutes shaking hands and meeting people. Sarah and Rebecca were hugging nearly every woman there and they spent a few minutes showing off their left hands to the giggling flock. Charlie came out last and he got as much attention as the rest of us, although he seemed shy about the attention.

Suddenly a shout cut off conversation. "What the hell's going on here? What's the matter with you people? Ain't you never seen a traveler before?" Nate strolled up, came within inches of me and growled into my face. "We got rules here, slick."

I was about to reply when Jake literally jumped off of me and wrapped his hands around Nate's neck, pulling him off balance and tumbling him to the ground. Nate twisted and landed heavily on his back with Jake sitting happily on his chest.

I laughed with the crowd and when the noise died down I said loud enough for everyone to hear, "You'd better be more polite or next time I'll find a *five*-year-old to seriously kick your ass."

Nate laughed out loud and I helped him to his feet. He handed Jake back to me, and I shook Nate's hand with all the enthusiasm I could muster. "It sure is good to see you again, old friend," I said warmly.

Nate smiled. "You too, buddy. You, too. C'mon, we'll get you guys to our visitors lodge, then I'll take you on a tour."

"Good enough," I said, as I shouldered my gear and set Jake down. Sarah came up beside me and took Jake's other hand.

Together we walked him down the street and up the hill. We waved to a number of people and a lot of people came out to shake hands and say hello. It was nice to be back.

On our way through the town, I noticed a lot of improvements. The homes were well-kept and there were lots of small garden plots in the lawns of many homes. A lot of homes had coops for chickens and areas for rabbits. We didn't have chickens at Starved Rock, so I actually began to hope we might get some eggs this trip.

One group of people caught my eye. There was a well-armed gaggle of what I assumed were teenagers sitting outside a building. They were watching us with undisguised interest and one of them, the leader, I guessed, looked over with as much insolence as he could muster. I didn't return the favor, figuring to leave well enough alone.

"Trouble, you think?" Charlie's barely audible voice reached me from behind.

"Maybe," I said. "We'll see what happens."

We reached about midpoint of the hill and Nate took us into a three-story building that looked like it once had been a business of some sort. It had been worked over and now looked like a decent place. Nate showed us our rooms and we stored our stuff. We talked for a minute and Charlie, Duncan, Tommy, and I decided to go with Nate on his tour, while the rest went to find old friends. Sarah took Jake with her and Rececca took Julia, so the kids were happy.

We walked over to Nate's place where he backed a large pick-up out of the garage. We climbed aboard and began our tour of the town.

Nate took us all the way down to what used to be Archer Avenue. We passed a thriving community, with several hundred occupied homes and places that looked like actual businesses. Charlie looked askance at Nate and he laughed.

"We trade, mostly. There's stuff to be had if you're willing to risk your neck getting closer to the city. But everyone gets what they need," he said.

I looked around and smiled to myself. *This is a nice place, but I think I'll take my lonesome lodge over fences and neighbors.* I looked back at Charlie and I could tell by the look on his face he was thinking the same thing.

We waved to a bunch of people and took in the rest of the town. The old ditch had been abandoned as a barrier and the new boundary was a highway divider fence that marked the new territories. It had the advantage of weight and portability. Six strong men could put up a fence relatively quickly.

I saw hopeful signs of life all around and everyone seemed to get along really well. I asked Nate about any internal troubles and he told me that he was surprised at how few problems there actually were. It was like people shrugged off the old complaints and got busy trying to live.

"We do have a new set of problems and I'm getting ready to deal with them," Nate said as he turned the corner to another part of town.

"What's that?" I asked as I watched a small boy helping his mother plant seeds in a backyard garden. It reminded me of Jake helping Sarah. He tended to try and eat the seeds.

"Well, there's a small group of young men who are eager to test themselves and have been causing trouble here and there. Picking fights and such."

"That wouldn't be a small group of well-armed kids I saw earlier?" I asked.

"The same," Nate said. "They've gotten bolder and there was a report of a possible assault, but nobody saw anything and they are sufficient in numbers and arms to intimidate any single person going after them."

I said nothing, but nodded.

Nate continued. "It's just a matter of time before someone gets killed and I was hoping to avoid those kinds of problems right now. We don't have a legal system here, everyone has been pretty much following the laws as we remember them, but we're thankfully short on lawyers."

"Want some advice?" I asked.

"Sure."

"Set up an official security team, made up of all able bodied persons in the community. Make a rotating schedule so everyone participates and above all, with a community this size, you need formal rules and regulations."

"Seems like a lot of work."

"Considering we've been shoved back a thousand years developmentally, I'd say you have little choice." I was hardly sympathetic.

"Thanks." Nate barely contained his sarcasm.

"My pleasure. Now you see why I'm on the frontier."

"Speaking of which, you never told me why you guys came back." Nate arched an eyebrow at me.

I shook my head. "I hate repeating myself, so I'll save it for later. We'll need to have everyone assembled for what I need to tell them."

Nate pulled the truck into his driveway. "Fair enough. I'll get the grapevine going. You all can relax for a while."

10

We spent the rest of the afternoon relaxing in Nate's house catching up and hearing about all the improvements the community had made. I was impressed with the aggressive moves to root out the zombies in the neighboring areas and to secure more and more zones. It felt like we had been just vacationing in our own little world compared to what was happening here. Nate assured me that we had earned the rest.

I did relent and told Nate about what we had learned about Major Thorton and his band of merry marauders. Nate cursed more eloquently than I had ever heard from him before and managed to stun even Tommy and Duncan into silence.

When he had finished, he looked pointedly at me and said in a deceptively calm voice. "So what are we going to do about it?"

I shrugged. "What choice do we have? We try to get there first. If we succeed, great. If he beats us to it, we make sure no one knows he destroyed it. The idea can remain alive, even if the document is not. We will use force if pushed."

Nate snorted. "I've seen you when you've been pushed. This should be interesting." He stood up and stretched, the rest of us doing the same. "I'm going to make sure the meeting gets rolling. We are meeting now at the old school gymnasium. We'll see you there in what, thirty minutes?"

"Deal. We'll be there. Let Sarah know where I am if you see her," I said, trying to work out a kink in my back.

Half an hour later, we stepped out into the growing darkness. The sun had set, but there was still a decent amount of light. We couldn't make out small details unless we were right on top of something, but we could still see fairly well. We walked two by two, Charlie and I in front with Duncan and Tommy bringing up the rear. We moved down the center of the road, heads moving to every sound, hands straying near pistols. We passed a few people on their way to the meeting and it was interesting to see how alert we were and how casual they had become. If I had to guess, I would bet most people within town limits were no longer arming themselves as a regular part of their day. I wondered if I would have given up my guns had I stayed here.

My wonderings were interrupted by a voice to my left. "Well, well. The big hero everyone's been talking about."

I looked over and saw the same kid I had seen earlier in the day. He was casually sitting on a porch swing, his hands in his lap. He was about six feet, maybe less, and had a wiry, lanky build, with slightly stooped shoulders. His long brown hair was held back by his ears and his aquiline features were accented by deep-set eyes. With his head down, his eyes were just pits of black.

I gave a hand signal to my friends and they kept walking, Tommy saying they'll see me at the meeting. I watched them walk to the end of the street, then they turned out of sight. I turned my attention back to the guy on the porch.

"You seem to know who I am, but I don't know you," I said, hooking my right thumb in my belt near my SIG. "Got a name or do I make one up for you?"

"Name's Dan Winters, not that it matters. I just wanted to see for myself who the big hero was. Our savior!" Winters said sarcastically, waving his hands in the air. He stood up and walked to the end of the porch. "I heard a lot about what you did and how you got the people to stick together. I even heard some interesting stories about what you may or may not have done south of here."

Winters came off the porch and walked out into the street. "I'm not so sure I believe what I have been hearing, because nobody is that bad ass. Nobody." Dan had come to a stop about five feet in front of me and he stood in a mocking pose similar to mine.

"Is there a point to this conversation?" I asked. "Because I need to go talk to some adults." I knew I was deliberately baiting him, but I didn't care. If Nate was going to have to deal with this idiot, I may as well get the ball started.

Dan bristled as most near-men do when their lack of age has been pointed out. "Point is, hero-man, that I think you're full of shit. I think all those stories are shit and the people who think you're so great are full of shit too."

He was pushing hard and I realized that he was nervous, like he was trying to get something over with before something went wrong. Too bad he didn't know what I knew. After Charlie, Duncan and Tommy had supposedly left, they circled back and made sure I wasn't going to be ambushed. I could handle idiot-boy on my own, but I was powerless against a bullet in the back.

I waited, not replying, and I could see Winters getting slightly more nervous as time stretched on. Finally, I heard the sounds I had been waiting for. On my right there was a strangling noise, like someone had just been put in a choke hold. On my left, there was stifled cry, as if someone had been hit, then silenced. Behind me, there was loud crashing sound, like someone had been bodily lifted and thrown to the ground.

I smiled at Dan and I could see his eyes widen as he began to realize this was not going as planned. I stepped up close as my companions dragged their victims through the yards and dumped them in the road. One of them started to get up, only to get pushed back by Tommy, who ended any further revolt by pulling his knife and shaking his head. His captive seemed fascinated by the large blade just a few inches from his face.

I stared hard at Winters. He seemed to recover his wits and was defiant once again. I realized there was little to be gained through talking to this idiot. I turned my back on him and his friends and signaled to my companions that we keep moving.

But Dan wouldn't let it go. "See you around, hero. You won this one, but maybe your woman or your kid won't win the next one." He sniggered to his friends who were loosely pulling themselves to their feet. His laugh turned to a cry as I wrapped my hand around his skinny throat and squeezed. His friends tried to intervene, but were knocked back with drawn weapons. This one belonged to just me.

I spun Winters to the ground and stepped back, watching him grasp at his throat and suck air. When he had recovered enough he bared his teeth and stepped up, looking to punch his way through. I sidestepped and landed a short jab to the side of his head, knocking him sideways and stunning him momentarily. He shook it off and charged, his head ducked low and his long arms outstretched to grab hold of me. I waited until he came close enough, then shoved quickly on the back of his neck, forcing him to the ground. I stepped away again before he could grab my legs and I waited again.

Winters got to his feet and advanced more cautiously this time, holding his hands up and looking for his opportunity. He must have learned to fight from rank amateurs and it made sense why no one had pummeled this fool earlier. He was too ridiculous to take seriously. But he threatened my family and that made him fair game as far as I was concerned.

I stepped in quickly and jabbed a left to his mouth, knocking his head back. Not waiting for him to recover I slammed a right to his head, knocking him to the ground. I reached down and removed his firearm, tossing it back to Duncan. I grabbed Dan by the hair and delivered three short, savage punches to his face, mashing his nose and splitting his lip. He tried to defend himself, but I knocked away his hands. I hauled him to his feet and held him by the neck. I forced him to look me in the eyes.

"You threatened my family, junior. That mistake you won't get a break from. If I ever see you near my wife or my son, I will kill you. I don't know how you and your idiot friends survived the Upheaval, but it sure wasn't through skill. But my friends and I? We are the real survivors. We're killers and we're good at our work." I brought Winters in quickly as I delivered a punch that started at my knees. I slammed him under the chin and he toppled back like a felled tree.

I looked back at his friends, who were being held on their knees by my crew. "Bring them," I said as I grabbed up a now unconscious Dan Winters by his collar and dragged him unceremoniously through the streets.

By the time we reached the school, we were more than a little late. Working our prisoners through to the gym, we opened the door to a surprised audience. Nate was speaking, but went silent as the four of us brought in our charges. Charlie, Duncan, and Tommy forced the trio to their knees again in front of the community, while I dragged Winters in and dumped him on the floor.

In response to the unspoken questions, I replied in simple terms. "He called me out, then threatened my family when his ambush failed." Sarah, who had been sitting in the front row holding Jake and waiting for me, flashed a very cold stare at

Winters. His life was forfeit on more than one front. "He got his only warning this evening."

Nate looked at us, then shrugged. "Solves my problem, thanks." I could see by the nods of approval in the crowd that this group of so called toughs had been making things difficult for a number of people.

Nate got the ball rolling. "John has come back and he has some information he feels you need." Nate was never one for long winded introductions. I personally was surprised that he hadn't cursed.

"Hey, everyone," I said, to a round of applause. I smiled and raised my hand, fairly certain I had not earned this praise. "Thank you for that. I am very happy to see many of you and I am especially glad to see many people I have not met, which means this community is growing and surviving." There was another round of applause. "I realize now that I should have come back sooner, but I will certainly remedy that situation in the future. Right now we have another concern and I wanted to talk to all of you to decide what we want to do about it."

I spent the next several minutes talking about meeting Simon and what he had to say about the situation in California. There were many dark looks as I gave the information and I could understand the source of their hatred. So many people had lost so much to this disease that having a group take such advantage and hold people in bondage and fear was anathema to them. I wrapped it up by letting the assemblage know what we had considered doing and why we had come up here. I wanted to know what the community thought about the situation and whether or not they actually cared as a group what happened to the documents of the Founders. If they figured it was a thing of the past and it was time to move on, then I was going to take a little vacation here and return home. But if they thought otherwise...

I didn't have to wait long. Nearly immediately people began to speak up, telling me we had to get the Bill of Rights and the Constitution. It was our duty as a people to save our heritage and preserve it for future generations. I thought that last one was a little over the top, but they were adamant. If someone could do something, shouldn't they?

I raised a hand for quiet and I presented the first problem as I saw it to the group. "So we're agreed that we should do something, with the probability being pretty strong that no one else really knows of this Thorton's plan. I figure he's not going to advertise it, although communications being as they are, they are getting better. So, we figure to get there first. Next question is who will go?"

That brought up the assembled short. While it was true they were all veterans of the war with the zombies, living in the communities had dulled their skills somewhat. If I had to guess, most hadn't been in training in months. If the zombies showed up, they could beat them back pretty well, but they might lose a few. One on one, I was confident anyone here could take a zombie, but taking a trek across over a thousand miles of the United States of Zombie, not a chance.

I smiled. "Well, since I don't have much else to do these days and you all are busy trying to rebuild civilization, I guess I should contribute in some way. I'll do it. Anyone else want to take a ride?"

There were a lot of nods of approval at this and a lot of men who wanted to raise their hands, but they were voted down by their better and probably smarter, halves. Tommy raised his hand, to the frown of Angela, and Duncan was actually a half step faster than Tommy. Charlie, of course, had his hand up and I was pleasantly surprised to see Nate's hand go up. In all, I had the crew I knew stood the best chance of making this run in one piece.

"All right," I said, heading over to Sarah and relieving her of a sleepy Jake. "We know what needs to be done. We'll start our planning tomorrow." The community filed out, each member taking the time to shake each of our hands and saying 'Thank You'. It was a nice gesture and a good indication that we were headed in the right direction as a people. We just needed to make sure we didn't let monsters like Major Thorton come out of the dark.

11

In the morning, we made our way down to Nate's house, where we would be planning the trip. Patty, Nate's wife, was just finishing up breakfast and we all sat down to an excellent meal. We made small talk over the food, talking about the things we had done over the year, the winter campaigns and such. It was nice to see how much progress had been made. In some areas, progress was still slow.

"How's the push to the city?" I asked, pushing my plate forward and resting a hand on Jake's head, after he had come to see what I was up to.

Nate shook his head. "It's still a dead zone. Two of Trevor's men went up for a look-see last winter and they said it was wall to wall zombies. Even with a thousand men, we'd never clear it before they thawed. It's still the source of a lot of zombies still haunting the secured areas."

"That bad?" asked Tommy.

"That bad," said Nate. "Ever hear of the town of Herret?"

Tommy shook his head. "First time."

Nate continued. "It was a small town located on the east side of Rockford. Got overrun a few months back. We had set up radio contact with them using the shortwaves, but all we could hear was someone screaming for help. Then we heard nothing. We checked the map and found that of the three towns that had been hit over the last summer, they were all in line from the city. So it's still a problem."

I moved Jake in the direction of Julia and he toddled off happily. I watched him go and turned my attention back to the table. "We'll deal with that later. Right now we need to figure out how to get from point A to point B and back without getting ourselves killed."

We talked for a while, ironing our strategies out and weighing the pros and cons of each. Duncan initially thought a boat trip was a good idea, being safe on the water, but it was pointed out that Niagara Falls was a bitch to sail over. Especially coming back. Eventually, we agreed to a land route and it had the advantages of being able to resupply more quickly, more options for escape, and it allowed us to see what was left of the country.

It was simpler to choose a vehicle for travel. Nate told me they had a large RV they had been using for extended scouting. It had been fitted with chain-link fencing over the windows and a reinforced roof with a sniper's fence. A plow had been attached to the front, hung low enough to keep the Z's from flowing under the RV. The whole thing had been raised six inches to allow for more clearance and retractable gangplanks allowed for roof access. It was diesel, so it wasn't as quiet as possible, but larger stores of gas could be found in trucks and distribution yards. It stood a good chance of taking us there.

The next part was harder. I knew I was going, but I needed someone else not to go. I motioned Charlie to come talk to me and we headed outside. Sarah and Rebecca looked at us quizzically, but didn't say anything.

Charlie was confused but came along. When we were outside, he asked me what was up.

I didn't waste time. "I want you to hang back from this trip, Charlie."

Charlie stared hard into my eyes. If I didn't know him as I did, it would have been unnerving. After a minute, he said, "Can I ask why?"

"I got a feeling about this one, bro. I got a feeling that if we both head off on this trip, our home won't be the same," I said. "I managed to get myself into this mess and I'll get myself out. But I would rest a whole lot easier knowing my old partner is watching the home fires."

Charlie turned thoughtful. "You think this Major fellow would come calling?"

I nodded. "If he's half the bastard Simon made him out to be, he might just want to be the only wolf in the woods. That means taking us out any way he can."

Charlie mulled that one over, then nodded. "If I was going, I'd want you to look after my family as well. All right."

I smiled and shook his hand. "Thanks, brother. I feel a lot better."

"Promise me one thing," Charlie said as we turned back to the house.

"Anything."

"Don't hog all the action. I get to kill me some scumbagstoo."

I laughed. "I hope it doesn't come to that, but I'll see what I can do."

We reached the house just as a teenage girl came running up. Nate spoke with her for a minute and then sent her on her way.

"News?" I asked.

"Yeah. That Dan Winters took off this morning, stealing one of the recon cars and making off with a bunch of food and ammo. Looks like he left with a couple of his cronies as well," Nate said.

"Good riddance, says I," I said, not giving it much thought.

"Maybe," said Nate. "I have a feeling that little punk will cause us trouble one way or the other."

We planned for a little while longer, then set up a time table. We would leave the day after tomorrow, giving us a full day and a half to gather what supplies we needed and fully plan our route. I had been through the country before, but I had a feeling I wouldn't recognize it now.

I went to visit my brother while I was in Leport and I was surprised to see how big my niece and nephew had become. Mike was very glad to see me, as was Nicole. We spent a good deal of time together and towards the end, I began to get the suspicion that Mike wanted to ask me something.

"Well, I need to get Sarah and Jake back to the house, they're heading out in the morning, going back to Starved Rock. It's been great seeing you all again." I gave the kids and Nicole a hug, then gave my brother one as well.

"John..." Mike began.

I looked at him. "What's on your mind, bro? You've been avoiding an issue since I got here. What is it?"

Mike looked at the ground, then looked at Nicole. Nicole broke the silence. "We were wondering if you had any room for another family out at your lodge."

I was taken aback. After Charlie and I had rescued my brother and his family from the Visitor Center at Starved Rock, I figured they wouldn't be in any hurry to return. "Of course, you're welcome. We have plenty of room. Get your stuff and we can take you on the boat back."

Mike gave me a big hug, then gave Nicole a hug and a kiss. Nicole hugged me and whispered "Thank you." in my ear. Sarah smiled and I found myself glad that my brother was coming with.

"Of course, there is a condition," I said ominously.

Mike looked at me, his eyes apprehensive. "What's that?"

"You have to train with Charlie to get your skills up. You're out on the frontier now and the only thing between you and living death is the skill and strength of your arm and the preparedness of your mind." I slapped him on the shoulder. "I ain't coming back to find you dead because you did something stupid."

Mike nodded and it seemed like he was looking forward to the challenge. I hoped he was, because Charlie took no prisoners.

We walked back to the house and Sarah and I spent some alone time together. Jake took a nap, which was convenient as hell.

Holding Sarah in my arms, I told her about the decision to keep Charlie back and she agreed with me, "Rebecca will be happy."

"I hope it all works out," I said, playing with a loose strand of her hair.

"Anything you need for us to do while you're gone?" she said, running a finger across my chest.

"When you pass the towns, pass the word on what we are doing and where we will bring the documents once we get them. Have each community send a representative here and we'll start the government process over."

Sarah sat up and leaned over me, her hair spilling across my face. "Are you serious?" she said.

"Very," I replied, running a hand down her back. "Once we get this thing settled, we're restarting our country. I've avoided it long enough, and we have to do something."

Sarah kissed me deeply, then rolled over, pulling me on top of her. "You have knack for hope, my dear. It's oddly arousing." She said as she settled herself beneath me.

"Indeed." I said as I kissed her, and then stopped talking for a while.

12

The next day I saw the loading of my family and my brother's family onto the boat. They headed off to a large crowd waving goodbye and as they pulled away, Charlie raised a hand to me, then made a fist, placing it on his heart. I repeated the gesture, knowing that he would defend to the death the families placed in his care. I would have done the same in his shoes. Mike waved goodbye for a while, then turned his attention back to his children, who were thrilled at being on a boat. Sarah held Jake up and they both waved goodbye. I stayed on the dock until the boat was out of sight, burning the image of my wife and son into my mind. It would be the image that I would draw strength from, should I ever need it.

Preparations went well and by nightfall the big vehicle was stocked with food, filled with fuel and armed with ammo. I was bringing my faithful AR, my ever present SIG and my M1A. The latter was to be used for serious fights. Tommy, Duncan and Nate were bringing their favorite toys as well. We were going to move out in the morning, keeping to the back roads. We were hopeful in finding more people out there, but after two years in the post Upheaval world, it was anyone's guess as to their state of mind. I had the feeling some were going to have to be brought back kicking and screaming.

I was standing on the dock, looking downriver at where my family went, when Tommy came up to me.

"I heard you were sending word that the towns should send up a representative, that we are going to start government again." He pitched a rock into the river.

"I did. Sarah got me thinking about it and I figure its time we did before too many 'Thortons" spring up and completely ruin what's left of this country. We need the good people to get up and fully make a stand. We need to wipe out the zombie threat and get our lives back once and for all."

"What's our role in that?" Tommy asked and I realized that Tommy and Duncan were at loose ends, looking for some definitive meaning to what they were doing. I had thought about it and had come up with a solution.

"To be honest, if we get the manpower, you, Charlie, Duncan, and I were going to lead the charge to get rid of the zombies once and for all. We'll turn over every rock, root out every Z we can find, and obliterate this damn virus once and for all," I said.

Tommy mulled that one over for a minute. "You know, a year ago, I would have thought you were crazy. But given how far we've come, you actually manage to give me hope that it can be done."

"Thanks. A year ago I would have thought I was crazy also, but since then I ...what's that?" I stopped midsentence and pointed to what seemed to be flickering lights coming up from the south on the far side of the canal.

Tommy stared for a moment then cursed. "Shit. Zombies," he said.

I realized he was right, the flickering lights were several pairs of bioluminescent eyeballs headed our way. Their path would take them up the hill to the overpass which would bring them down into the town. How the hell they got past the guard tower was a mystery, but irrelevant now.

I ran back to the town, stopping at Nate's to yell into his yard "Zombies reaching the bridge!" I bolted down the street towards the guest house where my gear was still stowed. Tommy was right on my heels and we both grabbed our favorite fighting tools.

Running out into the street we nearly collided with Nate who was rushing our way. He was armed with a .45 and a crowbar.

"What the fuck?" he growled, running alongside us to the intersection that would bring us to the long bridge that crossed the river.

"Tommy and I were on the docks when we saw the little dancing lights of zombie eyes across the way. They were headed for the hill to get across the water," I said, running at a steady pace. We passed several onlookers, who ran when Nate yelled out at them.

"Get inside, zombies inside the perimeter! Spread the word and arm yourselves!"

We reached the bridge and began the long run to intercept the zombies. I hoped like hell there weren't any of the little fast ones. Fighting them during the day was bad enough, but at night it was ten times worse.

We crossed the highest point and started down the other side. At the bottom of the hill were about ten dark shapes moving up from the shadows of the brush. I shouted to get their attention and to keep them from spreading out too far. I wanted them to come to us. I had no desire to go chasing down a zombie in the dark in the brush.

Nate and Tommy and I spread out as we slowed down and approached the zombies. There were eight of them, not too difficult a fight for the three of us. Their glowing eyes locked on us and the group as one sounded a chorus of moaning that echoed over the hills of the town.

Nate reached the zombies first and drew a bead with his .45. The heavy gun barked once and the nearest zombie's head turned inside out. Nate fired again and dropped a second. I had pulled my SIG out at this point and was firing. I killed two in short order, then heard Tommy open up on his side. We all retreated a step as the remaining three zombies moved around their fallen comrades and came towards us, oblivious that they looked death in the face. We all fired as one, the crashing volley reverberating over the hillside. Three zombies dropped in their tracks, staining the road with dark fluids.

I held up a hand and walked forward, looking for further signs of more enemies. I waited at the road's edge and listened intently. Sure enough, there was a dragging sound and the snapping of underbrush. I fished out my flashlight and shined it into the bushes. I caught a flash of grey moving behind the shrubs and I backed away, waiting for the inevitable.

The zombie fell through the bushes with a crash, then slowly began dragging itself to its feet. I could see why it was slower than the rest, one leg had been broken and was forced into a weird angle, keeping it from its speedier brethren. I shined the light in its face and noticed its neck had been torn open, explaining why it wasn't groaning. Its eyes were also not glowing, so this one would have been a nasty hunt in the dark if it had been whole. I lined up a shot and fired as it straightened to take a charge at me. It toppled back into the bushes, spreading out as if it had decided to lounge there all day. I turned the light off and listened again, but in the quiet I heard no movement.

I walked back to Nate and Tommy and they were just finishing up piling all the corpses for a fire.

"That the last of them?" Nate asked.

"Don't hear any more, although you might want to send out some searchers to make sure that wherever these got through, they're aren't any more on the way," I said, holstering my SIG.

"Got that, right after I kick the shit out of whatever guard let them through without warning." Nate grumbled.

"There is that," I said, looking over to the dark guard tower. Whoever let this happen just opened a fresh can of whup-ass.

We walked back over the bridge and found ourselves facing a crowd of about ten men with rifles trained on us. When they saw who we were they lowered their weapons, although there were questions in their eyes.

Nate spoke up. "Clean-up tomorrow! Check the lists to see whose turn it is. Search team beta needs to cross the river tomorrow and do a sweep of the whole area. Search team Alpha needs to check the guard tower first thing in the morning and find the breach."

There were nods as people packed up their weapons and headed back to their homes. I was impressed with the efficiency of these people and told Nate so. He waved off the compliment.

"We do what's necessary. We're all the fence that keeps the demons at bay. You taught us that, John," Nate said. "You insisted everyone train for battle. If we didn't have the barriers, we'd still have the fence of arms."

I was glad to hear it and very glad that this community was destined to survive. All we needed to do was to make sure the country survived so we could make up for the mistakes of the past.

In the morning, we piled about our battle wagon and pointed it south. I sat next to Nate who drove. Tommy and Duncan sat at the little kitchen table and cleaned and sharpened weapons. Boxes of ammo were open and extra magazines were loaded.

Nate fired up the big RV and looked over at me.

I nodded and said, "Strap yourselves in, its gonna be a bumpy ride."

13

(TWO WEEKS AGO)

Major Thorton was bored. They had been on the road for several days and had passed several small towns. None of the towns had been inhabited and Thorton was itching for some kind of action. Any kind of action.

The convoy had been following Route 6 out of California and had made their way to Ely, Nevada. There they picked up Route 50, which according to the maps, should take them all the way across the country. But they had to make some jogs through some more inhabited country, so Thorton was confident something would happen soon.

There had been the occasional dead walker, but the convoy chose to ignore the minor threat rather than stop moving. They had been making pretty good progress, all things considered. With most of the world dead, the road crews were not out to clear the debris from the roads that accumulated every spring from thawing hills and falling rocks. Several times the convoy would stop while men cleared the way.

The last action the Major saw was during one of the stops, a lone zombie was working its way up the road and was nearly on the men before they spotted it. In the scramble to get away, the zombie lumbered on, focused on one lone trooper who raised his weapon to fire, only to have it knocked away by Thorton.

"Don't waste ammo, dumbass," Thorton said, waiting for the zombie to get closer before he stepped up and shoved his boot in its chest. The zombie flew backwards, over the roadside and down the mountain. Before it was dashed on the rocks below, the tumble down the terrain literally knocked the zombie to pieces.

The Major had glared at his men. "Use your brains. It's the only thing that separates you from them."

That was four days ago. They had crossed most of Nevada and were coming up on the town of Beaver. It was thought that they might try the interstate and see how things were before continuing on side roads. Riding in from the west, Major

Thorton could see the I-15 interstate as it loomed above him and the outskirts of the small town. The sign read a population of over two thousand, but in surveying the quiet streets, Thorton had his doubts.

He signaled his driver to slow down, to take a look at things. The town didn't seem too much the worse for wear, but Thorton knew that any town close to an interstate had a high likelihood of infection. They followed West Center street into the town and there was some evidence of problems. There was a car that had crashed into a tree and the inside was covered in old blood.

As they travelled further into the town, there were some homes that had dirty rags hanging from the mailboxes, reminders of the futility of hoping that the disease could be contained and controlled. As they passed by, Thorton began to get a familiar feeling between his shoulder blades, a feeling that told him something was wrong about this setup.

They turned up North Main Street and Thorton signaled a stop. He had seen the Sheriff's office and wondered if there were any weapons to be recovered. Stepping out into the street, he adjusted his belt and signaled to the truck behind him that he wanted three men to accompany him. Lt. Tamikara got out of his vehicle and two other men came at his beckoning.

Major Thorton walked over to the three men. "Let's take a look at the police station, see if there is anything worth taking." Thorton looked down the streets and back at Tamikara, who was looking at him. The other two men headed for the police station.

"Sir?" asked Tamikara.

"What is it?"

"Do you feel anything strange about this place?"

Thorton looked around. "Yeah, I do. Can't put my finger on it, but there's something seriously wrong here."

"I agree. Do we need to stay?" Tamikara, normally emotionless, actually seemed nervous. Thorton was somewhat amazed.

"No. Something is telling me to get the hell out of here," said the Major.

The two men who went to the police station walked out, each holding a shotgun and what looked like some ammo. Neither was talking and they both looked shaken.

"What's up with you two?" snapped Tamikara, his own nervousness showing.

The first private spoke up. "Sir, you better go look for yourself."

Morbidly curious, Major Thorton walked over to the station and cautiously peered in. He wasn't scared, knowing he was more than a match for any dead thing and most, if not all, live things. But the unknown was a different factor and his warning bells were screaming at him right now.

He looked inside and didn't see anything seriously out of order. There were papers on the floor and an overturned chair, but nothing else. He looked down the dark hallway and could see cell doors at the end of the hall. Moving cautiously, he slowly followed the hall and stood at the end, fully taking in the grim scene before him. In the cells were about fifty people, all huddled together. Men, women, children, all tucked into little positions. Dead babies were held by their dead mothers and dead fathers wrapped their protective arms around their dead children. Curiously, all the bodies were as far away from the bars as possible. Thorton was confused about that until he looked down and saw what had happened. Around the cages were hundreds of footprints, dark and foreboding. Zombies had trapped these people here and paced outside the bars until the trapped people died from hunger and thirst.

Ken backed away, leaving that hellish scene of torment and hopelessness. He walked back down the hall, more intent than ever to get away. He had seen some nasty things, but this was up there with the best.

Walking out of the building, he saw many faces turned to look at him. He waved his hand dismissively, then shouted for everyone to mount up. When the trucks were rolling again, he told his driver to head north. The entrance to the interstate was up that way and he wanted to get out of this town.

As they headed up Main Street, a though kept nagging at Thorton. What happened to the rest of the town? If those fifty people were the last of the living, this place was a couple grand zombies short of an explanation. It was possible that the remainder of the town had melted away into the countryside, but there should have been something. It was just strange and kept getting stranger.

The convoy passed the last of the businesses and started the slow curve to get to the highway. On the left was Beaver Valley Hospital and even from a distance of two hundred meters, Thorton could tell it had been hard hit. Burn marks above blown out windows told the story of a fire out of control, while crashed vehicles told the tale of people rushing with their sick loved ones to the emergency room before they knew what horrors they were transporting.

As they curved around the building, Major Thorton looked hard at the hospital. Sure enough, there was movement. About forty small shapes detached themselves from the shadows of the building and headed out across the open field which separated the hospital from the vehicles. They were moving fast, much faster than they should have been.

"Shit. Kids, coming up on our left." Thorton was about to radio to the vehicles behind him when something on his right caught his attention. A man and a woman were racing out from a house on side street, carrying what looked like backpacks. They were waving their arms and shouting, hoping to get a ride. Thorton looked over at the approaching horde and back at the two, mentally calculating distance and time and who might reach them first.

He reached a decision. "Speed up." He turned and pulled a standard AR-15 from the rack and watched the other two vehicles speed up as well, leaving the couple racing for their lives ahead of a pack of hungry zombie kids.

"Stop here," he ordered, getting out of the vehicle and stepping to the side. He sighted his rifle and fired once, hitting the running man in the leg. The bullet smashed into the man's thigh, flipping him over and leaving him on the ground. His woman screamed and ran back to him, pulling on him and trying to get him to stand up to run again. The zombie children raced closer, some of them leering in anticipation.

Thorton fired again, striking the woman just above her left knee. She and her husband fell to the ground, unable to run any more. Major Thorton lowered his rifle and watched with interest as the zombies closed the distance on the struggling pair. One hundred yards, then seventy five, then fifty.

At thirty yards, the man proved he was down but still a fighter. He pulled a gun and giving his woman a final kiss, placed the gun against her head and pulled the trigger, surprising the hell out of the Major. Still full of fight, the man fired a dozen shots at the man who shot him, causing Thorton to duck for cover and scramble back into his vehicle as bullets whipped past him.

As the zombies came within reach, the man fired his last shot into his own mouth, blowing the back of his head off and falling lifeless at the feet of the zombies who quickly tore him and his wife apart, ravenous for fresh meat.

Thorton threw himself into his seat as his driver pulled away, sullen that his fun hadn't been so much fun and his men saw him scramble for cover from a man who proved to be game to the end.

In the second vehicle, Captain Tamikara smiled to himself as they continued driving to Interstate 15.

The interstate seemed to be a good bet as they pulled onto the main road. There were cars here and there, but nothing like the jams that clogged the streets around most cities and towns. The cars that were there were off to the side and abandoned, indicating that they had simply run out of gas. Debris and personal items were scattered around and Thorton kept an eye out for anything that might be useful. The cars they didn't even bother checking for leftover gas.

On the right of the convoy was Fishlake Forest and Thorton briefly thought about camping there for the night, figuring the trees would serve as a decent natural barrier, but that would require him to actually discomfort himself, which Thorton thoroughly believed beneath his dignity. The fact that his dignity had taken a serious blow just moments before was already forgotten.

Travel went fairly swiftly and Thorton and his men started to get the notion that they would be able to take the highways most of the way across the country, saving a lot of time and trouble. The simple truth that the convoy had been on the road for a week and had not experienced any serious threats should have been a warning, but such was the arrogance of the group that they believed themselves to be possessing better luck than most.

The joy ride came to an end after they crossed into Colorado on I-70 and came near Grand Junction. The gridlock became much worse and Thorton could see many cars that showed signs of violence. Two accidents had snarled the majority of the cars and the steep embankment showed signs of cars that had tried to get off the highway and go around the mess. Several were rolled over and upside down at the bottom. More than a few cars had active zombies in them, clawing at the windows and struggling in their seatbelts. Whole families had been turned and it was weird to see a family of four twisting in their seats, acting for all the world like they had decided to take a zombie holiday, wound up in traffic and now needed to use the bathroom.

Thorton radioed back to the second truck. "Send two men up to see if we can get around this." He was not happy, but he was practical. The road curved around a hill and Thorton wanted to see if the logjam was just here or if it extended beyond.

The two men moved forward and with a nervous glance back at the safety of the trucks, weaved their way into traffic. The cars were close together, with barely enough room to walk through. The panic had caused the motorists to drive four abreast on a three-lane road, using up most of the available room. The soldiers walked quickly past the occupied cars, fingernails claw at windows while dead faces pressed themselves against the glass, snapping at the food just out of reach.

As the men kept moving, they noticed that some of the vehicle's occupants were dead, but not zombies. They were usually lying together, huddled into little balls. Bloody handprints covered the windows and it was not difficult to figure out that these families had been trapped in their vehicles, not able to get out and slowly dehydrated while the dead moaned and clawed at the windows. What sort of desperate last hours that must have been, slowly dying while ghouls leered and slavered for flesh just inches away? What kind of feeling of failure did parents feel when they helplessly watched their children die, crying for relief?

The men kept moving and they reached a point where the attacks on the occupants had become much more vicious, cars with broken glass and blood splattered everywhere. Body parts that had been ripped off were scattered about, a large number of them fingers and hands. Many cars had been abandoned as people ran from the attacks, further jamming the traffic. Here hands grasped the air as the men approached and hungry eyes followed their every move.

Looking for an alternative route, the men looked to the side of the road, but one glance over the side rail tossed that notion. The land dropped quickly and at the bottom of the hill was a crowd of around fifty zombies. They were simply milling about, drawn to the scent of death from the road, but when they saw the men looking down at them, they groaned their hunger and tried to scramble up the hill, but it was too steep.

One of the men realized that the zombies stuck in the cars couldn't reach very far. Jumping up onto a hood, the soldier scrambled over the car, avoiding the rotting hands that grabbed at him as he passed. The other soldier realized he was being left behind and recognizing the value of the idea, quickly jumped up on another vehicle and proceeded to move forward.

Back in the first truck, Major Thorton was waiting impatiently, but smiled as he saw the men climb up on top of the vehicles. *Gonna have to promote that little smarty*, Thorton thought to himself. He adjusted his belt, which held his favorite firearm, a Smith & Wesson Model 629 in .44 magnum. It was a custom job in its previous life and had a three inch barrel, ported to help recoil. Thorton had relieved it from its previous owner, who had used the large handgun to turn his head into a bowl.

The men reached the corner and disappeared for a moment, reappearing again as they made their way back. They seemed to be moving faster than they had been heading out and Thorton was curious until he saw the large horde of zombies working their way through the cars in pursuit of the soldiers. It said something about the discipline Thorton utilized, as these men had not stayed and fought, but used their heads and ran from a fight they couldn't win, saving their butts and their ammo.

The men made it back to the vehicles just in time for the major to order a turnaround of the vehicles. They drove quickly away from the advancing horde, but Thorton didn't want to backtrack any further than he had to. So when the road leveled out, he ordered the trucks to head off the highway and off road it in the direction he wanted to go. He was unaware of the second horde that was at the bottom of the hill waiting for him as he moved his men closer to the slaughter.

The men who scouted and knew what they were getting into, screamed at Captain Tamikara to radio to Thorton, that they were headed to disaster. Tamikara relayed the information but received, "Thanks. Keep moving," as a reply. Tamikara was sure Thorton was going to get them killed, but he had no choice but to follow. If he broke off and went his own way, he would be killed by Thorton if he lived and ever caught up to him again. The Captain shook his head and wondered for the millionth time why he ever hooked up with this lunatic.

For his part, Thorton finally saw the danger and realized he had made a bit of a mistake. But as he looked at the horde, he realized they were hanging around the hill and were away from the flatter part of the land. "Gun it." Ken said to his driver and relayed the same message to the trucks behind. They bounced precariously over unseen obstacles, but managed to get past the majority of the horde before the zombies had the wit to turn and start after. Two of them were directly in front of the truck and were mowed down where they stood. The struck zombies smashed to pieces and gooey bits of ghoul stuck to the windshield. The driver never slowed and slewed the truck around a large group, sideswiping several of them and sending them flying in the opposite direction. The rest of the horde, which had begun chasing the trucks, groaned their frustration as the fresh meat quickly drove away.

Thorton smiled, noting the danger in the mirror. It was a close call to be sure, but as long as the vehicles kept moving and didn't hit any obstacles and get stopped, they would pull through. The last vehicle, not keeping as close as they should have, wound up slamming into several zombies and running over several more. They bounced over the bodies and nearly lost control, but the driver kept his head and swerved around the growing horde. As they pulled away, several zombies spun along the ground and struggled to get up with broken legs and arms. Some didn't get up at all.

Driving away from the zombies, Thorton's driver had his hands full finding a route suitable for a truck that wouldn't damage the undercarriage. After a particularly nasty bump, the Major growled, "We need to find a road."

The driver nodded and pulled to a stop in a small open area. The highway could be seen to the north and Grand

Junction just beyond. The driver pulled out a map and quickly scanned where he was and where they wanted to be. "Sir, we can get on Route 50 and take that around Denver, where we should see less of what we just went through," he said.

Thorton glanced at the map. "How soon?" he asked.

The driver looked at the map, checked his bearings and said, pointing East. "Five miles that way."

"Go." Thorton knew the horde behind them would be catching up if they stayed much longer and they had no idea what they were going to meet in the country. If Grand Junction was infested and it was likely as hell that Denver was, then there was probably hundreds, if not thousands, of zombies roaming the countryside in search of something to chew on.

The convoy moved slowly through the country, passing small ranches and homes, each one abandoned and desolate. Thorton idly considered spending the night in one of the homes, but they were too close to the towns for comfort and he knew the sound of the engines would draw out many more zombies than were currently here. Sound carried far in the open country and he could already see stirrings on the horizon and near the dark draws. It was past noon and they were going to have to find a defendable place to spend the night.

In a short time, they came across a road, which after a brief check of the map took them north to an intersection. At the intersection, the driver stopped for a second, then turned right. His faith was rewarded by a bullet-marked sign labeled Route 50. Thorton looked over at his driver and said, "Well done." The driver beamed.

The radio crackled to life. "Sir?"

Thorton picked up the receiver. "Go ahead."

"I just checked the map and if we stay on 50 we'll be able to take it all the way across country and avoid most cities. There's a bunch of towns, though." Tamikara's voice came through loud and clear.

"Well, at least we won't have to worry about supplies then, will we? Thorton out." Ken put the radio down and looked over at his driver. "Very well done," he said. "Congratulations, you're a corporal now."

Ken's driver preened at the praise and promotion. He was already thinking about what he was going to do with his extra share of spoils, should they come across any. That was the way it worked in Major Thorton's army. The higher the rank, the higher the percentage of loot and the sooner they got to the women. The rank and file privates had a long wait for their turn.

Route 50 was fairly deserted, despite being a well-maintained road. They passed several cars, but they were empty and had nothing of value or interest. One had a zombie teenage girl tied up in the back seat, duct tape across its mouth, an indication that a family just couldn't let go of their loved one, even though they knew how deadly it was. The zombie just eyed the trucks as they rolled past, impotent in its bonds.

The first town they approached of any size was Gunnison, but as they rolled through, it was clear the town had been abandoned. No attempt had been made for defense and the stores had been looted. They stopped briefly at the gas station and were rewarded with several gallons of gas from the underground tanks. A summative scouting of the town revealed nothing of value and Thorton did not want to spend the night in a defenseless place. There were no suitable buildings for keeping the zombies out and ammo was to be used for emergencies, not just popping the odd undead.

After Gunnison, the convoy reached Solida, which needed to be skirted. The town was ringed with a tall chain-link fence, but there were hundreds of zombies roaming the streets. Thorton guessed that they managed to keep the infection out, but didn't know they had it within until it was too late.

Lincoln Park, Pueblo and La Junta were pretty much the same story and the men of the convoy began to wonder if there was any area of the country which had successfully resisted the zombie hordes.

As the sun began to dip lower, the convoy approached a town with the name of Lomar. The population sign said there were supposed to be eight thousand people living in the town, but given the level of activity that could be seen, there were far fewer. But it was a live town, which made it very special in this part of the country.

Thorton grabbed the radio. "We need to be straight military. Pass the word." He then opened the back window which gave him access to the back of the truck. "We're approaching a live town. Act like real military and this will be easy."

Ken adjusted his belt and holster and made sure his uniform was in place. He brushed off his medal bars and checked his look in the visor mirror. *Should be good enough to get in, at least.* he thought. After that it was all up to the town.

The town was a sprawling affair and as they moved in, they could see that the area had been hit. Dozens of small homes had been destroyed and every one of them had a dirty white flag hanging limply from the mailbox. The center road was fairly open and the trucks only had to go around a few vehicles. There were zombies in the homes, but since they seemed to be contained, there was little danger.

Things got interesting as they approached the northern end of the town. A barrier, which from a distance Thorton thought was brush, turned out to be piles and piles and piles of furniture. Every house that could have been looted of its furniture seemed to have summarily done so and it had been unceremoniously dumped to build this barrier. Chairs, tables, dressers, china hutches, entertainment consoles, everything that could be used was. The convoy drove along this interesting obstacle and the Major had to smile at the ingenuity of the people. Use what you have until you don't have it anymore. People in Western states were like that. They were practical to a fault.

Following the pile of stuff, the convoy turned in to another area and moved along the road at a quicker pace. This area had been cleared out and several of the homes had gardens planted in what used to be their front lawns. The obvious signs of life encouraged the men in the trucks.

The trucks moved along the road and stopped at an earthen barrier which encircled this part of the town. An old box truck served as a gate and two semi truck trailers were upended to make guard towers. As the convoy approached, Thorton saw increased activity as the town became aware of the trucks. He was acutely aware of the men in the towers who held high-powered scoped rifles at the ready. If trouble came, they would have to be first.

Major Thorton motioned his driver to stop and he got out of the truck. He signaled for Tamikara to join him and the little Captain hopped out of the second truck. He waited for

Tamikara to catch up and together they walked up to the barricade. At twenty feet from the gate, they stopped and hailed the men in the towers. Thorton kept his hands behind him, somewhere he had heard military men do that sort of thing. It had the effect of accenting his shoulders and neck, making him look even more imposing than he already was.

In a matter of minutes, the box truck rolled aside and a group of four men walked out to meet the visitors. They were stereotypical western men: thin, sharp-eyed and rough. These were men who had seen bad winters and cruel summers. They were used to accepting what life had to throw at them and rolled with the punches.

"Afternoon. My name's Brent Rowdan. Who might you be?" Brent's eyes roamed over Thorton's uniform, halting briefly on the medals and the sidearm.

Thorton was aware of the scrutiny. He shifted and placed his hands near his sides. "Major Ken Thorton, United States Army, at your service. We're glad to see you folks alive after the mess."

Brent shrugged. "Given the choices, wasn't much we could do. We lost a good portion of the town, though." He pointed to a large pit off in the distance.

"How many of you are left?" Thorton asked, looking over the onlookers.

"'Bout a hundred, give or take. I ain't counted recently, you understand." Brent said.

"I'll get to the point. We're on a reconnaissance mission to determine whether or not there are usable assets in a given area, specifically any military personnel who may have left post or are defending an area. Tamikara remained silent next to him.

"We would like to spend the night here, if we may, then push on in the morning," Ken continued.

Brent cocked his head. "Not meanin' no offense, but how many men are we talkin' about?"

"Is there a problem?" Thorton asked, his suspicious nature rising quickly.

"Not at all major," said Rowdan. "Just thinking about supplies and trying to feed all of you."

Major Thorton smiled and used his winningest smile. "Don't worry yourself. We will have everything we need." The look in Thorton's eyes would have any sane man reaching for a gun.

But Brent just shrugged and signaled for the truck to be moved back and the three military trucks rumbled through the entrance.

Brent's eyed drifted back to his assembled men and one of them, an older gent, just shook his head. Brent wandered over to the old man and after several heated moments of furious discussion, Brent's shoulders slumped slightly in defeat. He had just let a viper in his home, now he had to get rid of it.

Inside the perimeter, the trucks moved to the center of the town, where a neat square could be found. The trucks stopped outside the town hall and the men spilled out of the trucks. They stood in squads and their NCO's issued quiet orders. Safeties were quietly clicked off and magazines covertly checked. Major Thorton and Captain Tamikara huddled together for an instant, then broke apart as Brent Rowdan and about twenty armed men approached the convoy. The men on both sides eyed each other warily as their leaders met again.

Brent was brief. "You all can camp here, there's still water in the wells for whatever you need. When will you be moving on?"

Thorton looked at Brent a full minute before replying. "All things considered, Mr. Rowdan, I am probably the last ranking officer in the military, which gives me the authority of the United States Government. Technically, this town falls under my authority."

Brent didn't look convinced. "Ordinarily, you'd be right. But since your authority comes from the U.S. Government, which don't rightly exist anymore, leastaways not that we've heard of lately, your authority applies just to military personnel.

"We got nothing against you men, long as you're peaceful, but if you're otherwise, I'd say you need to move on."

Thorton looked at Tamikara, who looked at his men. "I understand your concerns, Mr. Rowdan. I really do. But you wouldn't turn out a group of men who just need a place to sleep for the night, would you?"

Rowdan looked ashamed. "I didn't mean to send you out now, but I do not agree with your authority over this town. I think you might know why."

Major Thorton narrowed his eyes and looked down at the smaller man. "Why would that be?" He was not used to being resisted and it rankled.

"You ain't military," said an older gent carrying a pump shotgun. "No officer I ever saw carried a revolver like that," he pointed to the magnum at Thorton's hip. "And your medals don't make sense. You got a Navy Cross and a Vietnam Pin, but you ain't Navy and too young to be in Vietnam."

Thorton chuckled. "Well, well. It was bound to happen sometime." He casually drew his revolver and fired it into the chest of the older gent who pointed out the flaws in the ruse. The heavy slug threw the older man back, dead before he hit the ground.

While the rest of the townsmen were shocked for a second at the unprovoked violence, the fake soldiers opened up with their weapons.

It was a slaughter. The townsmen had no chance to react and were cut down mercilessly. Tamikara dispatched three men to deal with the men in the towers and spread the rest out to sweep the town and get rid of any resistance.

"Round them all up and bring them here." Thorton ordered, standing over the dying bodies of the town's defenders. "If they fight, kill them."

In half an hour, the inhabitants of the town had been rounded up. There were many cries of dismay at the bodies of the men who had been shot and many of the women were crying. There were only five men who survived the assault and there were thirty-five women and twenty children who survived as well. Thorton looked over his prisoners and a pretty young girl caught his eye. He smiled. His bed would be warm tonight.

The prisoners were on their knees in the grass, facing the killed defenders. Women held their children and those without children held each other. Thorton stood in front of the dead and addressed the survivors.

"I am Major Thorton and you all belong to me. Whether or not you survive the night depends on how accommodating you are." A snicker arose from his men's ranks. The anticipation in the faces of the fake soldiers was evident and many of the women cringed, knowing what was in their future.

"To make you more accommodating, I have an incentive program." He nodded to his captain, who signaled his men. The men moved through the prisoners and took the children away from their mothers. Every child under the age of ten and over the age of two was taken away. They screamed for their mothers, who were kicked back when they tried to fight off the soldiers. The children were placed into the bed of a truck, with the older ones being told to take care of the younger ones.

Once they were quieted down, three men stationed themselves onto a picnic table that had been moved close to the truck. The men pointed their weapons at the canvas walls of the truck. There were several shrieks from the women.

Thorton spoke again. "If anyone resists, these men open fire. If anyone tries to escape, they open fire. If any of my men is harmed, they open fire. If I am displeased by *anything*, they will open fire. Do you understand?"

Defeated, there were several nods of agreement. Thorton smiled. "I'm glad we understand each other." He stepped forward and grabbed the arm of the girl he had picked earlier. There was a moment of anger that passed over her eyes, but she looked at the truck and submitted without a word. "You're with me. Consider yourself fortunate. I'm real kind to those who like me."

Thorton dragged the girl over to the nearest house and called over his shoulder "First squad, take the north side of town, find anything that we can use. Second squad, you're up for weapons and food. Third squad, you get to go first."

There were whoops of joy at this proclamation and some groans. But louder than both were the cries from the women who were chosen to service the conquerors. Women were dragged into nearby homes, businesses and alleyways to be assaulted. Clothing was ripped off, backs bent over counters and chairs, while hands clawed at the dirt, the floor and bedcovers. Death and pain had come to Lomar.

When one squad was finished, another would begin, so each woman was raped not once, but at least twice. The prettier ones were raped several times, leaving them broken when the men were finished. Supplies were stolen from homes, ammunition hordes were confiscated and useful tools were taken. Cries sounded from the truck in the center of town, scared children who just wanted their mothers and were forced to hear their parents' screams of pain and humiliation. The men who guarded the truck taunted the children, pointing out to them cries that could be their parents and laughing at the screams of rage and terror.

In the morning, the soldiers brought the women back to the center of town, many of them trying to hold their dignity together with strips of clothing. The mothers ran to the truck and their children were released to them. Tears of joy and concern flowed from both mother and child. The soldiers jeered at the children and women, then aimed their attention at another atrocity. Around the square, from various branches of the cottonwood trees, swayed the bodies of the surviving men. Thorton had the idea to hang them, tying a rope around each man's throat and lifting him a few feet off the ground.

Thorton was in a good mood. He had enjoyed himself thoroughly with his own prisoner and had left her tied to the bed he had raped her in. Since he had slowly broken her neck as a parting gift, she was in no condition to complain.

Thorton had his men mount up and as they pulled out of the town, he had the gate torn apart. He then set fire to the first row of homes near the gate. As the flames climbed high, black smoke rolled up in the morning breeze, sending a huge plume of black smoke up into the lightening sky.

That ought to attract a few zombies to this place. Thorton thought to himself as the truck rolled out east. He couldn't care less about the survivors of his assault on the town. He had been satisfied and he had caused a great deal of misery on other people. It had been a good night. The fires backlight the trucks, throwing red onto the faces of the men who bothered to look back. They were unaware of the hate-filled eyes that followed them, tearfully damning them for what they had done. It was a look that would repeat itself again and again.

Ken Thorton stretched in the cab and looked out the window. The sign that welcomed him to Kansas had no idea what kind of devil it was inviting to visit.

14

BLAM!

"Jesus, Nate. He's right there."

BLAM!

"You know, he's not even moving."

BLAM!

"C'mon, Nate. The guys are watching."

BLAM!

"Finally! When was the last time you fired a gun?" I stepped over to the railing that Nate had rested his rifle on and peered at the scene across the waterway. A mother and her son had been treed by a roaming zombie and they were well on their way to dying in one form or another when we happened across the situation. Nate had decided to ride to the rescue and steadied himself for what should have been a single shot. The zombie had been only fifty yards away, an easy shot for any of my crew. But Nate, living as he had been with the community and spending his days training, seemed to have let his firearms skills lapse.

Nate stood up from his rest and glared at me. "I'm not sure when I may have shot last, but I'm gettin' a good idea as to when I'm shootin' *next*." He threw a single finger salute to the rest of the crew, who were standing over by the RV.

I laughed to ease the tension as Tommy came over to where I was standing and watched as the pair climbed down from the tree. I had my own rifle at the ready in case any other zombies had been attracted by the shots. The mother and son went to the small canal's edge and drank deeply, likely their first drink in a couple of days. When they finished, they returned to their vehicle, threw us a wave and drove quickly off. They knew that shots were likely drawing more undead to the area, so it was better to keep moving and get to a safer place.

I returned the wave and continued to watch the treeline.

"Four shots," was all Tommy said.

"Yep," I replied.

"You could have nailed him with your SIG, couldn't you?" Tommy asked as he tossed a small stick into the water.

"We all could have," I sighed. Long range pistol shots was something we had practiced, the logic being you never knew what kind of situation you might find yourself in, with or without your rifle. You just had to know your gun, know your sights and adjust accordingly. Charlie had gone to the trouble of notching his front sight, marking the lines where he could make thirty, forty and fifty-yard shots. Past that, it was a game of artillery with a semi-auto.

In this case, it was about forty yards from where we stood to where the zombie had been. In a way it worried me a little, but a logical part of me realized that Nate was just out of practice, that he would regain his skills the longer we were on the road.

At least that was what I hoped for as I headed back to the RV. I climbed aboard and plopped myself down at the kitchen table which had a few maps on it and a couple of legal pads with pens tucked in them.

Duncan came in behind Tommy; he had been poking around a small group of houses just up the way. He was carrying a lumpy garbage bag and at my raised eyebrow he let me know what he found.

"Trade goods," he said with a grin.

"Really? What kind?" Trade items were always welcome. We had found that having needed items went a long way to establishing good relationships with communities that might be more isolated than others. In a way, I felt like early explorers coming into contact with native tribes.

"Charmin."

"Oooo... nice. Save a few rolls for us, hey?" Toilet paper was a very valuable commodity.

"Already have. I'll stash this stuff in the back locker." Duncan worked his way to the back of the RV and disappeared out of sight.

I opened up my map and felt the RV start up. Nate was driving and I was pretty sure he didn't want company. I think he might have been embarrassed by his shooting, but it was something he was going to have to come to terms with. If it didn't improve, I was going to have a hard time trusting Nate to cover me in sticky situations. With the rest of the crew, there was no doubt. We all knew our rifles inside and out, we knew what ammo they worked best with and we knew exactly what the bullet drop rate was for them. Same thing with our pistols. It wasn't a pride thing, it was survival. Above our makeshift shooting range back at the Rock, Charlie had posted a sign that read, "What if you only had one shot to save your friend's life?" We took it seriously. I guess in the safer communities, you tended to forget the things that go drag in the night.

Tommy sat down across from me and peered over the maps. I handed a notepad to him and said, "We need a route through Ohio, away from major cities and roads."

He nodded. "Roger that. Duncan show you what he found?"

"Toilet paper, right?" I didn't look up from my map of Indiana.

"No, he found a radio too."

I looked up. "What kind?"

"Portable short wave. Got its own hand crank generator. Looks like an emergency one."

"That's cool. We'll have to see if we can reach anyone with it."

"Yeah, we'll try that later. How are we headed?" he asked.

I was figuring on staying with Route 30 if at all possible, since it skirted most of the major cities. It would drop us off in Baltimore, which would allow us a short jog into DC.

Tommy looked over his maps. "If we stay on 30 through most of Ohio, we could head south and pick up 40, which would take us straight to DC."

That sounded better than my plan. "Major cities?" I asked.

"A few, but it seems to roll around pretty well. You know, it's funny," Tommy said.

"What's that?" I asked, taking a quick drink from my water bottle.

"I never really realized how many small towns there are out there until we started going over these maps. I mean, there's a lot of people out there," his hopeful expression turned dark. "A lot of zombies too, I reckon."

I shook my head. "Worry about it when they're in front of you, not before."

Tommy shook his own head. "You're right." He glanced forward. "Gonna talk to Nate soon?"

I scooted out of the seat and picked up my pad. "Right now, as a matter of fact."

I went up to the front of the RV and sat in the copilot's seat. Nate glared ahead as he navigated his way out of Ford Heights, a real crap hole of a place even without the zombies. Boarded up homes were everywhere, garbage all over the place. Several dead men stumbled out of buildings, but they could have been live junkies for all the difference it would make.

I handed a piece of paper to him and he grunted as he took it. I decided on a different tack.

In my best Darth Vader voice, I said "When I left you I was but the learner, now *I* am the master."

Nate, a die hard Star Wars fan, couldn't stop himself from grinning. "You're a real smart ass, you know that?" I could see dozens of cars stalled out on the road as we passed under Route 396 and a line of cars backed up to the highway. Interstate 80 was up there and it was as useless to us as rubber bullets.

I grinned. "Gee, you think?" I swiveled in the chair and tapped his arm. "Stop here."

Nate slowed the vehicle down. "Why here?" he asked. One side of the street was wooded with a few homes tucked away. On the other side was a small strip mall, with a copy pace and restaurant taking up most of the space.

I checked the mirrors and headed for the side door. "Check it out. Gun shop by the pizza place and the nail salon." I pointed to the small store nestled in between pepperoni and pedicures.

"All right," Nate said. "I need some back-up ammo, if you find any."

"Will do."

I nodded to Tommy to follow me and motioned for Duncan to cover us from the roof. We left the RV and scooted over the road to check out the small business. We avoided the cars in the lot and headed straight to the store. The front window had been smashed in and the door was broken as well, so I didn't think we'd find anything, but it never hurt to look.

I picked up a chunk of glass and tossed it into the store, hoping to stir any waiting Z's. Not hearing anything, I nodded to Tommy and went in first, SIG already out. The store was very narrow, barely ten feet wide. The counter area ran the length of the store and took up almost all usable space. Every case had been smashed in and there was dried blood on some of the glass, indicating that people had been desperate enough to smash the case with their bare hands.

The cases were empty as were the ones on the wall. We moved farther back and that's when Tommy nudged me and pointed to the door that led to the back room. A pair of feet were stretched out, with the rest of the corpse still hidden. I moved closer and took a quick look in the back area and saw it was a really small gun range.

Bet the neighbors loved that, I thought, looking around the corner at the owner of the feet. He was a black man, about six feet tall, but his age was impossible to determine. He had been shot three times in the chest, likely trying to defend his business from looters. He was still wearing a holster, which based on the shape, once held a Government Model 1911. A quick glance around the office showed a lot of scattered papers, but nothing of value.

I stepped out and shook my head at Tommy, who nodded and started back to the door. He took two steps then stopped, staring at something near the floor of the display cases.

I tapped him on the shoulder, but he crouched down and pulled at a handle partially hidden under the lip of the case. A drawer came out and we were excited to see a bunch of different magazines for various guns. Tommy put about ten AR-15 mags in my backpack and I put a bunch of Glock and SIG magazines in his. We moved down the row of cases, pulling out the hidden drawers. We found gun cleaning kits, animal calling lures and a bunch of adult magazines. In the last drawer we found some ammo, but not a lot. There was two boxes of .223, one box of .38's and three boxes of .45 acp. We took it all, figuring to trade the bullets we didn't need for stuff we could use.

My pack was full, so I carried the ammo in my left hand, keeping my right free to use my gun. Tommy and I scrunched our way through the broken glass and out into the parking lot. We threw a wave to Duncan on the roof of the RV and scampered over. Rounding the front of the RV, we ran smack into a trio of zombies.

These guys must have come through the woods to check out the shiny intruder to their world. They were about the same age, roughly teens and looked relatively fresh. In the back of my mind I figured these guys had been surviving until one of them got sick and infected the others. At the sight of Tommy and myself skidding to a halt, the trio groaned loudly as one and advanced on us.

I threw my gun up and shot the nearest one in the face, snapping his head back and dumping him to the ground. Tommy shot the next one just as quickly, pausing for a microsecond to aim his shot. A dark hole appeared in the forehead of the ghoul and its' dead eyes rolled up into its head as it collapsed. I was lining up the third for a shot when a rifle cracked from the roof of the RV, hammering the last one to the ground with a blown-out skull. Apparently, Duncan wanted a piece of the action, too.

We climbed aboard and Nate quickly got us under way. A few dozen zombies were climbing out of homes and businesses, making their way over to our position. I personally didn't like the odds, so we beat the hell out of there.

I put the ammo into our storage locker and went back to sit next to Nate. I handed him a box of .38's and he grinned like a kid at Christmas.

"Hey, thanks! I didn't think you'd find anything in there." Nate exclaimed happily, losing his previous funk.

"No problem," I said. "Actually got some for the AR's and a 1911, if we ever find one."

"Trade it, if someone wants it."

"There is that. What town is next?"

"Check the map. I didn't live here."

"Lazy grouch." I blocked Nate's swing at my head and opened up the map and looked it over as we passed a few subdivisions. I didn't need to see the tattered white flags to know this area was as dead as the next. Empty homes and empty cars told the tale as loudly as a concert. This close to the city, these people didn't have a chance once the Z's spread out. Once again, I was amazed that we had managed to survive the worst of the Upheaval, although the trio we just killed was a potent reminder that this conflict was far from over.

Looking quickly at the map and getting my look-see bearings, I figured we were about to cross the Illinois/Indiana border into Dyer. I flipped the road atlas to Indiana and checked for the population of town to get an idea of what we might be heading into.

I looked at the number and winced. Over fifteen thousand. I exhaled and Nate looked over at me.

"Fifteen thousand," I said.

"Great."

"I'll tell the guys," I said as I headed to the back areas. Duncan was sharpening a knife and Tommy was still looking over a map. They both looked up as I cam into the kitchen area.

"Dyer up ahead," I said. "Population was fifteen thousand."

"What about now?" Duncan asked, sheathing his blade.

"We'll know in a minute. Heads up," I said, taking my carbine out of its place and checking the camber.

They both retrieved their long guns and readied themselves on both sides of the RV. I went back up to the front and positioned myself next to Nate. A thoughtful gent had made a portal in the windshield which could be opened to allow front firing. It saved me the trouble of trying to lean out the side window and possibly get grabbed from behind.

We followed Route 30 as it wound around a bend and straightened out. Slowly coasting down a small hill, we eased into the center of Dyer, which had several roads intersecting in one place, making for a huge intersection. Brick buildings surrounded us and there were a couple of state-line cigarette shops within view, as well as a gas station. The road we wanted to head down was directly ahead, down a hill and under a viaduct.

Unfortunately, that road was occupied by about a thousand zombies, whose heads turned as one to see the big vehicle lumbering through their town.

Nate and I ducked down and I signaled to Tommy and Duncan in the back to get out of sight. Zombies will be attracted to movement, but if they don't see or smell prey, they aren't likely to attack. If they can't see the driver of a car, then they will generally let it pass. Tinted windows were very handy with zombies. Since we were high enough, we were able to duck down and stay out of sight. They could still inspect the vehicle, but if we could keep them from swarming, we wouldn't have to stop. If we got stopped and they thought there was food inside, it was going to get ugly in a hurry.

Nate had the worst of it, since he had to try and drive from the floor. He was cramped up and waiting instruction as I moved further back to guide him out of sight.

"Keep it straight," I whispered, watching as we moved into the zombie horde. The RV was barely moving, but we were making progress. I could feel the RV shift a little under my feet as we ran into zombies, pushing them out of the way with the plow in front, knocking them into other zombies. Glancing out the back window, we left a wake of tangled arms and legs.

"To the left. Left. Your other left!" I whispered hoarsely and winced as we nailed a Z head on. The RV lurched slightly as we ground the ghoul into the road.

Nate shook his head as an apology and corrected the big vehicle.

"Turn it back more. More. Good. Hold it—run it back a bit—hold it... okay, let it straighten. Okay, good. Now to the right, keep going." I tried to steer us around the larger groups of zombies, kind of like steering a ship through an ice flow.

We kept this up for nearly twenty minutes and I could see the raised arms as we passed the crowds. They seemed to sense that something was wrong with a big vehicle moving on its own, but they were too stupid to connect the dots. Which was fortunate for us since there were enough of them to stop us cold if they swarmed all at once.

The zombies weren't the only problem. We had to steer around abandoned cars, which added more stress to our trip. Luckily, we managed to get through the worst of it, then the way cleared for a bit.

"You can get up now," I said, returning to my seat. Nate levered himself back into the driver's seat and shook his head at me.

"Let's try not to do that again," he said, looking at the shambling horde behind us.

"With the hill, there was no way to reconnoiter. Be grateful we managed to get through unseen."

"That is true." After travelling for about twenty minutes, Nate looked over to the right and pointed at what appeared to be a middle school. "Looks like there might be survivors," he said as he pulled in to the school's parking lot.

I looked over the building. The windows looked to be reinforced from the inside and the doorways I could see were all blocked from the inside as well. It was close to the hordes we left behind, but any survivor was worth making contact with.

I moved back to get my gear and ran into Tommy and Duncan.

"What's up?" Duncan asked, checking the magazine in his sidearm.

"School looks like it might have survivors, or at least have been a place where people holed up. Probably nothing, but worth checking out." I took my faithful pickaxe out of the closet, checked my knife for clearance, and made sure my pistol magazine was full. Tommy went through the same checklist before we stepped outside. There were a few zombies across the road and they started moaning when they saw us, but since there was a fence between us and them, they weren't any real danger.

We moved up to the building and saw the front door was completely blocked on the inside. Circling quickly, we moved around the building and checked out the other entrances. All of them were blocked, but based on personal experience, I had to figure they had to have an easy way in and out. The windows near the ground floor were all blocked and covered over, so they wouldn't have been used. I started to look up and that's when I saw the door for the roof access by the gym. Following the progression of floors, I figured that in order to get in, I had to get on the roof. Looking around with new knowledge, I saw a dumpster out of place by the building and a sturdy wooden box on top of it.

I tapped Duncan on the arm and he scampered over to the dumpster and climbed up. Tommy and I kept our rifles at the ready, me pointing at the roof and Tommy making sure we weren't surprised. When Duncan stood on the box the edge of the roof was just over his head, making easy access for a live person, but impossible for a zombie. He climbed up and with a quick look around, signaled us to follow.

We looked for signs of violence on the roof, but finding none we went over to the door and tried the handle. It opened easily and we all stepped back as the door swung wide with a squeak. Training my rifle at the dark opening, I flicked on my combat light and stepped into the dark. I stayed to the right to give Tommy a clear line of fire and Duncan brought up the rear.

We descended into the gloom and found ourselves in a power room. I guessed this was a custodial room based on the mops and cleaning supplies scattered about. I didn't see anything that indicated the presence of zombies, so it was So Far, So Good.

Descending another small flight of stairs brought us to what looked like a P.E. teacher's office and we approached another door. I assumed this one would bring us to the gym. We doused our lights and stood by the door, listening intently for sounds of activity. We had made it so far without detection and didn't want to be shot for popping up in the middle of a council meeting or something.

Hearing nothing, I opened the door slowly and stepped out of the way as Tommy brought his rifle up. Nothing appeared out of the gloom and we could see fairly well, thanks to the skylights in the gym ceiling. There were piles of clothing, food and water bottles, tools and equipment. I saw bags of seeds and dirt, mixed in with bags of rice and flour. In one corner were weapons of various types, from hand axes to what appeared to be spears, of all things. Baseball bats were in abundance and there were modified hockey sticks as well.

There was still no sign of violence, so we moved to the door and the common area. Opening the door, we looked into a vast dark room, with no lights at all and vaguely familiar smell. This seemed to be where they had their meals, judging by the stacks of full garbage bags in the corner. Still no signs of violence, although there were some unidentifiable dark streaks on the walls. We moved near the office area and someone had written "Armory" on the glass of the office. I nodded to Tommy who went to take a look. He emerged a few seconds later and shook his head.

I started to get that old familiar creepy feeling in the back of my head and figured if this place was occupied by the living, we should have known it by now. We moved around the hallways, checking each classroom. Every single one showed signs of occupancy, with sleeping areas, stacks of clothing and food supplies. Not a single one showed violence, though. It was if the whole place had simply up and walked away.

Duncan shook his head at me and I nodded. He was feeling the same creepiness about the place as I was. We followed the hallway as it went around the whole building and found ourselves back in the commons. We didn't find a single person or a single reason for the place to be empty. We went up to the second floor and found more of the same. But the last room had something and Tommy was the one who found it.

"Hey, come here," he whispered. He was holding a sheaf of papers that looked to be some kid's drawings.

"What do you have here?" I asked as he handed the pictures to me.

"Some kind of answer, I think," he said.

I looked at the pictures. The first one showed what seemed to be a family of four, but the little boy's face in the picture was colored green. The second one showed the little boy jumping at his father and there was lots of red crayon used in that picture. The next picture showed the school and just the mother and the daughter. *Guess we can figure what happened to the dad and son*, I thought. The next couple of pictures showed people living in the school, which seemed normal, but the last picture made me cringe. It was a close up of a zombie face, complete with black lips and bared teeth. The yellow eyes and green skin really set it off and I had a pretty good idea of what might have happened here.

I showed the picture to Duncan and he winced. "Not pretty. Wonder if that was her mother."

I hadn't thought of that. Not a good thing for a kid to see, but it was a rare thing to find anyone not scarred by the Upheaval.

"What's that at the bottom?" Duncan asked.

I looked and there appeared to be some sort of writing at the bottom. It was just a string of the letter 'E', whatever that was supposed to mean. I put the pictures down and we moved back into the hall. Duncan was ahead of me and at a dead stop, so I bumped into his back.

"What?" I whispered, looking left and right.

"I saw something move," he replied, aiming his rifle down the hall. The signs on the walls indicated the media center was that way. There was more light up here because the windows weren't covered and I could see a window through the double doors that led to the library. I was about to kid Duncan when a shadow moved across the window.

"Roger that. I just saw it too." I brought my rifle up and watched the door window closely.

Tommy sidled out into the hall and saw us with our guns up. He covered the opposite direction and asked, "What's up?"

"Movement in the library." Duncan moved forward and headed to the doors. I covered him and Tommy stayed back to watch the hallway. We moved silently across the carpet, checking the classrooms quickly but finding nothing.

About ten feet from the door, I realized the doors opened outward, so anything in there could easily get out if the way wasn't blocked. We closed the distance and that's when our luck ran out. Duncan was so focused on the door that he didn't watch where he was walking and managed to kick a small truck across the floor and into the door.

BANG! went the truck and all of us hunched down as if we had been struck. We froze in silence and Duncan shook his head in apology. I waved him off as a new sound emerged from behind the doors.

It was an eerie, high pitched noise, like someone was playing with a mangled chew toy. It was a wheezing sound and very unnerving. I looked over at Duncan just as his face fell and backed up a step.

"Oh God. We gotta go," he said as he continued to back up.

"What? What aren't you telling me?" I said, gripping my gun tighter.

"Remember the picture? Remember the letters on the bottom?"

Then it hit me. The letters were the sound that particular zombie made, the sound we were hearing right now. The sound coming from behind those doors.

Just as I stepped back, the door burst open. About ten zombies fell out of the opening and more were behind. In front of them was a small girl, about ten years old and as dead as they come. But she glared at us with yellowed, glowing eyes and her blackened lips were split to reveal dark and bloodied teeth. She saw us and quickly moved forward, her fetid breath wheezing through her teeth, causing that high-pitched song of death. Behind her, several zombies got to their feet and moved forward, not making a sound. To a person, they had all had their throats ripped out, compliments of the little demon in front of us.

"Go. Now," I said as I turned and bolted at Tommy. Duncan didn't need to be told twice. He pivoted and ran and Tommy led the way as the horde came after us. The little girl zombie was by far the quickest and she moved with a speed that was scary. It didn't take a rocket scientist to figure out how all these people died. Probably the kid was a rescue that came in infected and when she turned, which was probably at night, she started tearing apart her saviors.

That revelation didn't help me run any faster, or give me a good position to fight her off. By the time I was done dealing with the little monster, the others, who I saw were fairly fast themselves, would be on me.

We literally jumped down the stairs and tried to secure the doors, but they had no handles at all and swung both ways. The delay in checking the doors was costly, because the little zombie slammed against them as we tried to find a way to secure them. I held the two doors and shouted at the others.

"Get out, don't waste your time grabbing anything. Just get to a safe position to cover me!" I yelled.

"Ain't leaving you, man. We don't work that way," Duncan said as he held the other door. Tommy nodded as he gripped his rifle.

"Get your asses out, I ain't planning on dying today. I'm just gonna time this to knock the little bastard on her ass and buy us some room." I didn't have much, as I could hear the other zombies falling down the stairs in their pursuit. The little Z scrabbled at the door and I could hear her frenzied wheezing as she tried to get us. "Go! Make a path for me, I'll be along in second."

Duncan nodded and pulled Tommy along with him. Part of me was touched that they were reluctant to go, but I was heartened they thought enough of me to figure I'd be okay. But I needed to give them time to get out and they needed to make sure I had a clear path to get away as well.

No sooner had they moved away then the door shook as the little Z ran into it again. I could see the top of her dead head through the small square window and for whatever reason, she chose that moment to stare up at me. I looked into those dead eyes and realized once again how people could fall prey to these things. Looking into those eyes was looking at death, both figuratively and literally. But they were lethal in their intent and that was what kept me from succumbing.

The little Z hissed at me and pounded at the door. Behind her the first of the horde was picking themselves up off the floor after they had fallen down the stairs. Some of them had broken bones, so arms were at awkward angles and some feet were twisted in crazy directions.

I had one shot at this so I waited on the other side of the door and watched as the little Z charged again. Just as she hit the door I kicked it with everything I had, slamming her back and into the feet of the followers. I didn't bother to check my handiwork, I just turned and ran.

As I cleared the gym doors I heard the sound of a door slamming open and the dreaded wheezing again. I ran as hard as I could across the gym and through the open P.E. office doors. I swung them shut behind me, but as the door nearly closed, a thin hand shot through the opening and began to pull the door back open. I bolted up the stairs and had the distinct pleasure of hearing that awful wheezing following me up.

I had no room to stop and fight and so I kept moving, charging up the next flight of stairs with that little demon right on my heels. I swore to myself that as soon as I got some distance and a little room, I was going to unsling my pickaxe and let that little bitch have it right between the eyes.

I jumped through the roof access door and flung it closed behind me, but sure enough, the little stinker hit the door just as I thought it was going to close and started squirming her way out onto the roof. I jumped down into the dumpster and in a spectacular display of agility, managed to trip off the dumpster and land sprawling onto the ground. I picked myself up as the dumpster banged again, this time with the wet sound of a zombie landing on its face. I looked over my shoulder to see the little Z getting back to its feet only to fall off the dumpster onto its face again. I didn't waste time and ran like hell to the front of the building, closely pursued by the zombie. If it wasn't the fastest zombie I had ever seen, it was pretty darn close.

I managed to get a little ahead of the Z and was vastly relieved to see the RV idling in the parking lot. I sprinted for the open door and dove through, letting Tommy slam the door shut behind me.

I lay on the kitchen floor panting heavily as the sound of little fists pounding on the door reverberated through the RV. I looked over at Tommy and Duncan and grinned.

"Thanks for the pathway. If I had to stop to open the doors, that little shit would have taken a chunk out of my ass, no pun intended," I said between gulps of air.

Tommy smirked. "Any more of those little monsters and we all would have been meat."

Duncan helped me to my feet and I slapped him on the back in gratitude. I went up to the front of the RV and sat next to Nate.

Nate looked over at me and arched his eyebrows. "No supplies or anything? I'm surprised. Was anything in there?"

I just looked at him and continued looking at him as a thump sounded on the windshield. I didn't avert my eyes when I saw Nate recoil from the nasty thing that was trying to gnaw its way through the glass of the windshield.

"Nothing too bad," I said. "Just some art work and school supplies."

Nate looked over at me like I was nuts, but his eyes drifted back to the horror that was clawing at the glass and snapping its teeth in frustration. I ignored the noise outside the window.

"Oh, yeah. There was some minor difficulty in securing any usable supplies, but I'm sure we could all go back in and sort it out," I said calmly.

Nate winced as the foul little Z started licking the glass in anticipation of the food it saw in the vehicle and I chose that moment to look over at the little zombie. I looked back at Nate and said, "Got any wiper fluid? You seem to have gotten a pretty big bug stuck on the windshield."

Nate actually sprayed the washer fluid and tried the wipers before he realized what he was doing and stopped it immediately. The wipers streaked the zombie spit all over the place and made a mess.

I shook my head at Nate and went to the side door. Duncan looked up from the back table and came forward with his rifle. I nodded and we both went outside. I did a quick look around and saw that the noise from the little Z had attracted the attention of several others, who were slowly making their way over to investigate. Duncan moved out to have a clearer field of fire should they get too close and I circled wide to make sure I had plenty of room when my target decided to charge me.

I was about twenty yards away from the RV and circling to the front of it when I saw it had gotten off the windshield and was starting to make its way back to the side door. When it saw me, it let out that weird hiss and charged at full speed.

Ordinarily, I would be nervous about taking out a Z this fast. But this little twit had just chased me out of a building, made me fall on a dumpster and dive for my life into a recreational vehicle. I was too pissed off to care that it was fast.

Bracing myself, I held the pickaxe high and waited for the Z to arrive, timing its steps with my swing. When it got within reach I swung as hard as I could, slamming the chisel end into its temple and sending it sprawling onto the pavement. I didn't wait for it to get up again, I followed it and struck it again as it slowly climbed to its feet. I was rewarded with a loud crack from its skull from the second blow and the zombie was very slow in getting to its feet a second time. I reversed the pick head to the pointy side and slammed the pick onto the top of her head with a snarl. Her dead eyes rolled up into her skull and she fell in a heap. Dark fluid leaked out of the hole in the top of her head and stained the pavement a sickly brown color. I walked back to the RV as Duncan shot the closest Z, tumbling it into the ditch by the road. Duncan's rifle cracked again and again, a signal it was time to go.

As I went to the RV, Duncan commented, "Why didn't you just shoot her?"

I sprayed my pickaxe with kerosene from an industrial sprayer we kept on the back of the vehicle. It misted the kerosene over a larger area and put out less to burn, so we weren't trying to constantly extinguish our weapons. I touched a lighter to the weapon and it flared briefly red, then went out.

I turned to Duncan when I finished. "This way felt better," I said.

100

We climbed back aboard the RV and Nate pulled us out of the parking lot and back onto our preferred route. We passed a lot of zombies and a lot of dead areas, some still having the white flags on their mailboxes, a reminder of a time when people held out the hope that the virus could be contained.

Back in the front seat, I looked over at Nate and sighed. He was savvy enough to say, "What?"

I used my most petulant voice. "I said, 'Let's use the waterways, it'll be safer,' I said. But *you* said, 'No, a land route is better for supplies.'" I shifted and tried to see around the zombie muck smeared on the windshield. "I wanted to be practical and get this done as quickly as possible, but noooo, you had to have your way, didn't you?"

Nate chuckled. "Cheer up. After this, how bad could it get?"

As we travelled down the road I feared for a meteor to hit the RV.

15

We passed several homes and dead areas and as we travelled I began to realize the enormity of what we were doing and how long it was going to take to even start trying to rebuild. There was so much devastation, so much death and so many zombies, I wasn't sure we would live to see it pass. I wasn't even sure we had enough live people left in the country to start clearing out areas in earnest. I looked at the map and saw hundreds of small towns and I wondered if the infection had hit all of them. Maybe it wasn't as bad as I thought. After all, we had found several towns making a stand in the small area we had been to. Maybe there were a lot more like that, just wondering what to do next.

I thought about Major Thorton and resolved once again to make sure a piece of crap like that would never take over. People needed hope, even a little, to make it through this nightmare and if you took that away then we were nothing as a country, nothing as a people, nothing as a species.

These happy thoughts bounced around my head as Nate maneuvered the big vehicle around stalled cars and dead intersections. We had a bit of a time getting through the Route 30 and Route 41 intersection since there were about three thousand zombies populating the parking lot of the two shopping centers. I looked over at Nate and he raised his eyebrows in a question that I answered with a flat "No."

He chuckled and continued driving. When we reached the intersection of Route 30 with Interstate 65, we had to find an alternate route. The intersection was jammed with cars and there was no getting around them. On the overpass I could see a long line of dead cars and hundreds of zombies roaming the freeway, too stupid to find an off-ramp.

We swung south on 53, but that took us past a huge hospital campus, which looked like it had been bombed. Every window had been broken out and there was evidence of fire damage from a dozen windows. We could see dark forms shifting from window to window and there were dozens out on the lawn. When they saw us they started moving in our direction and some actually fell out of higher windows, just to land broken on the ground below.

We swung down a side road while I scrambled to find another route on the map. I directed Nate down through a blighted subdivision, then back to the interstate. We took a turn back north on Colorado Street and found our way back to Route 30. That little side trip cost us about an hour and a half and it was getting darker. We were going to need to find a safe place to stop for the night. We drove for a little ways and I motioned Nate to pull into a place on the right. It was Deep River Water Park and I figured it would be as safe as anywhere and not likely to be a place that saw a lot of people seeking shelter.

Nate pulled the big vehicle up to the visitor center, but I pointed at a spot closer to where they seemed to have been doing some construction before the Upheaval.

"Why there?" he wanted to know as he moved the RV around.

"We can probably find some gas for the rig in the tractors and trucks over there," I said, moving by the door and my gear.

"Good one," Nate said, working to get the RV as close as possible. "Where are you headed?"

"Tommy and I are going to check the area out, you can look for gas with Duncan." I beckoned Tommy out of his chair. Duncan was already buckling on his weapons.

Tommy and I moved quickly away from the RV and to the first building, which looked to be a concession/restaurant kind of place. We had to break a small window on the door to get in, which was a good sign that the place hadn't been open when the world ended.

We went inside and searched around, but didn't find any zombies. We found a good supply of canned goods and a few boxes of something that might have been hot dogs at one point, but neither of us was brave enough to guess. I found some candy bars that hadn't expired yet and Tommy and I both enjoyed a Three Musketeers each.

With his mouth full, Tommy remarked, "You know, before I had a real sweet tooth, but now it's been so long since I've had chocolate, this seems almost too sweet to eat."

I nodded. "Me too, but I notice neither one of us stopped from eating the whole thing."

Tommy smiled a chocolatey grin at me then turned serious. I put the box of candy down and brought up my carbine. I had heard it, too. Something was moving in the back room and it sounded like it was headed our way.

I moved to the door of the restaurant seating area and peeked in. I couldn't see much because of the lack of light, so I waved Tommy over and he held open the door while I looked around with my flashlight. Nothing seemed out of the ordinary.

But then I saw movement. One of the chairs shifted slightly. Then another, closer this time. Then another, even closer. It was as if there was a ghost slowly making its way across the room.

For a wild second I thought about invisible zombies, but then laughed at myself for being so stupid. But *something* was making those chairs move and it was headed our way. I could see a large black opening which might have been the kitchen and there seemed to be some sort of light in there, but I wasn't about to go charging in until I knew what was coming at me.

Tommy looked at me and I waved him over. I pointed the flashlight at the chairs and sure enough, one of them shifted very close to us. Tommy jumped and brought up his rifle, flicking on the weapon light and aiming it at the ground. I could understand his reasoning. If it wasn't above, it was below.

Looking down, a pair of red eyes flashed out of the dark at us and Tommy nearly fired when I said, "Hold it." I bent down and held out my hand and a skinny little black cat scampered out of the darkness and started rubbing its head on my hand, purring loudly in the silence.

"Hey, little buddy. Where the hell did you come from?" I stroked the little cat's back, feeling its ribs and thin frame. I had no idea how it got in here or how it managed to survive, but it had to have come from a home recently, since it didn't seem feral. If it had been, it would have bolted when we opened the door.

Tommy relaxed and moved to the kitchen doorway, scanning the area with his rifle before going in. He came back out holding his hand by his nose and coughing.

"There's a door open in the back, which explains how this little guy got in. There's a ton of dead meat in there, so the smell is horrible." Tommy coughed. "But there's some stuff that we might be able to salvage, although it all seems to be in huge cans."

"We'll see what we can take. We can always trade it if we need to." I went back through the door and went over to the pool access area. We stepped out and looked around, taking in the multitude of water slides, wave pools, wading pools and a big lazy river. The water had turned green with algae and smelled rather badly, but it would have been fun in its day.

We also saw the seven zombies that had come around the building and had managed to cut off our escape back to the RV. I imagine they had come from the subdivision across the way, since there were no other homes around here. They had apparently come through the public access gate and upon seeing us standing there sightseeing like fools, decided an evening snack was in order.

This put us in a bind, since we didn't want to fire any shots this close to night. The sound would attract every single ghoul from the surrounding area and I had every reason to believe there would be plenty. So we had to take these guys out ourselves and do it without firing a shot. Damn.

I looked around and spotted a possible solution. Retreating quickly, I bumped Tommy on the arm to get his attention to follow me. Tommy was taking a few practice swings with his favorite melee weapon, a length of duct-tape wrapped iron pipe, with fittings attached to the end that made it look like a medieval mace. It crushed skulls without bursting them open, so the wounds were cleaner, but just as devastating.

I moved over to the small bridge that crossed the lazy river. It was about ten feet wide, not ideal, but it would have to do in keeping us from getting surrounded. There was a fence that blocked off access to the river, which helped a little. Tommy followed quickly and as I turned to make a stand, I noticed our little furry friend had beat a hasty retreat to some concealing shrubbery. I slung my carbine across my back and took out my pickaxe. It still smelled of kerosene.

The first of the zombies came lurching at us, stumbling slightly as it encountered the rise in the walkway. It was a man about my age, with a bald head that had tears all along the back. His head was down, but I could see him looking at us from beneath heavy eyebrows. As he took another step, Tommy moved in and swung at it's head, knocking it to the side and over the fence. The zombie hit the brackish water and disappeared beneath the surface.

"Nice one. You been working out?" I asked as I readied for the next one.

"Yeah, a little," Tommy replied. "I figured you and Charlie shouldn't have all the fun."

I took an overhand swing at the next one, burying the point of my pick into the top of a smallish woman's head, arching her eyebrows and killing her with a surprised look on her dead face. I shook out my weapon then grabbed her by the arm and leg, heaving her at the mass of undead charging us. The woman's body collided with three of the others, causing them to stumble and fall. The remaining two walked around and came at Tommy at once, causing a tactical dilemma. I swung at the same time he did and we managed to slam the zombie's heads together like a couple of overripe coconuts. They went down in a heap and we stooped quickly to move them into the path of the remaining three who had gotten up from the one I had tossed earlier.

The first one, a middle aged guy who was missing a lot of flesh from around his eyes, came stumbling along and actually managed to get a hand on my shirt. I shoved the pickaxe into his mouth and heaved him into the fence, flipping him over and into the water. Thankfully he let go as he fell. The next one was on top of me before I could get a good swing in and I had to block his attack with the handle of my pick. He snapped and snarled at me, grabbing at my arms and trying to pull me in for a chew. I twisted, lifting him off his feet and slammed him into the fence. I could hear his vertebrae snap on impact and he fell to the ground on useless legs.

I moved forward and killed it with a strike to the head, leaving him hanging on the fence. Tommy was finishing off his attacker with a blow to the neck

I took a minute to catch my breath and Tommy did the same.

"You know, its not that I'm out of shape.," he started.

"I know." I finished for him. "The end of the adrenaline rush really sets you down." We heaved like a couple of aging boilers and when we recovered we hustled back around the building. The sun was setting quickly and I really didn't need to spend the night out here. A small shadow detached itself from a bush and scampered over to us as we stopped to check around the side of the building.

"Well, hello, Skinny. Nice of you to lend a hand back there," I said to the cat that had rejoined us who was now rubbing himself on my legs.

"Cat probably has fleas and worse," said Tommy as the cat rubbed against his legs as well. He did reach down to scratch between the cat's shoulder blades.

"Coast is clear...wait. Damn." We were fifty yards from the RV and a stupid zombie was stumbling around like it was looking for the bathroom. It figured to be a teenager, by appearances. I was just about to rush it when the cat ran out from cover, stopped and meowed at the zombie. The Z spun around and locked onto the cat, which then proceeded to stay just out of reach by scampering forward every time the teen reached for it. The cat kept this up, leading the zombie away from us and into the construction zone. I had to know, so I silently followed and bless me if the little cat didn't lead that dumb zombie into a construction hole. The cat climbed out easy as you please, but the zombie was in for good.

If I didn't know better, I could have sworn that little scamp had a big shit-eating grin on its feline face as he came back for more pets.

Tommy summed it up nicely. "If I hadn't seen it, I wouldn't have believed it. That cat is coming with us and if anyone says different, they'll have to take it up with me."

I couldn't have agreed more. As we got back aboard the RV to clean our weapons and secure for the night, I couldn't help but wonder what else we were going to see on this trip.

16

The convoy out of California had been on the road for nearly three weeks. They had spent considerable time moving around large population areas and combating zombies when necessary. Considering the distance they had travelled, it was a marvel that none of their number had been killed.

There had been battles and some communities were not as welcoming as others had been. Major Thorton was savvy enough to realize when he was holding a losing hand and didn't press the issue. When some communities showed a preference for fight it was a wiser choice to hold back.

The overall picture Thorton got as he crossed the heartland was there were more survivors than he originally had anticipated, but the lack of effective communication kept them isolated from each other. A few communities had set up runners, but for the most part, they were self reliant. This worked well for Ken, as he intended to make sure no other power came into being after he took over the governing of the country.

For the moment, he was enjoying a little rest and relaxation. He and his men had fought a number of zombies around the St. Louis area, so much so that he had been forced to take his convoy off the designated path and head around the city area. When they reached the river, Thorton realized he had to find a way across as the river was higher than he expected.

Fortunately, the Mississippi is crossed by several small bridges and the group managed to find one in short order. After the crossing, Major Thorton and his men found themselves in a state park, Pere Marquette and were taking a little rest after their weeks on the road. The park was in pretty decent shape and the hotel on the premises gave each man a room to himself and a bed for the first time in a while. There was plenty of water, thanks to the river and the woods provided a good amount of fresh meat. The men had explored the area and had not found much in the way of zombie activity. Down the road a little bit were some homes and a couple of businesses, but they had been looted and destroyed.

Right at the present, his men were combing through the forest preserve and the Major was enjoying a moment on the grand porch of the lodge. His captain was out with the men and Ken was appreciating his surroundings. *Wouldn't this make a great place to start the new regime?* He thought to himself. *Good place, plenty of resources and if the map is right, damn near in the middle of the country. Just about perfect.*

Thorton's ruminations were interrupted when a very wet and nasty looking creature stumbled into view. It apparently had been hanging out in the river area and finally motivated itself to see if it could get a meal with all of the activity of the men thrashing about in the woods. Water dripped off decaying limbs and the clothing it wore was simply in tatters. From this distance, it looked like pieces of skin were coming off with the water as well.

The Major looked around to see if there was anyone nearby he could order to get rid of this creature blocking his view, but of course, everyone was out of sight.

Naturally, he thought. *Oh well, gotta do some things myself.* He heaved his heavy frame out of the Adirondack chair he was lounging in and walked over. The zombie, seeing potential prey, let out a gurgling moan and managed to spew water in the major's direction, not endearing itself at all to the living man.

Ken stopped at a woodpile and selected a suitable club, not wanting to waste ammunition if he didn't have to. The wood was for the large fireplace inside the lodge, so the logs were about four feet in length and about four inches in diameter. Ken hefted his weapon and turned back to the zombie.

The ghoul was much closer now, moving steadily on squishy feet. Thorton could see its wet progress across the parking lot and again wondered where it came from, since zombies tended to avoid water for some reason.

Moving in, Ken readied his weapon in a baseball stance and waited for the zombie to get closer. Just as it was in range, he swung the heavy club. The log whispered through the air and would likely have knocked the zombie's head clean off if it had connected. But the zombie fell at the last second and the log passed harmlessly over its head. Overbalanced, Ken spun around and fell on his back, his log spinning away harmlessly.

The zombie, seeing its prey suddenly closer, doggedly crawled forward, grabbing Ken by the ankle and trying to bring it in for a bite.

Thorton was not about to be brought down by a single zombie. He shoved his other booted foot into the zombie's face and held it off while he drew his weapon. He was going to have to be quick, because the second he moved his foot, the zombie was going to snap forward and bite him. Taking aim at his toes, Thorton suddenly released the ghoul's head and fired at the same time. The heavy .44 caliber bullet slammed into the zombie, blasting apart its head in a spray of bone, brains and zombie bits. The now fully dead ghoul slumped to the ground and Ken shook his ankle free of the dead fingers.

The sound of the shot brought several soldiers running to the scene with guns drawn, but all they saw was their leader getting to his feet with a dead, wet zombie nearby. Thorton holstered his weapon and glared at the assembled men.

"Thanks for nothing. Where the hell were you morons?" he growled, staring hard at a small man on the far right.

The man blanched at being singled out, but managed to stammer out, "We were watching the trail. Captain Tamikara ordered us to keep an eye out for roamers while he and three others checked out a survivor sighting."

"Survivor sighting? Here?" Major Thorton turned thoughtful.

"Yes, sir. The captain got a report from a scout party that there might be a couple of survivors up on the hill overlooking the rivers," the soldier offered.

"What's up on the hill?"

"Haven't been there myself, sir. I heard from another man that there was an old government building up there and that might be where they sighted the survivors."

Thorton looked up at the landscape. "Come with me. I want to see this place. The rest of you get rid of this mess."

"Yes, sir!" came the chorus.

Thorton and the soldier walked over to the trucks and boarded the closest one. They drove along the park's main road, dodging deadfall trees and branches and slogging through erosion washes. Everything a normally running park would have crews to remove blocked the passage of the big vehicle.

In the end, what should have taken an easy ten minutes to the top of the hill wound up taking a half an hour. By the time they reached the top, Major Thorton was short on patience and feeling rather frustrated. He stepped out of the vehicle and forcibly shut the door behind him. The slamming door startled a series of birds who protested as they soared to the skies. He paid them no mind as he looked over the facility. It was a small building, roughly thirty feet on a side, made out of poured concrete. It had two small windows and a single steel door. A large radio tower stretched upwards and the entire building was surrounded by a barb-wire topped chain link fence. A small sign near the single gate simply read "U.S. Government Property–No Trespassing." The area was much more overgrown than the surrounding park, suggesting that this little area had been abandoned years before the Upheaval. What its purpose was, Thorton could only guess.

The major walked around to the front of the building and looked inside. It contained what appeared to be three rooms. The first had a decaying couch and a couple of broken chairs. The second room was the galley kitchen with a small bathroom and shower along the back wall. The third room was the bunk area, long abandoned. The place was dusty but the elements had been kept out and the concrete had kept out the most persistent of creatures from getting in. The place had been cleaned out, obviously by its previous occupants and the lack of debris and other castaways usually left behind when people left places in a hurry suggested to Thorton that this place had been occupied by former military.

What the place was for and what it was doing in the middle of the state park was still a mystery. Thorton was curious, but not that curious and was about to holler for his driver when the man stuck his head around the corner of the door which led to the kitchen.

"Sir?" The soldier, named Cody Ransom, seemed excited about something.

"What is it?" Ken didn't hide the impatience in his voice.

"You gotta see this, sir."

"I don't have time for games, what is it?"

"Sir, this one I have to show you."

Ransom's insistence got Thorton's curiosity aroused again and that won out over impatience. He followed the private through the kitchen and into the bunk area. There were three bunks, suggesting a rotating shift of some sort between three men, doing God knows what in this empty place. That in itself wasn't as curious as the stairwell in the back corner that led down into the ground.

The opening was simple and was easily covered with a metal door. The floor rug had been pulled back, exposing the trapdoor into the secret of the bunker.

"Well, well. What have we here?" Thorton asked out loud, peering into the darkness.

"It's interesting, sir. Follow me." Ransom stepped down the small spiral staircase, quickly dropping out of sight. The Major was thoroughly curious and quickly followed. His heavy bulk caused the stairway to squeak in protest. At the bottom of the stairs was a room roughly the same size as the bedroom upstairs. A table and chair sat over by the side wall and a large desk occupied the far wall. A strange metal cabinet sat next to the desk, but the equipment on top of the desk got Thorton's attention.

In the light of Ransom's flashlight, Ken could see a large radio transmitter. There were numerous dials and switches, a microphone for broadcasting and three sets of headphones. Everything looked in excellent condition, despite its age and Thorton could only wonder as to why it was here.

Back in the late 1940s, the US military was coming home from Europe and Asia with a lot of ponderables and what ifs regarding the security of the United States. It was decided that a communications network needed to be set up securely from coast to coast, unreliant on local power grids and manned by military personnel. The mission and purpose was to provide communication to troops and vital personnel in the event of a nuclear attack from a hostile nation. An electromagnetic pulse, generated by an atmospheric nuclear explosion, would effectively cripple a nation by knocking out its power and communications. The military had it in mind that if such an event were to happen, they would be in a better position to coordinate a counter attack if a system of communication was still active. Across the nation, small structures were built and manned in remote areas, outside the normal prying eyes of the public. Men were stationed in theses places and rotated in and out on a three month rotation. These little buildings had their own power sources and were capable of transmitting messages hundreds of miles to the next station. What was not generally revealed, however, was that these stations had a darker secret. They were designed not only to be able to send messages, but to be able to listen in on nearly every wavelength used by professional and amateur airwaves. Essentially, these places were the listening posts of the nation, keeping an ear out for subversive activity and for reporting to the authorities any activity of a suspicious nature.

These listening posts were highly useful during the Red Scare days of the 1950's and 1960's, but as other methods of communication developed, they began to fall by the wayside. In 1968, the program was quietly scrapped and the system was shut down. But several posts still remain and some, undisturbed.

"Well, it's interesting, I'll give it that, but why are we down here, looking at a pile of old equipment?" Thorton asked.

"Sir. I thought the same thing," Ransom answered. "But then I did this." The private reached out and flicked a large black switch on the side of the metal cabinet. The dials of the radio suddenly glowed with life and dozens of red and green lights lit up under frequency dials.

The major took a step back as he realized what he was looking at. Something he hadn't seen in nearly two years.

"Holy shit. There's power here." He said quietly. "But how?"

"Sir? Remember that little dam we drove over to get to this side of the river?" Ransom asked, walking over to the stairwell and turning on the light switch. The room was bathed in a yellow glow as an ancient light bulb slowly came to life. Thorton marveled at the bulb as Ransom continued. "I would guess that little dam has been providing power to this little station since they built it and no one ever figured out where the generators were."

"Freaking amazing," said the major. "Well, let's see what this thing can do."

"Yes, sir," said Private Ransom, sitting down at the desk and placing the headphones over his ears. He sat there for a few minutes, adjusting a few knobs and dials. After a about ten minutes, Ransom took the headphones off and looked up at the major.

"There's a lot of chatter out there, sir, more than I thought there would be," Ransom said.

"Let me hear." Thorton took the headphones and put them on. Over the airwaves, he could hear dozens of people talking to each other, mostly discussing mundane things like planting food and foraging for supplies. Some talked about trying to set out for the cities for stuff, others talking about how bad the zombies seemed to be in their area. On other channels, he overheard some people who were getting desperate, hoping someone would come to the rescue as zombies broke down their defenses. He chuckled at that, then looked over at the panel. There was a "Transmit" switch and he pointed to it as he took off the headphones.

"Think these people would hear me if I hit that switch?" Major Thorton asked his private.

Ransom shrugged. "Can't see why not. If we can hear them, I imagine this place was set up to transmit as well and have the power to do so. How are these people talking to each other, anyway?"

Ken gave a wry smile. "If I had to guess, many of them are talking on CB radios, with a few short waves thrown in for luck. This little device seems capable of sending a message out to all of them, although I sure couldn't tell you how." He ran a large hand over the large black box humming quietly. "Interesting. I will have to see how this can be of use to us. For now, monitor these broadcasts and I'll get a report from you later."

"Yes, sir. Oh, by the way, sir?" Ransom asked.

"What is it?"

"Could you see if the rest of the place has power? My flashlight batteries are at half at best."

Thorton laughed. "Sure thing." He walked over to the stairwell and ran his hand along the wall. Sure enough, there was a light switch and not really thinking anything was going to happen, he flicked the switch. An old bulb weakly came to life, but it was enough to light the room and both he and the private stared at it for a moment before Thorton went back upstairs.

In the small living area, Thorton looked around and figured this would be a very useful system to have in place, if he could find out where the other stations were. Chances were pretty slim they would be untouched like this one, but it was possible. The possibilities were pretty encouraging, but he didn't have the manpower at present. Still, it was helpful to know there was a communication network available.

Outside the small bunker, Ken walked back to the road and stretched his legs a little, looking around at the forest and listening to the small sounds that nature generously provided. Insects were making their presence known and in the distance, Thorton could hear a couple of squirrels chattering away as they bounced around from tree to tree. It was probably April, but no one would be sure for a while. Hard to believe they had been on the road for nearly a month and likely had a month more to go, but overall, their progress had been pretty good.

Major Thorton was enjoying the quiet when he began to hear the sound of a truck laboring up the road. He was pretty sure any vehicles nearby belonged to him, so he casually leaned up against the building and waited for the truck to arrive.

It didn't take long. A few minutes after he had leaned on the wall, one of the trucks came around the bend and up to the top of the hill. Ken could see his captain in the passenger seat and was amused when he saw the puzzled look on Tamikara's face. The truck swung into the small area and parked next to the one already there. The captain swung out of the cab and walked over to Thorton.

"What are you doing up here?" he asked without a salute or so much as a 'sir'.

Thorton's face flickered with irritation, but he hid it well, tucking it away for future use. "Discovering a lot more useful things than you, I'd wager," Ken said, enjoying the not-well-hidden flash of anger on Ted's normally impassive face. Ken had been suspecting for a while that his captain was on the verge of a break and he was going to have to deal with that soon, before he managed to recruit others to his side. As it was, he had no idea if Tamikara had been recruiting all along.

The captain shrugged. "Possibly. But you might want to hear what I have found out from one of our guests."

Thorton's eyebrows raised. "You caught a couple? How interesting. Let's see."

They walked over to the back of the truck and flipped over the edge of the cover. Two of the patrol soldiers got out and stepped aside for the two young men who jumped out afterwards. They were dressed in casual clothing, jeans and sweatshirts and each carried a heavy backpack. Both were wearing belts that had knives and guns, but they were careful to keep their hands away from their weapons. Both of them looked around and the taller of the two, a lanky kid with longish brown hair, roughly six feet in height, addressed Major Thorton.

"I take it you're in charge," he said.

Ken took a moment to answer. The kid looked capable and he held himself in a way that indicated possible flight if the opportunity presented itself. Thorton stepped closer, looking down at the kid, who returned his look without fear. *You will be fun to break*, Ken thought to himself. He looked over at the other kid, who seemed to be of a similar age, although not as sure of himself. He was shorter than the first and had longish, dirty-blonde hair. He kept looking around at the assembled soldiers, eyeing their weapons and looking back the way they had come. A runner if he had ever seen one.

"My name is Major Ken Thorton. You have already met my captain, Ted Tamikara. You and your friend will come in out of the sun and explain what you are doing here and where you came from. I have a lot of questions you will need to answer." Ken believed in establishing relationships early and determining who was in charge. He noted as he said this last there was a small frown on the taller kid's face. Typical, Thorton thought, as he went back to the door of the building.

Tamikara was right behind him and looked around as they entered the small building. "What is this place?" he asked.

"Later. I want to talk to our friends, first," Ken said. He motioned to the pair to sit on the aged sofa while he and Tamikara remained standing. He signaled for the other soldiers to wait outside.

"So let's begin with you." Thorton looked down at the blonde kid. "What's your story?"

The kid looked over at his companion, then looked back to the major. "Not much to tell. We've been on the road for a while, coming south from the suburbs of Chicago, avoiding the dead and living off the land. Our car crapped out about a week ago and we managed to find a small bass boat which has been taking us down the river. We were looking for some supplies when your men found us. That's it."

Thorton digested this for a moment, then said, "Okay, you're useless. Outside."

"W-What?" The blonde stammered.

"I hate repeating myself. Go outside. Your information is useless," the major motioned for the kid to leave and he stood up slowly, looking back at his companion. His friend shrugged and the blonde went outside. He was immediately grabbed by the soldiers and secured, his cries shut off by a sharp punch to the face. He slumped and was trussed up to a tree, just within sight of the big window in the building. His friend jumped to his feet in protest, but kept silent as Tamikara smoothly drew his Browning Hi-Power and aimed it at his head.

Thorton didn't even bother to look outside, as he already knew what was happening. He affected a bored look and addressed the other kid.

"What's your story?" he asked in exactly the same way he had asked earlier. The brown haired kid sat sullenly, but realized he was a prisoner much more quickly than his companion, who still slumped against the tree he was tied to.

"We came from a community that had established itself along the canal near the outskirts of Chicago. About a year and a half ago, maybe more, a guy had banded a bunch of people together and they set up a new town, taking it over from the zombies. There's a bunch of people there now and they are all trained to kill zombies if they need to. Everyone has a weapon and everyone knows how to use it. There are crops for food and we all pitch in to work. About a year ago, the same guy went south to some other towns that had survived and were in trouble. Rumor is he took on about thousand zombies on his own, but I ain't sure about that. He went to one of the state centers to see what happened to the military and the government."

Thorton looked over at Tamikara. "Sounds like a real bad-ass." he chuckled.

The kid spoke up. "You have no idea. He could easily take anyone you have to offer and the crew he runs with are first rate killers."

Ken's pride took a hit. "I imagine I could deal with him if I had to."

"Pray you never have to. He and his crew ran through my gang like we weren't even there. If it wasn't for the fact he was in a hurry, he probably would have killed us all."

"Why was he in a hurry? What is his name?" Tamikara asked, intrigued by this mystery man.

The kid looked them both in the eyes. "His name is John Talon and he was in a rush to stop you."

"What are you talking about?" growled Thorton.

"John knows what you are trying to do. One of your prisoners escaped last winter and made it to where John has his home. He talked to John and John went and talked to the community he set up and they decided he and his crew should try and stop you." The kid was talking freely now, seeing his friend still slumped over at the tree.

"Stop us from doing what?" The major was concerned now, hearing that a prisoner had escaped so long ago.

"Taking the Constitution," came the reply.

The admission was like an icy punch in the gut. If someone knew what he was doing, he was going to have to step up his plans, especially if it came to a race to the capital with a very capable individual. If this person was allowed to talk to other communities, it would take some force to bring them into line. He was going to have to be creative.

A notion occurred to Ken and the more he mulled it over, the better he liked it. He turned his attention back to the kid.

"You said John went to the community he had started. He doesn't live there?" Ken asked.

"No," the youth answered. "He and his friends found a place in Utica, on the river. Place called Starved Rock. His wife and his kid live there. "Rumor has it he managed to save his son from the Upheaval and kept him alive through everything else. His first wife died and his second is one he met when he had saved a bunch of people in a school or something."

Ken smiled. *Too perfect*, he thought. *Exactly the motivation to come home.* He looked over at Tamikara and smiled. "Better and better. Two problems solved."

Ted looked curious but kept his attention on the kid. He wasn't sure what was going on in Ken's mind, but he was sure he was not going to like it.

"How did you get here? Your car stopped working, I believe you friend said."

The kid's eyes flickered to his still unconscious friend tied to the tree. "We hit the river and managed to find a boat. We were working our way down river and had just loaded up on fuel and supplies when we ran into you."

"Lucky me," said Thorton, meaning every word. "By the way, we never got your name."

"Dan. Dan Winters."

"Well, Dan. You've been much more helpful than your friend, although I am curious as to why you seem to be choosing to sell out your so-called savior and friend." The Major said.

"He's not my friend, but I respect what he's been able to do. Fact is, we were going to try and head back to see if we could rejoin the community," Dan said, starting to regret what he had spilled so far.

"Well, we'll see about that. You have given me a lot of useful information, especially on how to deal with your benefactor and I am grateful to hear of where he lives and all, but I do have a concern over your loyalties. I will need to talk to my—HEY!" Thorton yelled as the coffee table suddenly flew up into his and Ted's faces.

Winters wasted no time. When he realized he had spoken too much to avoid the same fate as his friend, he came to the conclusion he had just condemned John and his family to these renegades. When the Major's attention was low, he had flipped the table up and bolted out the door, slipping around the corner and running flat out for the woods. The soldiers holding his friend had no time to react as he ran past and dove into the trees.

Thorton and Tamikara ran from the building and quickly looked around. Ted spoke first to the soldiers.

"Find him! Eliminate him! Go!" he shouted. The men ran off, leaving the two who were guarding the prisoner.

Thorton addressed them. "Take him down to the river and up the road until you spot a zombie. Cut his tendons and leave him to get eaten. Go."

The men nodded and cut down the groggy prisoner, dumping him into the back of the truck and driving off on their deadly mission.

Tamikara and Thorton listened to the sounds of pursuit as they watched the truck pull away. The major spoke first.

"We need to talk about how this harms us. Let's get back to the lodge," he said.

Tamikara nodded. "What about the men?"

Ken waved a hand dismissively. "They know to come back successful or not at all. That kid's a dead man. Besides, they know where the lodge is and I don't feel like waiting."

The two climbed back aboard the truck and lumbered away, forgetting about Private Ransom, who was about to stumble on some very interesting information.

Back at the lodge, Ken talked to Ted privately.

"I want you to take ten men and head north. I want you to find this 'Starved Rock' and kill everyone there. From there, I want you to head to this community Dan was talking about. Take over and wait for me to get back from DC. From what I have heard, this sounds almost too good to be true." Ken settled into a chair at a table in the main room. He kept his right hand in his lap, near his holster, unsure of what his captain might do in response.

Tamikara considered it and realized there was an opportunity for him to supplant Thorton once and for all. *Let the fool go after the Constitution. If he gets it, he can be shot as soon as he shows his big head in Illinois.*

Ted smiled. "Of course. Not a problem. I'll select the men and we'll be off in the morning."

Thorton smiled back. He knew Ted would take men that might be more loyal to the captain than the major and that suited him just fine. He then turned serious. "Don't fail in this, Ted. I need that John Talon out of the way, if he's as serious as that idiot said."

The captain shook his head. "How hard could it be?" he asked.

17

Dan Winters ran. He had to get to his boat and make a run for it at least across the river. He couldn't go south now because they would be waiting for him on the river. But his conscience was starting to get real itchy and he began to feel like he needed to go north. Right now, he just wanted to get away.

"There he is! Get him!" Shots whipped past his head as he crashed down the long slope towards the water. The men above him were clearly unused to a hard chase and Dan was able to keep ahead of them. He had kept his weapon, but he knew if he stopped and fought, he would be outflanked and killed in a short amount of time. The greatest danger would be the few precious seconds he was going to need to get the boat untied and started, but if he could gain a few seconds, he might be able to make it.

As he reached the bottom of the slope pretty much on his ass, Dan stretched his long legs and ran like he had never run before. While taking shelter behind a tree, he looked for his pursuers and saw them just halfway down the slope, dim shapes through the leaves.

Praying for luck, he took out his handgun and fired as best he could with shaking hands. Four shots and then he was running again, not even looking to see if he had hit anything. The men on the hill shouted and ducked for cover, giving Dan a few seconds to get away. But when more shots weren't forthcoming, the soldiers continued pursuit.

Winters ran for the water's edge and then ran upriver to where his boat was moored. He slashed the rope with his knife, then threw the boat into the water, launching himself into the back end. Muttering a quick prayer, he yanked on the cord and the engine to life, then died.

Cursing, Dan primed the motor, prayed again, then tried again The motor coughed again and then died. Dan primed it again, all the while realizing he was drifting closer to his pursuers.

Yanking the cord again, Dan ducked down as a bullet careened off his gunwale and ricocheted into the sky. The engine coughed, sputtered, wheezed, then roared to life, surging forward and nearly tipping Winters overboard. He corrected himself and sent the boat running upriver as bullets whipped past and churned the water around him. He fired his own weapon over his shoulder at the assembled men on the shore, causing them once again to duck.

Just as he was about to round a bend to relative safety, Dan pitched forward as a sledgehammer slammed into his back. He managed to keep a hand on the tiller and steered himself away from the fight.

Back on the shore, the men saw Winters fall and figured him for dead. They reloaded their spent magazines and started the long walk down the river back to the lodge, congratulating themselves on a job well done.

Dan knew he was in a bad way, but he couldn't go for help. He shoved a towel onto his injured back and strapped his backpack on as tight as he could, trying to stop the bleeding. The bullet hadn't gone completely through, but was lodged in his back near his shoulder. His right arm was nearly useless, but he had to keep going. He had to get to Starved Rock and warn the families there they were in danger because of his stupidity.

After he and his friends had quit the community, they had found nothing but hardship. They had lost one of their number in a bad town crawling with little fast zombies that had chased them to the river. They managed to escape, but just when things seemed to go well, they turned bad again. After a month of living hand to mouth, Dan had regretted acting like such a fool. He and his companion were just about to turn north anyway and ask forgiveness when they had been caught. Now Dan's big mouth may have condemned several people to die, but it wasn't going to happen if he could help it.

Winters travelled until nightfall, then beached himself on a small island. It was safer than trying to find a place on shore. He settled into a feverish sleep, sweating and fidgeting.

In the morning, Dan woke up to find the sun full on his face. He had slept longer than he wanted to and his shoulder was stiff as a board. It was a struggle to get up and even harder to start the motor, but he managed to do it, crying out in pain as he fell back when the motor kicked to life. His shoulder was a mess of dried blood and the towel was stuck to his back, but the bleeding had stopped. Dan gritted his teeth and continued north.

A week later, a man tending to cattle held on an island in the middle of a river discovered a small boat grounded on the south side. He surely hadn't seen it before, but approached it cautiously, since there appeared to be a bloody hand hanging over the side. Looking in, he saw a man, barely old enough to shave, slumped in the bottom of the boat, hardly breathing. Carefully lifting him, the man brought the injured kid over to his boat and took him swiftly across the river to the landing on the other side.

Taking out his radio, he called ahead and received a reply, telling him to hold tight and wait. The man took the delay as an opportunity to look over the injured man, giving him water and trying to see the extent of his injuries. He appeared to have been shot, a curious thing, but the wound looked old, several days at least. Ten minutes later, a large man appeared from the woods, making no more noise than a shadow. He was well-armed and took in his surroundings every few seconds, making sure all was well in his vicinity.

The second man spoke. "What have you found, Mike?"

"Well, I was over checking on the livestock when I found this jasper in the boat on the...whoa!" Mike jumped back as the standing man drew his weapon and trained it on the head of the man lying down. The prone man's head had turned at the sound of voices and was instantly recognized by the newcomer. Mike drew his own weapon in response and stood up next to other man. "What's going on?" he asked, pointing his own weapon at the wounded man.

Charlie James knelt down by Dan Winters and spoke coldly. "If you can hear me, you'd better give me a reason for not killing you right now."

Dan opened his eyes and tried to think through his fever-racked brain. All he could muster was, "They're coming for you."

Charlie looked around, his brow furrowing. "Who? Dan, don't crap out on me now. Who?"

Winters took a few deep breaths. "Thorton." More breaths. "He knows where you are."

Charlie cursed. It was what he and John had feared. "Where did you escape? When?" Charlie was impatient and concerned all at the same time. He opened his canteen and splashed some water on Dan's face. "You gotta talk to me, kid," he said sternly.

Dan seemed to revive a little with the water. "Seven days. Pere Marquette." He slumped into unconsciousness, unable to speak anymore.

Mike looked at Charlie. "What do you want me to do?"

Charlie looked down at Dan. "Take him to the Visitor Center, I'll get Rebecca down to look at him. After that, get yourself armed. We got a fight coming." Charlie looked at the lodge and the surrounding area. For all he knew, the fight was already here.

18

We'd been on the road now for about three weeks. Normally a trip like this would take two days at most. But that was when the world was normal and the highways weren't choked with abandoned cars and rotting corpses all over the place. Some of those corpses were still walking around, many of them weren't.

When we had reached the outskirts of Fort Wayne, Indiana, it was clear we weren't going to be able to follow our designated path. Route 30 had become a tangled mess and I was amazed we had been able to follow it as long as we did. But in parts it was obvious that it was the major road and people had tried to escape using it. Spots of it were clear, but enough was jammed with cars so we didn't even bother to try. We were forced to go further south, which was fine by me. We would have had to eventually turn south anyway, so this route was as good as any other.

The map indicated that Route 40 was a straight shot to Washington, so we decided to try our luck with old number 40. Things had been going pretty well, all in all. We had discovered that away from the major population centers, people had managed to survive. The smaller towns joined with the larger ones and with increased numbers they managed to keep the zombies at bay for the time being. We still passed many, many dead towns, but the ratio seemed to be two or three dead towns for every live one. I had a lot more hope than I originally had at the beginning of this trip and I began to think we might pull this one off.

At every live town we came to, we explained who we were and what we were doing. It was gratifying to see the overwhelming majority of people supported us and wished us luck. We had a lot of volunteers to come help, but I always politely refused. I told them this was a job for a small team or an army and we had nothing that resembled the latter. At each town, we discussed communications and many of them had some form of speaking to each other. Many were nothing more than car batteries hooked up to CB radios, but they worked and that was the key. I had to think of a way to try and communicate with all of them, but nothing I knew of had that kind of power anymore.

We spent three luxurious days in a small town in Indiana and I say luxurious because they happened to still have power. The electrical plant was nuclear and since they managed to figure out how to keep the thing running and closed all non-essential lines, my crew and I actually managed to take a hot shower for the first time in forever. Tommy said he was grateful for the water as well, not for him, but for me, since he claimed I didn't smell so good.

We crossed into Ohio after having an interesting run through Richmond, Indiana. The people there were living ten feet off the ground. Every man, woman and child had up and moved literally ten feet in the air. They had suspended bridges between buildings, created walkways that allowed them to move freely about the town, all without touching the ground. Baskets of earth had been hauled up to the tops of flat roofed buildings and they planted their food up in the air as well. All this was well and good, but there was a snag that we could see from our perch on a distant hill. The ground was crawling with zombies. All kinds, large and small, milling about, groaning at whoever happened to be seen at that particular moment. The noise was impressive, but even more so was the fact that the people didn't seem to notice the grim sea beneath them. They had adapted their world and were content with the living arrangements. We just went our way. It was none of our business and the odds were long against us. Besides, if we did somehow manage to get rid of the Z's, they'd probably be mad at us for making them waste all that effort. People were weird.

According to the map, the town we were approaching was Lewisburg and for some reason I can't explain, I started to get a twitchy feeling in the back of my neck, like something was going seriously wrong somewhere. I couldn't shake the feeling and it stayed with me all day. I spoke to Nate about it, but he just told me to stop being an old woman and concentrate on the job. Good old Nate.

The road we wanted to take led us right down the middle of the town and at first glance, there didn't seem to be anything about. The road turned down a small valley and we passed what appeared to be a subdivision entrance that went back up a hill parallel to the one we were on. Some fairly large homes were tucked away back there, but even at this distance, we could see signs of the Upheaval.

We moved slowly up the next hill, learning from our past not to rush too quickly into areas we couldn't see. The road was lined with old oak trees, flexing their branch tips to the spring sun. On the left side of the road was an old farm, on the right was an old cemetery, full of weeds and tired gravestones.

I still didn't see much movement, so I just shrugged at Nate and gestured to him to keep moving. We glided into town and I looked carefully around. I didn't see any serious signs of violence, so it may have been that this town just up and left for more secured living. We passed an old courthouse, with its front door framed in WWI artillery pieces and an auto-body shop with wide open bay doors.

We bumped over a couple of sets of railroad tracks and Nate pulled over to the gas station sitting on the corner.

"We're not empty, but a couple of our gas cans are, so I'm going to see what I can come up with," he explained, easing the big rig under the station's awning.

"Sounds good. I'm going to have a look around, see if I can't come up with any supplies," I said, moving to the gear locker.

Tommy and Duncan came up from the back. "What's up?" Duncan asked, looking out the window at the quiet town.

"Nate's going to see about some gas for the rig and I'm going to see about some possible supplies. Wanna come along?" I asked, shrugging into my backpack. My SIG was always on me, as was my knife. I picked up my AR and pickaxe.

"Sure," Tommy said. "I could stand to stretch my legs." He grabbed his gear and Duncan did the same. We each snared an empty duffle bag to put supplies in and with a quick look out the window, stepped out of the RV.

We quickly fanned out into a triangular pattern, moving eastward on a cross road that ran parallel to the railroad tracks. There were a number of businesses along that front I wanted to take a quick look into, especially the pharmacy midway through the block, since medicines were in constant short supply. We moved past a small ticket station next to the tracks and I looked around to see if there was any more evidence the town had been hit by the virus.

We moved deeper into the town, weapons at the ready, but not seeing anything to cause alarm. I guess that was why I was nervous. I didn't see anything wrong, yet the whole setup *felt* wrong for some reason. I had the distinct feeling I was being watched, but I couldn't be sure. If it was the undead, they would have attacked the moment they had the chance. If it was a hostile local, they had plenty of opportunity to plant a bullet between my eyes. That thought didn't make me feel any better, but the fact that nothing had happened yet was probably the thing that was bothering me the most.

I broke the silence to the other two: "You guys got a feeling about this place?" We moved further up the street towards the businesses. I could see a subdivision in the distance, rows upon rows of cookie-cutter homes. The entrance was across the tracks again about a quarter mile up the road.

"You mean like something is seriously wrong here and we're just too stupid to figure out what it is?" Duncan asked.

"Or the proverbial shoe is about to drop and we're right underneath it?" Tommy added.

"That would be the feeling, yes," I said, grinning to myself. I looked around as the wind picked up, rustling through the budding trees. Bits of debris flitted here and there and something hit my foot. I looked down and saw that a small white towel had snagged itself on my boot. I kicked it off and it fluttered in the wind, just like a little white flag. Little white flag...

I turned to say something and my mouth dropped. Between us and the RV were probably fifty ghouls, shuffling steadily at us in the increasing winds. The RV itself was surrounded and I had a fleeting hope that Nate had made it safely inside. If he had, he could stay there until his supplies ran out, since they had no way of getting in. If not, rest in peace, old friend.

From the subdivision to the east, zombies were coming out from between every house. Down the street, dozens of zombies were moving out from alleyways. All of them were focused on one thing and one thing only. Us for lunch.

"Ho-lee..." Duncan started.

"Shit," Tommy finished.

"We need cover," I said, looking quickly around. I thought briefly about getting on top of the little train station, but the main body of advancing Z's had already reached it. I looked at the row of houses across the tracks, but zombies were over there as well. Where the hell did these guys come from? It reminded me of something, but I didn't have time to think about it.

"This way!" I said, bolting for the pharmacy. It was the nearest building and would at the very least afford some cover and reduce being attacked from all sides. Tommy and Duncan didn't hesitate, they were right on my heels. That was one thing living on the frontier taught you. If a trusted member told you to do something, you did it immediately. Your survival depended on it.

As we ran, I heard the horn of the RV and stealing a glance through the pack of undead, I could see several unmoving zombies stretched out near the RV. Nate was probably okay, safely ensconced in the RV. Hopefully he would be able to pull our butts out of the fire one more time. I was glad to see he wasn't dead.

Right now, though, I had to save my ass and those of my friends We sprinted to the store and dove through the door. I moved ahead into the darker back area, checking for threats, while Duncan and Tommy threw shelves and counters and everything not nailed down in front of the door to block the way. I made it all the way to the pharmacy counter when the first zombie hit me. I was coming around the condom display and angling back by the stock room when a dark shape reared up out of the vitamins and took a swing at me. I ducked under the outstretched hand and brought the butt of my carbine up to smash the zombie in the face. The blow knocked it back into the zinc supplements, its nose flattened against its face, giving me time to move my carbine to my left hand and draw my SIG with my right. Little brown pills flew everywhere as I exploded the Z's head into pieces.

"You all right back there?" Tommy yelled from the front of the store.

"Fine," I yelled back. "Just seems to be only one of them."

"They're here!" Duncan yelled and suddenly there was a loud crash, like an ocean wave hitting a coastal barrier.

"Damn! The whole barricade moved! We need cover!" Tommy shouted as he and Duncan frantically threw more debris on the pile. I could see dozens of hands and faces reaching, grabbing, biting, trying to get past the barricade.

"Give me ten seconds to find the route upstairs!" I shouted back as I kicked in the door to the stockroom. Upstairs was our only hope. We needed to control their access, or we were dead meat.

"We can give you five!" Duncan yelled, firing his rifle into the mass of ghouls. He had no chance of stopping them all, he was just making more of a barricade.

I slid past boxes of school supplies and shelves of adult diapers. A lot of stuff was on the floor, but I had no time to see if any of it was useful. I found a door and yanked it open, but it led down into a basement. The stairs just led down into blackness and there was a decaying odor wafting up, telling me exactly what waited for me down there. No thanks.

I heard a loud slamming and a 'Dammit!' from Tommy coming from up front. I had to hurry. Cruising down a row of shelves behind the pharmacy counter area, I stopped as my flashlight caught something sticking out of the shelves. Grey flesh reached out and I nearly fired a shot, but a realized that the zombie had to be standing on the other side of the wall to reach like that. Tapping the arm with the barrel of my rifle, I knocked the severed forearm and hand off the shelf and it thudded to the floor.

Strange place to store a snack, I thought as I stepped over the tidbit and reached the end of the row and found another door. It was tucked away in the corner and was positioned in such a way as to make it impossible to open without being directly in front of it. Crap. I had room to open the door, but had no retreat on either side.

I opened the door cautiously and shined my light on the stairs heading up. Good so far. I stepped up and shined the light up to the top, but all I could see was a banister and what looked like a table. I turned back to tell the guys when I heard a small wheezing noise at the top of the stairs. I brought my flashlight back up quickly and lit up a small zombie, probably an eight-year-old. He was staring down at me and his ashen face was twisted in a vicious snarl, his teeth exposed through a torn cheek.

He wheezed at me in that particular way young zombies had, curious and creepy at the same time.

I brought up my rifle just as the little bastard *launched* himself down the stairs at me. I had no chance at a killing shot, so I backed up quickly and let him slam himself onto the floor at the bottom of the stairs. Hate-filled eyes locked onto mine as he slowly lifted his body off the floor. I targeted those eyes and fired a killing shot right before he charged.

I grabbed a handful of his dirty shirt and hauled the lifeless body out of the way. I had no time for regrets, I needed to clear the damn upstairs. I could hear more shots being fired and I knew I had used up whatever time the guys downstairs could give me.

I sprinted upstairs and quickly looked around, seeing a small apartment dwelling. The kitchen was a mess and there was dried blood here and there, indicating more zombies, lucky me. I cleared the kitchen and small living room, then worked my way down the hall. Two small bedrooms were clear, but the door at the end of the hall was closed. I moved quietly to it and tapped softly on the door.

When I listened at the door, I heard nothing, so I was about to open it when the door shook hard, rattling in its frame. Something on the other side was pounding up a storm and by the way the door was shaking, it was big.

I watched for a second, seeing if the door would hold and when I was sure it would, I went back to the stairs to get my friends.

I was on the ground floor and halfway through the row of shelves when Duncan and Tommy came barreling around the corner.

"Go! Go! They're right behind us!" Tommy shouted, waving his hand at me to turn around.

I didn't need to be told twice. I spun around we ran up the stairs and back into the apartment. I let Duncan clear the landing, then I threw the table and chairs down the stairs to stall the horde, which was just reaching the door at the bottom of the stairs. Tommy ran down the hallway and Duncan and I were right behind him. He moved into the room on the left and we followed, slamming the door closed and looking for something to brace against it.

A quick look around revealed this room was not going to be a safe haven. It was a boy's room, probably belonged to the little Z I just wasted. There was a plastic race car bed, a little pressboard desk and dresser, a plywood toy chest and a fishbowl that had some brackish water, but no fish. Absolutely nothing that would hold back the advancing hordes.

As we caught our breath, we could hear crashing sounds as the zombies fought their way past the table and chairs. In hindsight, I probably should have tossed down the fridge as well.

"Find an exit," I told Tommy, realizing for the first time this room had no windows. "Bust up that desk," I told Duncan. "We need splinters, anything with an edge." Duncan pulled his close quarters weapon, a modified war hammer and set to work with gusto.

I went to the door and listened, hoping against hope that the zombies might lose us and leave or at least leave few enough behind to be dealt with easily. I could hear shuffling in the hallway and the attention was focused on the twit banging away on the end of the hall. I then heard something that chilled me cold. A small scraping sound, then a click. I realized instantly what had happened.

The damn zombie had turned the doorknob and opened the door!

I relayed the information to the other two and they just looked at me for a long moment. This changed a lot and I hoped like hell it was an isolated incident, otherwise it meant a whole new dimension to zombie fighting. If they could turn a doorknob, they could problem solve, which meant one very frightening thing.

They were starting to learn.

"God help us," I whispered.

"No shit," Duncan replied as he brought me some splintered desk legs. We stuck the pointed ends into the space between the door and the door jamb, putting four of them to good use. The hinged side we left alone, because it wouldn't have helped.

I looked over at Tommy, who was busily ripping a wall apart. He cursed as he struck brick, then cast his eyes on the floor. He looked at me and I shook my head.

"We're right over the store area, which would drop us right into the middle of it," I said, pushing hard on a makeshift wedge.

"Dammit." Tommy looked around, got his bearings, then stood on the small chair to punch a hole in the ceiling. "If it's bricked up here, I have no plan."

"You'll be fine," I said. "Just find us room to get through, a vent, crawlspace, attic, whatever."

"Yeah, I just hate getting drywall in my eyes."

"Poor baby," I retorted.

"Listen you two—" Duncan started, but his eyes drifted to the door and his voice died away. I looked down and saw what he did.

The doorknob was starting to turn. Slowly, slowly, but it was turning. I grabbed the knob to stop it and the door shook as the dead on the other side groaned loudly and threw themselves against it. The wedges held, but Duncan had to pound them in with the war hammer because they had been loosened.

Tommy tore at the ceiling with both hands as the pounding increased. I leaned against the door to hold back the horde and felt the staccato drumbeat as a dozen dead hands flailed in the opening. Duncan waited with his hammer to pound back any pegs that worked loose.

Suddenly, the door heaved inward and all of the pegs clattered to the floor. I pushed as hard as I could against the door, avoiding the hands and arms that struggled to get around and grab hold of anything they could reach.

"Shit!" I yelled. "Tommy! We need an exit, NOW!"

"Just a minute," Tommy sing-songed back.

"Haven't got a minute!" I shouted, heaving against the door. Duncan was pushing hard as well.

"Your dilemma is important to us. Please hold and our next available representative will be with you shortly."

"The one good thing that came out of the Upheaval and you ruin it." At least the end of civilization had taken telemarketers with it.

I heard crashing sounds behind me as a zombie pushed its nasty head into the opening and tried to squeeze into the room. The door pressed against the sides of its skull, causing the graying skin to crack down the center and peel back away from its eyes and cheeks. Those milky eyes rotated a bit before they settled on me. Another hand came through the doorway and grabbed at my arm.

"Not a chance, pal." I cursed, leaned against the door with my shoulder, and drew my SIG. I put the barrel in the Z's eye and blew it to hell. The body slumped to the floor, but just as I pulled the trigger I realized I had managed to block the door from closing. This was turning out to not be a good day.

"We're good!" Tommy yelled above the din.

I looked over my shoulder and saw a pair of hands sticking out from the hole in the ceiling he had made.

I glanced down at Duncan. "You first."

"You can't hold this door by yourself," he said and proving his point, a sudden heave by the zombies nearly opened the door by a foot, but we managed to thrust it back.

"Grab that wedge and shove it under the door," I said, pointing to the stick by his foot. Duncan complied and saw what I wanted him to do. He grabbed the other three and pounded them under the door as well. It wasn't much, but it would have to buy us a few precious seconds.

"*Come on!*" shouted Tommy from above, the hands shaking furiously.

"Go!" I said to Duncan.

Duncan impressed the hell out of me by stepping away from the door, bringing up his rifle and firing five times through the opening. Thumps against the door proved his accuracy.

"Thank me later," he said as he stood on the small chair, grasping Tommy's hands. In an instant he was up through the opening, then two more hands appeared. I let go of the door just as the zombies fell against it again, cracking it open and surging into the room, falling down over their dead companions. I leaped for the hands, knowing if I missed I was dead.

Thankfully, strong hands grasped me and I was pulled up through the ceiling with both men lifting me, zombie hands literally sliding off my boots as I passed from their clutches.

I stepped down onto support beams, realizing that this was an unfinished part of the attic and we could still fall through the ceiling if we weren't careful.

I looked over at the two men. "Thanks," I said.

"Anytime." Tommy said. "But we aren't safe yet."

"Right. Let's look around and see if we can't find a way out of here." I moved carefully into the attic, stepping around a brick chimney and heading over to what looked like a window.

Below us, the dead groaned at the hole that ate their dinner, unable to comprehend what had happened. They could likely still smell us and hear us, but they had no way to pursue. Thank God.

The window was nailed shut and painted black, but a tap with my knife handle cracked it quickly enough and I looked out the hole at the side of the building next to this one. I peered down, seeing there was no way we were going to make it down three floors without injury, so jumping was out. The building next to us was four stories, so we couldn't escape that way, either.

The cracked window let in a decent amount of light, enough to see the other window on the far end of the attic. Tommy worked his way over there and popped a hole in the glass of that window. Looking around, he smiled back at us.

"Good news," he said.

"What's that?" I replied.

"Got a fire escape here."

"Any bad news?"

Tommy looked out again. "Quite a few Z's out there, but they look to be moving towards the other side of the building."

"All right. Well, let's hope they stay true to form for a bit and don't look up. Let's get the glass out as quietly as possible, then we'll make our way up to the roof. These buildings are close together, so we should be able to make it back near the RV, or someplace where Nate can get us," I said, pulling out my pickaxe to pry out the glass in the window.

"Think Nate's okay?" Duncan asked, wincing as a piece of glass cracked under my work.

"He'd better be." I said, trying to mask my concern for my friend.

We worked quickly, making an opening big enough to escape and in short order we were on the roof. I jogged over to the front and looked down.

Holy Mother of God. There had to be two hundred zombies down there, trying to get into the front of the pharmacy. We had to move fast, because if one of them happened to see us, we were in a serious race.

From the distance to the next building, it was clear we had to go away from our objective. The building next door was too tall to try and get onto the roof. And the building after that was a two story, so it was useless to try and gain any ground that way. The building on the other side was the same level, so it was a quick jog and a jump to get to the next building. The one after that was a full floor lower and further away to boot.

But desperation leads to determination and I jumped first, after throwing my backpack and pickaxe over ahead of me. I aimed for a roof access to break the fall, missed completely and wound up rolling ass over teakettle across the roof. I stood up to see Duncan and Tommy laughing at me, then I got to laugh as the two of them did the same thing.

We had one more building to go and fortunately, it was the same height. Unfortunately, it was also about twelve feet between the buildings. Gritting my teeth, I took a long running start and sailed over the opening, skidding to a stop about halfway across the roof. Tommy went next and I stood near the edge to grab him if he went short. He didn't and we both waited for Duncan to screw up the courage to move. It took a while, but he finally did it, pumping his arms like a piston and breathing like a steam engine. He launched himself like he was flying and did a graceless belly flop onto the gravel roof of the building.

Tommy and I covered our mouths, convulsing with silent laughter at the sight, made worse by the dire consequences of getting caught. Kind of like getting the giggles at a funeral. Duncan salvaged as much pride as he had left and flipped us both off.

Wiping my eyes, I looked over the back of the building and saw the way was clear. We scrambled down as quickly as we could, unbelieving in our luck.

Or we would have, had Tommy's melee weapon not hit the side of the ladder opening as he went down. The entire fire escape resonated with the impact and it vibrated for a second, sending waves of sound out into the air.

Duncan and I froze on the ground as Tommy slid the rest of the way down. He looked at the two of us, shrugged and said, "Dinner bell."

"Jesus," was all I could say as I ran down the alley, the two of them in tow. We had to be careful to attract as little attention as possible. There were hundreds of Z's out there, possibly thousands and we were on our own with just what we were carrying. I had a vague feeling of déjà vu as I sprinted past the rear of the pharmacy.

At the end of the buildings, I looked carefully out and around, hoping to see no one and that was exactly what I didn't see. Dozens of zombies were on the move and they were coming out from all over, galvanized by their brethren to hunt food they thought was nearby. I looked over at the gas station and I was both relieved and furious at the same time, if such a thing was possible. I knew Nate was okay, but only because the RV was missing.

"What the hell?" Tommy asked, sticking his head around the corner.

"Are you kidding me?" Duncan chimed in. I glanced back at him since he hadn't even bothered to look. He just shrugged. "Hey, I'm a team player."

"Hang on," I said. "Nate wouldn't leave unless he had to, or he figured it was absolutely necessary." I went on. "He saw us run into the building, but knew there was no way we were getting out the front. If he moved, he can draw attention to himself and away from us." I pulled my radio. "And we get hold of him, thusly. Nate, you alive? Over."

The radio came to life. "Holy fucking shit, you idiots made it. I figured you probably would, but you had me scared there, boy. Where the hell are you? Over."

"We're in the alley behind the buildings. The Z's haven't found us yet, but it's just a matter of time. Whoops, over." I ducked back behind the corner of the building as two zombies stumbled into view. I hoped like hell they hadn't seen me.

"Can you head north on that 40 road for a bit?" Nate said. "I'm down by a small garbage truck company. Over."

"How far is 'a bit'? Over."

"Half mile. Tops. Over."

"On our way. Talon out." I put the radio away and turned to the other two, who were swinging weapons at my head. I dove forward into a roll and came up with my rifle at the ready, just in time to see Duncan flatten a small teen zombie and Tommy level a larger male. Both crumpled without a sound.

The two wiped off their weapons and turned to me. "We gotta go, I'm thinking," said Tommy.

"Roger that. Weapons out. We keep moving. Shoot it if it's in the way, otherwise, just run past. Follow me." I pressed my carbine into my shoulder in a low-ready position.

We moved out at a quick jog, running along the main road. After about forty feet, we could hear the moans of the dead as they spotted us and gave chase. I looked back once to see if there were any little fast ones to worry about, but there didn't seem to be any at the moment. We would know in a few minutes after they had outstripped their contemporaries.

We moved down the road and headed east, passing a few older, Victorian-style homes that seemed to be in nearly every small town in America. Each one we passed we gave a once-over and in every case, the homes seemed fine. The only evidence that there was any problem was a few homes looked like they had been left open after their inhabitants had left.

After a couple minutes of jogging, Duncan got my attention.

"Zombies on the left," he said.

"Got it, just keep moving," I said, angling away a bit to get past them.

Tommy spoke up. "Fast ones, coming up from the rear."

I looked back. Sure enough, four little quick ones were running ahead of the others. They weren't at a full run, but were way quicker than older ones would have been

"Let's get some distance from these others, then take them out," I said, moving a little faster. Tommy and Duncan kept up, although we were starting to get a little winded.

After about another fifty yards, I slowed to a stop and turned around, taking aim at the little Z's who were barreling down on us.

"I got the one on the left. Call it," I said to Tommy and Duncan.

"Got the middle," Tommy said.

"Got the right," Duncan said.

"Whenever you have the shot. First one down takes the leftover," I said, lining up the little kid's head. In another life this casualness would have horrified me, but a lot had changed since the end of the world.

I was aiming my shot when Duncan fired first, knocking down his target and swinging his aim to another. I fired once, sending a little girl tumbling forward. Tommy fired, shifted his aim, then fired again. His second shot was true and finished off a small boy. Duncan waited a second, then kneeled quickly and fired, blasting back a Z, nearly flipping it completely over.

"Took you two," Duncan said over his shoulder.

"My front sight is a liar, thank you very much." Tommy said defensively.

"Later, gents. We got more company." I pointed to another horde coming down a side street, with more spilling out of various homes and businesses.

"Man, this is like a bad dream," Duncan said as we started running again.

"I don't have dreams anymore." Tommy said darkly as he brought up the rear.

We ran down the street, passing a small corner strip mall. There was a cleaner's, a White Hen and a thing called the Black Cow. I guessed the last was an ice cream place. On the far side of the strip mall was a restaurant and veterinary office. Several cars were parked in normal places, making me wonder yet again what the real story behind this town was.

I looked up the road and finally saw the RV. Nate was flashing the lights and doing everything he could to get our attention. We ran towards the truck and I glanced back the way we came.

Nearly a thousand zombies were headed our way, some much faster than others, but all of them were making good progress. I'd need a wall, twenty men with two hundred rounds of ammo each and whole boatload of luck before I would even attempt to try to take this town back. That or a deep freeze and sledgehammer.

We ran up past a second abandoned ice cream parlor called the Creamery and we were fifty feet from our sanctuary when a group of fast-moving zombies ambushed us in the parking lot of the business.

There wasn't time to fire a weapon, they were on us that fast. There were five of them and had any of us fired, we might have hit each other. It was pure hand to hand.

I punched one of them to the ground, holding it down with a foot on its neck while I elbowed another in the head, spinning it away from me. A third got hold of my vest and lunged in for a bite at my stomach, thwarted only by the AR magazines in my front pockets. I tangled my hand in its greasy hair and viciously wrenched its head around, snapping its neck. The second one was on its feet and after me again, coming in low and fast. I stepped off the one on the ground and drew my blade, a simple Buck Nighthawk Tanto. I liked this blade because it could punch through sheet metal and skulls with equal enthusiasm. As the zombie neared, I pivoted away from the snapping teeth and plunged the knife hilt-deep into the back of its neck. The powerful blade sheared through its spinal cord and paralyzed it instantly. I turned my attention to the one on the ground, who had crawled up and was rearing its head back for a bite on Duncan's calf, Duncan being occupied with a squirmy Z who refused to hold still and die.

"No!" I yelled, reaching down and grabbing the zombie's ankle and hauling it away from Duncan. The ghoul twisted around and blackened teeth streaked at me like a striking rattler. I swung my blade up hard and slammed it under the chin of the zombie, burying it in the brain pan of the monster. The zombie looked surprised for an instant, then slumped dead.

I pulled out my blade and quickly searched for new threats, not seeing any but watching Duncan and Tommy finish off their enemies. I quickly wiped my blade off and picked up the rifle I had dropped in the fight.

"Thanks, man. I owe you one," Duncan said, cleaning off his knife.

"No score, brother, you know that," I said, clapping him on the shoulder.

Tommy spoke up. "More coming." He pointed down the street. "We gotta get out of here." His sleeve was torn, but I didn't see any bites.

"You're right. Let's get the hell out of this town," I said, running over to the RV. We would clean up later, right now, we needed to get away to relative safety.

We jumped inside and stowed our gear, stripping away any clothing that might have zombie virus on it. Tommy took off his shirt and I was relieved to see he didn't have any bites. Duncan had a welt on his leg, but that was the worst of it. I was very careful removing my vest, since the little Z had gotten its mouth on it.

Nate moved the RV out of the town, heading out again on Route 40. I slumped in the passenger seat and looked over at him.

"Well, that was a bust. Did you manage to get any gas?" I asked, hoping for some good news.

Nate grimaced. "No and they jumped me so fast I left an empty can behind. So we're going to need another one from somewhere."

I sighed. I guess this confirmed my suspicions about the place, but something was nagging the back of my mind and wouldn't let go. I mulled it over for a bit and when the answer hit me, it was like a ton of bricks.

I called Duncan and Tommy up to the front. They had changed clothing and were in regular duds.

"What's up?" Tommy asked, dropping into a kitchen seat. Duncan plopped down beside him.

I looked at both of them. "Remember when we were walking, we had a bad feeling about the place?"

"Yeah, what about it?" Duncan asked.

"What was your feeling on the situation?"

Duncan looked up. "Let's see. We were moving through what looked like an abandoned town, but when we got away from our safety, suddenly there were Z's everywhere."

"Right," I said. "What did you think right when we saw all the zombies?" I knew what I thought, but I wanted to see if they shared my sentiments.

Tommy spoke up. "I remember thinking we had just walked into a trap." His face suddenly fell. "Oh, man." He said.

Duncan looked stricken as well. "If they laid a trap, then here's a whole new ballgame."

I nodded. "It goes in line with the doorknobs," I said.

Nate piped in from the driver's seat. "What about the doorknobs?" I explained and Nate responded in typical fashion with eloquent cursing. "Well, that just about finishes off a shitty day," he said, angling the big rig around a car in the road.

Something in the tone of his voice tweaked my attention and I turned back to him. Tommy and Duncan were lost in their own thoughts regarding what we had just lived through and what we had learned.

"Something on your mind, hoss?" I said to Nate.

"Well, since you asked..." Nate stretched his arms one at a time before he went on. "While I was waiting for you numbskulls to figure out how to get out of the mess you got yourselves into..."

I narrowed my eyes but let it go.

"I was remembering all those communities we saw who were communicating through CB radios. So I decided to turn ours on and see what I could hear."

I was surprised. "We have a CB?"

Nate pointed to a small compartment above his head. I noticed in a similar opening the cat we had rescued was lounging. Tommy had named it Zeus, since it liked to look down on all us mortals.

"Anyway," Nate continued, "I turned the thing on and worked my way through the dials, listening in on a couple of conversations, but unable to respond, since their signal strength was low and they wouldn't have heard me anyhow."

I kept silent, wondering where Nate was going with this.

"But things got real interesting when I hit what used to be known as the Public Announcement channel," Nate said.

"Do tell." I prompted.

"Turns out there was a fella doing a broadcast, sending it out over the airwaves, talking about how everyone should accept the new order of things and he is gonna be in charge and we all had better toe the line if we didn't want to suffer, yadda, yadda, yadda."

"Really? Where could he have been broadcasting from?" I asked.

Nate looked over at me. "I thought the same thing, but then I remembered an old retired Army guy talking about how he spent a year of his life being bored to death in a listening post *inside* the US. Turns out the Army was taking a lot of paranoia seriously and set up listening and broadcasting posts all over the US, usually in out of the way places. They were set up to be nearly self-sufficient to minimize contact with locals. I wonder if this guy found one of those places, figured out how to turn it on and was sending a message out to all us low-life types."

I remained silent, thinking how useful a tool like that could be for organizing communities to strike out against the zombies.

"Anyway, I was about to shut him off when something really weird happened," Nate said.

"What could have been weirder than that?" I asked, stretching my legs up onto the expansive dashboard.

Nate looked over at me. "He mentioned your name."

19

Brother, you could have knocked me over with a cool breeze at that moment. I stared at Nate until he started to get uncomfortable.

"What?" I finally asked, not believing what I had heard.

Nate replied, "I said things got really weird when he mentioned your name."

Tommy spoke up from the kitchen table. "Who is this guy and how the hell did he hear of John?"

Nate shook his head. "You're not going to believe it, but it was none other than our good buddy Major Ken Thorton."

I went from disbelief to downright amazed. My mind worked overtime. How could Thorton have heard of me? I remembered Simon mentioning he had heard of me when he was a captive in California, but had Todd spoken to Thorton about me? Why would he in that situation? It didn't make sense.

"What was Thorton saying about me.?" I had to know, this was incredible.

"Thorton was announcing to the airwaves that you were a traitor to the country and you were not to be trusted. In fact, he came out and said that anyone who helped you would be punished by death. He said your mission to stop him was illegal and you were trying to take over the country for yourself." Nate nearly spat out that last.

This just got more and more incredible. "How did Thorton find out what we were doing? Who could have told him?" I asked out loud, more to myself than anyone else.

Duncan spoke up. "You don't think he found our home and forced the information out of our families, do you?"

At first my blood went to ice thinking Thorton might have tortured my friends and family to get information from them. But as quickly as my rage surged, it dissipated just as fast. "No," I said. "He's the type to gloat if such were true. My guess is he found out about us from someone who had been with us, knew what we were doing, and got caught out away from safety. I wonder who the poor bastard was?"

"What do we do about it?" Tommy asked. "This guy seems to have the upper hand, information-wise."

I shrugged, not really sure myself. "We see if he makes another broadcast. If he does, maybe we stand a chance of talking to him."

"What do you think you'll say?" Duncan asked

"No idea," I said, meaning it.

We rode for a ways down the road, avoiding towns and contact with anyone, just looking for a quiet place to spend the night. It was interesting that we managed to keep moving east, always east.

Nate finally pulled up into a state park area, just outside of Dayton. He parked close to a small pond, giving us access to water and providing a little security. If we got overwhelmed, we could always retreat through the water. When we came to a stop, Tommy climbed up on the roof with his rifle and binoculars and spent a good half an hour watching the surrounding area, looking for any ghouls that might be inclined to come over for a look. Nothing made your day look gloomy than a zombie clawing at your window first thing in the morning.

After he came back down, the four of us sat around the kitchen table, munching on a little dinner and discussing the events of the day. The zombies managing to turn doorknobs was a hot topic and in the end, we decided to see if it happened again. If not, it could just have been a freakish incident. The ambush had us more worried, because that was not something that could be dismissed as easily. That was group behavior focusing on a common goal and not a good thing. Again, we had a lot of questions and not enough answers. Would only large groups of zombies work together that way? Or would smaller groups hunt in such a fashion? We'd have to be more careful than we'd been before to find out.

When our conversation turned to Thorton, the mood got considerably darker. We believed nothing had happened to our loved ones yet, but there was that nagging doubt. How had Thorton heard about me? I had no clue. I was feeling pretty glum when Tommy reminded me of a simple fact.

"Charlie's not a fool and he knows about Thorton and his men. If they came calling, they'd pay a heavy price before they got past him. I doubt anyone would want any more after that particular kind of hell," he said.

I thought about it for a minute, then had to agree that Tommy was right. Charlie would be on alert and would shoot first. I freely admitted the man was a ghost in the woods, despite his size. Anyone trying to tackle him on his home turf would be dead before he knew what hit him. We'd lived long enough in the park to know every rock, canyon, tree and gully.

Reassured, I suggested we hit the sack. We had more long days ahead of us and we had to start thinking about our plan of attack when we reached the capital.

In the morning, after a restless night because my mind kept wandering back to my wife and son, I climbed up onto the roof to take a look around. The small lake at our back was as still as glass, with morning steam rising off the water's surface. The woods were alive with sound, making it pretty clear there were no dead wandering around unwanted. I listened carefully to the sounds around me, turning an ear to the wind and closing my eyes, sorting out the sounds that drifted my way, identifying them, placing them as normal or not normal. Charlie had taught me that particular method of listening, using it as a means of hunting. Find the sounds that fit and the ones that don't. After a while you'll know whether or not you're alone, or if you have company you need to take care of. It worked well in the dark..

Not finding anything out of the ordinary, I went back down to find Duncan had awakened and Nate as well. Eating a granola bar for breakfast, I spread out a map of Ohio and looked around for passage around Dayton. I saw a bunch of lines and circles on the map that weren't there yesterday and I looked up to see Nate looking at me from across the table.

"Sorry about that. I had a notion last night and spent some time sorting it out," he said.

"What kind of notion?" I asked, looking at a heavily circled area outside the town of Fayetteville.

"Thorton's broadcast had to have come from somewhere nearby. Those government stations were set up all over, with overlapping ranges so nothing could get by on any frequency.

But listening is different from broadcasting and if the government wanted to keep these things quiet, they had two options. Hide them far away from prying eyes or hide them in plain sight. In this area, they had to be away from sight. Given the range of most radios and equipment I'm familiar with, I'd say Thorton has to be somewhere within a hundred miles of us, give or take twenty.

"Before you get any notions," Nate cautioned, "Thorton has you outmanned and outgunned. Chasing him down would get you killed"

I shook my head. Nate knew me pretty well. "Why did you circle Fayetteville?" I wanted to know.

"Best guess as to where he might be. I imagine he found one of these stations and was able to determine where others might be located. He's probably jumping from one to the next, sending out his message, impacting as many people as he can." Nate said.

I thought about that one. We had to find a way to shut him up before he managed to demoralize half the country.

"You don't think there might be a way to link those stations, be able to send out a broadcast over a wider area?" I asked, thinking about a general message.

Nate pondered that for a bit. "Might be possible if you had someone at each station, but we don't have enough men for that. Not sure about the power of those stations, either. I'd know more if we were able to take a look into one."

"Fair enough," I said, looking down at the map. "We need to think about a route around this town. It's too big for a run through."

"No problem. Have fun with that. I'm going to stretch my legs a bit and look around." Nate pulled on his gear and stepped outside. Tommy watched him go, then took out his rifle and climbed onto the roof. I'll bet Tommy didn't even think about what he was doing. We were so used to backing each other up it was second nature.

Duncan strolled out of the back, yawning and stretching his arms. He popped his neck, then dropped down to do about forty push-ups. His morning routine was pretty close to mine, although I tried to do pull ups on the roof access ladder for variety.

Duncan thumped me on the back as he passed by, settling into the driver's seat and staring idly out the front window. I buried myself in the maps, pausing every now and then to think about Jake and Sarah, wondering if I was doing the right thing.

My reflections were interrupted by a strange voice coming from the front. It wasn't Duncan, so I looked up. He had opened the compartment with the CB in it and turned it on. He had been flipping through the channels when a voice came through loud and clear.

"Good Morning, Americans! At least what's left of you. This will be my last broadcast from this area as promised, until I can reach everyone at the same time. I have some system linking to finalize, then I will be able to speak to everyone. Right now, anyone who has heard me in the past can hear me now."

I looked over at Duncan. So there was a way. Interesting.

The voice continued. If it was actually Thorton, I expected a more threatening presence on the airwaves. His voice was somewhat nasally and higher pitched than I thought it would be. It deflated him somewhat, making him more vulnerable in my estimation.

I moved up to the passenger seat as Tommy thumped on the windshield, wanting Duncan to open the driver's side window so he could hear too.

"As I have stated before, being the sole military authority left, I am declaring martial law in the United States, with myself as the authority until such time as a new Congress and President may be elected to lead. Some of you might be tempted to question my authority. Be advised that such defiance will be considered treason and the punishment for treason is death. Anyone helping someone commit treason will be subject to death as well. As of right now, anyone helping John Talon or someone associated with him will be considered committing treason as well."

I looked up at Duncan. "Guess that means you," I said dryly.

Duncan grimaced and flipped the radio the bird.

The voice continued. "John Talon is not to be trusted and avoided. He is a known outlaw and is currently under a mission to destroy the founding documents which made our country great. As an officer in the United States Army, I am duty bound by oath to prevent him from succeeding."

I had taken just about enough. I grabbed the microphone, not really sure if he would be able to hear me and clicked the send button.

"Christ, what a load of bullshit," I said, actually speaking to Duncan.

The voice went nuts. "Who said that? Who the fuck said that? I am in charge and I will make whoever said that suffer!"

I smiled at Duncan. This was better than I hoped for. I hit the button again. "I said that, you murdering, child-raping fake."

The radio was silent for a second. I wondered if I had caused Thorton a case of apoplexy.

The voice came on again, low and deadly. "I will ask one more time, then I will find you and make you suffer. I'll carve you into little chunks and feed you to the zombies one piece at a time."

I found myself getting angry and less diplomatic than I normally would have thought. "This is John Talon, the so-called traitor. I am guessing I am speaking to Ken Thorton, a self-proclaimed major in the military, while never actually having been in the service. I am sure I am speaking to the same man who ran a concentration camp in California, enslaving survivors and forcing them to hear their babies cry, see their women and children raped and kill them out of hand. The same Thorton who thinks he can run the country after destroying the original Constitution and Bill of Rights. Did I miss anything, you worthless coward?"

This time, the delay was longer and I was pretty sure Thorton was kicking himself for setting up the relays so everyone could hear us. When he did get back on, his tone was much more controlled.

"Well, John. You seem to think you know a lot about me. But that sword has two edges. For example, I know you set up a community in Illinois and you left behind your wife and son to try and stop me. Where was it? Oh, yes. Starved Rock. Interesting name, that. I sent ten of my men up there to make an example out of dissenters, just so you know. If you hurry back, you might arrive just in time to see my Captain put a bullet in your son's head. By the way, Dan Winters says 'hi'."

My emotions spun. I was first afraid Thorton had already been to Starved Rock, but when he said he dispatched men to go there, I was both relieved and terrified. Oh, God. Jake, Sarah. What had I done? I gripped the microphone so hard the casing cracked. I struggled to control my emotions. Charlie, Charlie, please be okay. Save my family, I prayed with everything I had. Anger then gripped me. *Winters, you bastard! When I'm through with Thorton, you're next!* I swore silently.

I clicked the send button. "If you have any way of calling your men back, I would do so. If they have made it to Starved Rock, they're already dead. I did not leave my family defenseless, as you will find out." I took a deep breath. "But for you, Thorton, I will not be merciful."

"Do tell," Thorton mocked.

"You and I will meet, Thorton."

"I look forward to it, Johnny."

"I will look back on it, *Kenny*." I spoke again before he could. "America! This is John Talon! I am trying to save our founding documents from this imposter. Do not let him into your communities! He is not military, he is a fake and his men are nothing more than criminals. Do not engage him or try to stop him!"

"You wound me, Johnny," Thorton said in a condescending voice. "Why don't you want people to stop me?"

I spoke coldly and deliberately into the microphone. "You're *mine* to kill. Talon out."

I put down the microphone and turned off the radio. My hands were shaking and I stood up, trying to walk away my rage and fear. I went outside, not caring if anything was out there. I walked to the front of the RV and kneeled down on the grass. I prayed like I had never prayed before. *Charlie, please, don't let them hurt my family. Please,* I prayed. *Not my family.*

I thought about my brother and his family and I prayed he was up to the task of defending them. My heart ached with worry over my loved ones. Unbidden, the memory of my nightmare came to my mind and once again, I looked down at my fallen friends, my dead loved ones, my son's lifeless face.

"NO!!" I screamed at the sky, clenching my fists in fury at a god who would allow me to survive the Upheaval, only to lose everything. I stood up, unable to contain my rage and heard sweet music to my ears. The wind carried the sound of moaning zombies who had answered my call.

I scanned the horizon, and saw three of them cresting a hill to the south. I smiled grimly in anticipation, welcoming the battle. I had given in fully to the battle rage I fought so hard to repress, lest it get me killed. The threat by Thorton on my family had finally released it from its prison.

I walked slowly to the group, letting them see me, letting them advance. I loosed my knife, wanting this to be close combat, welcoming it. The rational part of my mind was screaming at me to pull my SIG, shoot and run, but I ignored it. The zombies moaned fiercely, I snarled in reply. The killer had awakened and wanted to smash and destroy.

I ran to the closest zombie, a severely decaying specimen and jumped in the air, bringing my fist back and punching as hard as I could as I came down. The Z flipped over and I landed in a crouched position as the next one, an older woman with flesh hanging off her arms, reached a slow, skeletal hand at me. I laughed and swept the arm away, swinging my leg out and catching it behind the knees, dropping it to the ground. The third was quicker, a younger guy with no scalp, but not quick enough by half. I reached through its grasping hands and grabbed it by the throat, sinking my fingers into its decaying flesh. I ignored the hands that grabbed at me as I turned it around and sank my other fingers into its eye sockets, spurting fluid out as the eyeballs popped. I reared my head back and roared as I brought my hands together, snapping its neck like a dry tree branch. I threw the motionless zombie onto the ground as the other two regained their feet.

I didn't wait for them both to attack, I kicked the nearest one in the knee, cracking the bone backwards and sending it tumbling down. I punched down with the knife, spearing the old woman in the back of the head, ending its life among the unliving. I tossed the knife away as the first one charged again and I dodged to the side, catching it by the wrist and spinning it to the ground. I kneeled on its back, amused at its struggles. I stood up, keeping one foot on it to keep it from getting up. When I had my balance, I stepped high with my other foot, slamming it hard into the back of the zombie's neck. I was rewarded with a wet snap and the ghoul went limp.

I looked for more adversaries, but there were none. Pity. I retrieved my knife and walked slowly back to the RV, each step bringing me back from the abyss, each footfall a step back to sanity. By the time I reached the RV, I was spent. My rage was dissipated, leaving only fear and apprehension. I went to the back and unhooked a bucket. Scooping up some water, I washed the zombie shit off my hands. I wasn't about to wash in the pond itself. When I had washed five times, I returned the bucket and sprayed a little kerosene on my blade. The metal burned brightly for a second, then faded. I extinguished it by plunging it into the ground.

After I put my blade away, I turned back to the RV. The simple tasks had brought me back to normal and I was ready to think more rationally. Inside the RV, I sat down at the kitchen table. I shook my head, trying to clear it. I had given in to my internal rage only once before, at the battle of Coal City.

Duncan sat down across from me, placing his hands on the table carefully, as if he feared making any sudden moves. I just stared down at the fake wood surface, trying to send my thoughts out to my wife and son.

After a few minutes, Duncan said quietly, "Next to you, Charlie's the best there is. He's got your brother as a back, not to mention Sarah and Angela and Rebecca. They'll be fine. I promise you."

I looked up slowly. I took a deep breath. "I know. But they can't prepare if they don't know what's coming. Even I can be ambushed. So can Charlie. So can anyone." I dropped my head down to stare back at the table.

Duncan was silent as Tommy came back down from the roof. He moved his wiry frame in next to Duncan.

"John?" Tommy asked.

I looked up. "What?"

"If you want to head back, I'm with you. This whole mission can go scratch if it means we lose our loved ones," he said.

I thought about that. Losing our loved ones. Losing everything we held dear. My mind made connections without my intent and I was reminded of an essay I read years ago about what happened to the signers of the Declaration of Independence. Various accounts abound, but the gist was they knew what they were getting into and they knew what the penalty might be for failure. They put their lives and the lives of their loved ones at risk because they believed in a cause greater than themselves. I thought about what we were doing. Was this a cause greater than ourselves? Was this the only chance our country would have?

On the outside, I had to think yes. We had to use the founding documents to forge a new future from the ashes of the Upheaval. We had to say once and for all we would fight. We had to have something to fight for and those documents would cement our belief that we were a country worth saving.

I must have looked calmer because Tommy looked at me quizzically.

"What?" he asked.

"We'll go on. We'll have to have faith that Charlie will be vigilant and be able to take care of things back home," I said.

"Are you sure?" Duncan asked.

I nodded. "If something happens, then we have a new mission."

Tommy and Duncan nodded. They knew exactly what I was talking about. If Thorton succeeded in hurting our loved ones, there would be nowhere on earth he could run to.

Our little powwow was interrupted by Nate slamming open the RV door. "Talon! Get your dumbass out here, *right now!*"

Confused, I got up and went over to the door, stepping outside and away from the RV. Nate was standing about fifteen feet away, taking off his weapons and gear. When he finished, he turned back to me and crossed his massive arms, glowering at me the whole time.

"Before you try to deny anything, shithead, I will tell you that I saw you take down those three zombies on the hill," he started.

I began to speak, but he interrupted.

"*Shut up!* I ain't done here. This is a lecture, not a fucking debate! When the hell did you get so damn stupid? You had firepower, but you still took on three zombies in close quarters!" Nate's voice rose. "What the fuck were you thinking? Are you trying to die? You got people counting on you here and people counting on you at home. You ain't no good dead, you hear me?"

My eyes narrowed. I walked up to Nate until I was staring him in the face. "You're out of line. You went out zombie hunting when Thorton came back on the radio. He and I spoke."

Nate's face softened somewhat. "About what?"

My tone hardened as I punctuated the words. "He and I spoke about how he knew about me and where my family lived. He and I spoke about how he sent ten men up there to deal with my family. He and I spoke about how I might get back in time to see his Captain kill my son."

I stepped even closer and dropped my voice. "So you might see where I would need to release a little anger, hmm?"

Nate looked down and I decided to step back. As I was turning away, he fired another shot.

"It doesn't change the fact that what you did was stupid. You can make a mistake too and get yourself killed. Then where would Jake be?" Nate asked.

I spun on my heel, my anger building again at the mention of my son. "I trust Charlie to do the right thing. Just like he trusts me to do the right thing. Could I have used a little better judgment? Maybe. But if I hadn't released that way, somebody really would have gotten killed. I don't need a lecture on tactics. Not anymore."

Nate looked hurt and then angry. "You think you're the best one out there, then?"

I stepped close again, keeping my voice low. "You're one of my best friends, Nate and I consider you a brother. I trust you with my life. I've trusted you with my son's life in the past. But if you're going where I think you're going, stop it now."

Nate stared hard at me. "Why?"

I was brutally honest. "You're not good enough. You used to be, but not anymore."

I could see the flash of pain cross Nate's eyes before it was replaced with anger and worse, pride.

"Think it's time we found out just who was best." Nate snarled, uncrossing his arms and flexing his big hands, stepping away to give himself some room.

Duncan and Tommy started from the RV, but I waved them off. I circled with Nate, keeping an eye on his feet and hands.

I tried to talk him out of it. "Doesn't have to be this way, Nate. We start fighting each other, Thorton wins."

Nate spat on the ground between us. "This ain't got nothing to do with Thorton. It's about respect."

I considered that, then abruptly pulled my SIG, firing a round in between Nate's feet. He jumped back and put a hand on his gun, but I stopped him.

"*Don't!* Don't make me kill you, Nate." I pointed the gun at his head. It hurt like hell to have to pull a gun on one of my closest friends, but I needed to shock him back to reality.

"We can't fight, Nate. You're still very good and one of us would get killed. How would either of us go on after that? I couldn't face your wife and tell her I had killed you in a stupid fight any more than you could face mine. I'm better than you because *I* always went out to face the zombies, *I* went to Coal City, *I* went to State Center Bravo. *I* brought those women back from the slavers in the dead of night. I've led the assaults to clear the land of zombies so families could live in safety. I've spent the last two years fighting nearly every day. I don't fear the zombies anymore, Nate. They're just a part of the landscape I have to deal with.

I holstered my gun. "But what I did was easy. You stayed behind and dealt with all the bullshit that rebuilding a community takes. You kept the people going, kept them fed, kept them trained so they could live. Your job was harder and I know I couldn't have done it. But we can't fight, Nate. We need each other to make this work. I clear the way and you bring the community in to retake what was lost. Without you, I'm just killing zombies for the hell of it."

Nate's eyes lost all their anger. He looked down, then back up at me. "Don't know what came over me. Guess I just worry about you, sometimes."

That was as close to an apology as I was going to get. I offered one of my own. "We're all stressed. Let's save it for Thorton." I walked over to Nate and offered my hand. He looked at it for a second, then shook it. I drew him in for a quick hug.

"Like a brother," was all I said.

Nate nodded. "Same here, man."

We let go and walked back to the RV. As we were climbing aboard, Duncan whispered to me. "Would you have shot him?"

I looked over at Nate, who was chatting with Tommy up in the front of the RV.

"Yes." Nothing more needed to be said. I knew deep down, fundamentally, my friendship with Nate just changed.

20

Thorton chuckled as he put away the microphone, but that was purely for the men who were in the room with him. Inwardly, he was seething. The broadcast had not gone as intended and John Talon had quickly usurped his plan. Major Thorton was hoping to continue his broadcasts, now that his men had figured out how to interconnect the radio stations and broadcast all at once. But most of his plans just got thrown in the crapper because of that miserable son of a bitch.

How dare Talon call him out? Thorton had never been threatened in his life and the thought of someone not being afraid of him was a new one. *When I catch you, you'll suffer. I'll kill you so slowly you'll think it's the new normal.* Thorton thought to himself.

Outwardly, it was another story. "Well, that wasn't quite what I had in mind, but it did serve a useful purpose." The Major said.

"Sir?" Corporal Ransom asked, moving one of the headsets.

"We know he's within hearing distance which puts him... where?" Thorton asked.

The other soldier quickly scanned a map, did some mental calculations, then drew a circle on the map. "Rough guess would be within this circle, about fifty miles," the soldier named Golat said.

Thorton scanned the map. "Best guess as to location?" he asked Ransom.

Ransom looked at the map, checked a larger map on the wall, then took the pencil and circled the top quadrant of the circle. "Up here, given where he came from. Makes no sense to be any further south. But I'm guessing."

Thorton nodded. "I had the same notion. All right, we're going to be pulling out of here soon, set up the relays like the others, then we're moving on." Ken walked over to the stairwell which led down to the ground floor. "Two hours," he said with finality.

Thorton climbed down the stairs and walked across the small living space, his face momentarily clouding with rage. He had never been insulted, never been threatened and did not know how to react to it. He wanted to smash something, destroy anything, just to vent his rage. After a few minutes, he calmed down, remembering his Captain's mission. *By now Tamikara should be getting close to Starved Rock. I'm sure Talon will appreciate his homecoming. That is, if I don't kill him first*, he thought.

As he started to feel better, he went outside and looked around. He was standing outside a small barn, tucked away behind a row of pine trees. There was one access road and his men were camped around the three trucks and two cars they had with them. They had picked up the cars along the way, using them for short range reconnaissance and scouting. This barn was one of several they had encountered that were not barns at all, but government listening stations. The giveaway was the radio tower, but that was not unusual in these parts. Several could be seen in any direction one chose to look. In each station, there was a map with the locations of all the posts, which allowed for Thorton and his men to use them for their purposes. Each station had its own water supply and power source. This one used two windmills to recharge a bank of batteries for power. In all, the system was brilliant and perfect in its secrecy. No one would look twice at a barn in farm country and Thorton was sure the rest were similarly camouflaged.

At his presence, the men rose to their feet, whispering to each other about what they were going to be doing today. Fortunately, none of them had heard Talon call out the major, so he didn't have to worry about any dissention or disrespect. It did bother him that other people might have heard and altered his ability to bring them into line, but that would not be a serious consequence. Already there were groups that were ready to swear their loyalty to him, survivors who did not have much to look forward to than the daily fight to live. If Thorton could bring some sort of order to their world, they were all for it. By last count, seven communities were willing to submit to his order, with the provision he provide security and some sort of future for them.

Thorton grinned. Naturally, such security came at a price. And the price was high, but the people were willing to pay for it. Fools for the fleecing.

As the camp began packing up, men were moving about, checking provisions and weapons, Thorton brought himself back to his current situation. How was he going to deal with Talon? Thorton mulled over a few possibilities, thinking about what and who he had on hand and what he knew about Talon.

Truth be known, Ken wasn't a very intelligent man. He had what could be described as animal cunning, but when it came to overall strategy, he was severely limited. He tended to react as an animal would, biding his time, waiting for an opening, then striking with brutal efficiency. He was limited in patience and refused to admit defeat, even when it stared him in the face.

Thorton decided that Talon needed to be punished and punished now for his impertinence. He had no idea where Talon might be, just a vague notion of the direction the man might be in. But those were details and he wanted results. Looking over his men, he decided that ten men should be sufficient to take out Talon and whoever might be with him.

He walked over to a parked truck and hopped up onto the lowered gate. His massive size seemed even more impressive and men slowly began to realize their leader had something to say. They quickly dropped what they were packing up and gathered around the truck.

Major Thorton addressed the men. "I'll get to the point. You've heard me talk about John Talon." There were many nods and some frowns. "Turns out he might be close enough to where we might get a shot at him." The frowns turned to grins. "I need ten men to head north and teach this fucker a lesson as to who's in charge. Who wants the job?"

Thorton was gratified that all men present raised their hands. They were a motley bunch of criminals and losers, but they never hesitated to fight, especially when they thought the odds were on their side.

The major looked over at one of his sergeants. "You're in command of this mission. Pick nine men and see me in ten minutes. Thorton jumped down from the truck bed. "Finish off this Talon and I'll make you a lieutenant," he said to the sergeant, who grinned evilly at the spoils to be his.

Thorton went back into the little barn to retrieve one of the many maps stored there. As he entered the building, he literally ran into Corporal Ransom, who bounced off the larger man and fell backwards over a chair. Thorton's flash of anger changed to amusement as he watched the soldier flip over the recliner and crash down on the other side.

Ken placed his hands on his hips and waited for the soldier to scramble upright. "Got a hot date with a zombie?" he asked sarcastically.

"Sir! Sorry, sir. Needed to tell you something right away, sir. Hoped to talk to you before you spoke to the men, sir." Ransom said quickly, brushing dust off his uniform.

"What is it, corporal?"

"Sir! Overheard a conversation between a couple of roamers, sir." Roamers was the soldiers term for people who just wandered about, surviving by living off the leftovers of the Upheaval. "They reported a recreational vehicle outside of Lafayette, heading east."

Thorton was skeptical. "What makes you think they saw Talon?" Even in a world where the dead walked, this seemed way too coincidental.

"Sir. They talked about passing a group of heavily armed men, people they said looked like they could handle themselves or anyone who got in the way. Said the leader looked like a cold-eyed killer, no question about it. Got to be Talon, sir."

Thorton was a bit tweaked that people might think Talon was tough, maybe tougher than him and he let his irritability show. "We'll see how tough he is. You have a map with his location on it?"

"Right here, sir." Corporal Ransom handed over a small map of Ohio, which had their location marked and a small town outside of Columbus circled.

Thorton took the map, glanced at it, then chuckled as he went back outside. "Excellent," he said to himself. Over his shoulder he barked "Set up for linking, we're out in two hours."

Corporal Ransom saluted Thorton's back and headed back to the radio unit to link with the rest of the system.

Outside, Sergeant Rod Milovich had assembled a crew to carry out the major's orders. There were nine men of various backgrounds, but all looked capable. They were lounging around the truck bed when Ken strode up to them. He signaled to Sgt. Milovich, who waved over his second, Corporal Tim Kazinski.

Kazinski was only six inches above five feet in height, but was nearly that wide in the shoulders. He suffered from a massive case of short-man-syndrome and made sure he compensated for his stature by being stronger than everyone else and more brutal to anyone who crossed him. In fact, he was only a little less sadistic than Thorton himself.

Ken spread out the little map and the three men leaned over it. "Ransom says he figures Talon to be here, based on some chatter he overheard on the radio. It makes sense to me, but I also figure our boy will not want to try and cross a major population center. So I figure him to head south. The roads lead to here." Thorton pointed to a little town called Harrisburg. "If you take Route three and haul ass, you should get there in time to set up a nice little ambush."

Sgt. Milovich and Cpl. Kazinski smiled and straightened up. This was the sort of thing they enjoyed. Inflicting damage without risk to themselves.

Thorton stopped them before they went back to gather their men. "Don't take risks. This one is a survivor and if you don't get him right away, you'll take damage." This was as close as Thorton was going to get to admitting Talon might be a bigger threat than he previously thought.

Thorton looked over the men as they tossed their gear into the truck and clambered after it, finding comfortable seats to check their weapons and prepare themselves. He nodded as they saluted him and watched as his sergeant and corporal climbed into the cab of the truck and started away. *Nothing will be stopping me now*, he thought as the truck moved out.

Turning back to the rest of the men, he shouted out his orders. "Pack it up! We're moving out! I want to be gone in two hours!" Thorton walked back to his own vehicle and checked his personal supplies. *Need to hit a supply station soon*, he thought, looking over his meager horde. *We'll see what the next stop on the map is.*

21

An hour and a half later, Thorton and his men were moving out along Route 50 again, passing several miles of unused and run-down farmland. Nature was taking back much of the land and Thorton could see a lot of growth of new tress and grass. Off in the distance, he saw a few tilled fields, indicative of someone making a go of it alone, but he wasn't interested in loners like that. They were all over and the fact they were alone and still alive made them very suspicious and very capable of defending themselves. Two of Thorton's men discovered that fact in Kansas and they nearly died as a result.

The first town they came to on the road was Allensburg and the initial impression Thorton got was pretty dismal. There were several homes along the main road, but if they had been abandoned during the Upheaval or years before, it was hard to tell. Some homes were boarded up, some were broken into, some were intact. There were several buildings and businesses, but the central industry seemed to be alcohol consumption, based on the number of bars the single main street boasted.

As the two trucks rumbled into the town, Thorton signaled a halt. There was a hardware store off to the left, a small gas station down to the right and a little way down the street, was a grocery store. It was the only building with a paved parking lot, Thorton noted. He climbed out of the truck and looked around. There was no zombie activity that he could see, so he figured the town was pretty safe. He went to the back of the truck and talked to the men sitting back there.

"You two," he said, pointing to the two nearest men. "Check out the hardware store, see if there is anything of use in there or for trade goods." That was a trick that Thorton had come up with for towns that were reluctant to open up. Offer them something and when their guard was down, that was the moment to strike. "You two," he said to another pair. "Head up the street and check out the grocery store. There might be something to restock with. Get moving."

The major walked back to the second truck and talked to the men there. "You three," he said, talking to the men who poked their heads out the back. "Run a quick check through the homes here, see if there is anything we can use. Make it quick. If it looks like it has been abandoned for a while, leave it. Go."

The men jumped out of the truck and headed back the way they came, looking to do a quick sweep of the homes they had already passed. The men from the first truck spread out and went to their various objectives, looking to finish as quickly as possible.

Thorton watched them go and turned his head north, thinking about the surprise that was going to be waiting for Talon. He grinned and turned his attention back to his men and the town they were in. Something was tweaking the back of his mind, but he couldn't put a finger on it. No matter, they'd be out of here in a little while anyway.

Private Ellis and Private Barnes walked quickly over to the hardware store. They liked missions like this because it gave them a chance to prove what they could do and perhaps get a chance at promotion. The building was a steel structure, with two small windows in front and two standard steel doors. The front doors were locked, so the two men walked around towards the back. Private Ellis noticed a set of skylights that were open, so if they had to, they could get in that way. Around the back of the building there was a dumpster turned over on its side and garbage was strewn all over. The ground was dark under the dumpster, like something that had been thrown away leaked oil.

Barnes reached the back door and tried the handle. "No luck," he said to Ellis.

Ellis shook his head. "Damn. Guess that means we gotta go on the roof."

Barnes looked at him. "What do you mean?"

Ellis stepped back and pointed at the open skylights. "We just have to get up there."

Barnes looked and smiled at the other private. "Nice one. Course, this works out well another way."

"What's that?"

"Locked all around means there's a good chance something worthwhile might still be in there."

"Truth. Let's get up there. Still got your cord?"

Barnes checked his pack. "'Bout fifty feet. That should be plenty," he said.

Ellis went over to the dumpster and grunting, heaved it back up onto its wheels. He pushed it over to the side of the arching structure and stood on top, trying to reach the skylight. He was about a foot short, so climbing down, he picked up a couple of stray cinder blocks and threw them up on the dumpster lid, hitting the side of the building with a deep booming sound.

Climbing up, Private Ellis was able to reach the skylight, so he grasped the edge and pulled himself up, hooking a leg in the opening and straddling the window as he pushed open the skylight to allow easier access. Barnes pulled his rappelling cord from his pack and secured an end to the bottom of the heavy dumpster. He then tossed the bulk of the cord to Ellis, who sent it down into the gloomy interior of the hardware store.

Private Ellis slid down the rope and looked around, letting his eyes adjust to the gloom. He was standing in the fasteners aisle, with nails on one side, screws on the other and a smattering of glue on the far end. He could see a center aisle in the store, separating it from the front rows and in the rear there looked to be a small office, flanked by a key making station. His attention was distracted by the rope wiggling and the bulk of Private Barnes blocking the light as he slid through the window. He didn't notice a dark shape move down at the front end of the store, slipping down a nearby aisle.

Private Barnes slid down quickly, landing heavily. He shook his hands and straightened sheepishly, then looked around as well. "Looks like this place has been home to just birds and bugs," he said, looking at a row of boxes damaged by rainwater which had fallen through the skylights. The air had a musty smell and there was evidence of a decent growth of mold on the rain-ruined boxes.

"Yeah, but let's see what we can find. Should be something good here." He started for the front of the store. "You check those aisles over there and let me know what you find. I'm going to check the front."

Private Ellis stepped away and Private Barnes limped slightly to the back. He discovered the battery section, so he grabbed a few batteries for his weapons' light and flashlights. He grabbed some more for good measure, stuffing them into his pack. He moved back along the wall, passing the gardening tools and sprinklers. He found the hunting section and saw there was still some ammo on the shelves. Jackpot. He grabbed a bucket from the gardening section and started to fill it with the ammo, from shotgun shells to rifle bullets.

Private Barnes was so focused he didn't hear the footsteps behind him and became aware only when a hand was placed on his shoulder. "Finished already, dude?" Barnes straightened up and turned around, coming face to face with a badly decayed zombie. Its skin was pulled tight around its skull, emphasizing the tears in its bluish skin. Its arms were thin, but as Barnes turned around, the hand that was on his shoulder was matched on the other shoulder by the zombie's other hand, which was missing three fingers and before Barnes could move or scream, the zombie's head darted forward to sink its black teeth into his face. The private cried out as the zombie hung on and bore him to the floor, tearing at his face.

Private Ellis was up front filling his backpack with seeds from a display case. These were always good for trade when they found a community of survivors and sometimes went in for goodwill. He had a handful of packets when he heard Private Barnes cry out. He stood up and shouted, "You okay?" When he didn't get an answer he started to move towards the back but found his path blocked by a large shape moving in his direction. Ellis dropped his pack and whipped his rifle up, but just as he was about to fire a searing pain exploded in his leg. He looked down and to his horror, saw a small zombie child furiously chewing on his calf, tearing off chunks of meat and drooling blood down its little chin. Private Ellis dropped his rifle as he fought off the little zombie, throwing it bodily away from him as he fell to the ground, unable to stand on his injured leg. As he fell, he saw the little zombie get back up and head back in his direction, followed by the large zombie. Ellis pulled his knife and waited for the little bastard to get closer, determined to take out the zombie that just killed him.

Private Hook and Private Gomez ran quickly down the street to the grocery store. They didn't want to be caught out in the open and didn't want to get cut off without a retreat in case the zombies swarmed them. That had happened in Missouri and all of them were still wondering what to make of the change in the zombies behavior.

Reaching the front of the building, Hook checked the door before declaring, "Locked."

Gomez nodded and they trotted around to the back of the store looking to see if the supply door was open. A quick check revealed it was locked as well.

"Ideas?" Gomez asked.

Private Hook thought for a second. "No time to pick it, let's go back to the front and break the glass."

Private Gomez nodded and the pair returned to the front of the building. It was a generic grocery store, with yellowing posters advertising sales inside. Some of the posters had fallen down, revealing a glimpse of the dark world inside. Gomez put his face to the glass and looked around for a long minute, checking to make sure there were no leftover shoppers looking for fresh meat from the butcher section.

With nothing to see, he nodded to Hook, who used the butt of his rifle to break the bottom section of one of the doors. Clearing the broken glass with his boot, he ducked under the center bar and moved into the store, rifle at the ready. A small in-store bank was in front of him, with a small teller counter and smaller office. Behind the bank was a long hallway leading to the checkout registers. As he moved slightly to his left, he scanned the frozen food section in front of him and the cereal aisle next to that. Nothing was moving and he waited for Gomez to catch up.

"Which way?" Hook asked.

Gomez pointed to the right. "Looks like there might be some canned goods that way. Let's check." The floor was littered with discarded goods, scattered hopes of survival. A corpse was lying in the corner, a blood streak on the wall and a skeletal hand gripping a can of beans explained what this person died for.

The two men walked carefully past the packaged meat section, avoiding the dark and rotting packages still hanging on the brackets. The rice pudding had turned grey, much to Hook's disappointment, since it used to be his favorite.

Gomez wiped his face as he moved to the next aisle. He hated these kinds of missions, where he never knew what was coming next. The next aisle could be full of zombies, just waiting to pounce. Give him a stand up fight with plenty of ammo any day.

They turned down the canned section and the shelves were nearly bare. There were a scattering of cans worth taking, so they put those in their packs. As they worked, Gomez stopped suddenly.

"You hear something?" he asked.

Hook immediately put down his pack and cans and picked up his rifle. "No. What did you hear?" he asked nervously.

Gomez shook his head. "I thought I heard a wheezing sound, like a dog or something?"

Private Hook relaxed a bit. "Could be. Might be one that got in here and is sleeping. Had a hound once that snored louder than my Dad's uncle. And that was a trick to do, let me tell you."

Gomez laughed softly. "Had a girlfriend who snored loud once. Denied it forever, but, hombre, she could shake the—wait. There it is again!"

Hook and Gomez listened and sure enough, they could hear a high-pitched sound, like a low pressure steam valve. It seemed to be coming from a nearby aisle. But in the building, it was hard to tell for sure.

Grabbing what they could, Gomez said, "Let's see if there is anything in the dried goods, like rice or pasta."

"Good plan," Hook agreed. "You remember which aisle?'

"Should be the far one."

"You go first."

"Jerk."

Private Gomez moved quickly to the end of the aisle and glanced around. Directly in front of him was the produce section, long rotted away. The air still had a sickly sweet smell of decaying fruit and vegetables and the floor had turned brown from the slime of the rotted food. Gomez swung out and trained his rifle at the dairy section and waved the other man forward. "Clear," he said.

Private Hook moved out and darted around the end of the aisle, scanning for threats before he nodded to Gomez. "Clear."

Private Gomez turned around and moved to the next aisle. As he glanced at Hook, he saw the other soldier's eyes get wide. Spinning around, he raised his rifle just as Hook shouted.

"Behind you!"

The cry echoed in Gomez's ears as he flicked on his weapon light to engage the threat. A fast moving zombie, probably no more than seven years old, was literally hurtling down the back of the grocery store, his teeth bared as his breath wheezed out of his mouth. His little bare feet pattered on the tile floor as he rushed to his prey. Gomez waited until he had a definite shot, then fired just as the zombie boy leaped into the air, the bullet passing harmlessly next to him.

The zombie was four feet from landing on Gomez, who raised his rifle to defend himself. At the last second, Private Hook fired, hitting the zombie in the head and spraying zombie brains all over Private Gomez.

Gomez wiped his face as best he could, hesitating a second to give the dead zombie a kick. "Stupid shit," he growled.

"Umm, dude?" Private Hook said.

"What?"

"Get your gun up, we got company."

Private Gomez looked and saw a sizable number of zombies moving in their direction from the Seasonal section. Their glowing eyes and pitiful moans made him sweat all that much more. "Oh, Jesus."

"Come on!" Private Hook grabbed his partner and bolted up the aisle, trying to head for the door. The pair skidded to a stop at the end of the aisle, nearly running into a second group of zombies that had come to the store to shop and never left.

"Shit! We're cut off!" Hook yelled, firing into the face of a nearby ghoul. "Get back!" He fired again, completely missing the horde and putting a hole in a bottle of soda. Orange mist sprayed over the zombies and some looked up as a citrus-smelling rain poured on them.

"This way!" Private Gomez sped back to the deli, darting around the case. He let Hook clear the opening before he and the other private started shoving a heavy stainless steel covered table over to the opening. Just before they got it there, they tipped it over, barricading themselves from the approaching undead.

Private Hook raised his rifle and took careful aim, killing the nearest zombie. Another took its place and as he looked, he could see many more coming from the far side of the store, their glowing eyes swaying slightly in the gloom. He turned back to Gomez.

"We got trouble, bro. There's a whole lot more of them than there are of us. I think we need to... hey, you okay?" Hook asked as he brought his flashlight up. Gomez was sitting on another table, holding his head with one hand while he tried to turn off his weapon light with the other.

Gomez looked up. "I feel weird, man. My head's spinning and my gut feels wrong," he said weakly.

Private Hook shined his light on Gomez's face. He could see dark streaks on Gomez's forehead, mingling with the sweat that was there, trickling down into Gomez's eyes. Private Hook knew immediately what had happened. When the little zombie died, the brains got showered over Gomez. When the private sweated, he got the virus into his eyes, giving it access to his bloodstream.

Gomez was infected.

Private Hook cursed. This was not turning out the way he had hoped. He fired at the horde again, killing a zombie who slid down the display case, leaving behind a dark stain on the grimy glass. The rest of the zombies pressed forward, reaching out, trying to grab at the two men. A short zombie was flattened against the glass, its facial features spreading out against the thick panes.

"Come on, let's see if we can get out of here." Private Hook grabbed Gomez by the arm, ignoring his cry of pain. Hyper-sensitivity to touch was a late stage symptom of the Enillo Virus, but if Gomez was complaining now, then the virus had indeed evolved and was faster than ever.

The two men stumbled through a back door, finding themselves in the meat cutting room. Hook left Gomez in a chair as a loud crashing came from outside. Looking out the window, Private Hook could see the zombies had forced the barricade and were spilling into the deli area, looking for thin-sliced humans.

"Think, think, think!" he muttered to himself, pacing back and forth. He searched around the room, but the quick glance he gave it didn't show him anything. Gomez groaned and Hook went over to his side.

"Hang in there, man," he said, knowing there was nothing he could do.

Gomez looked up. Already dark circles were forming around his eyes. His feverish skin was slick with sweat and his breathing was labored.

"I can feel it taking over," he whispered, slumping his head down onto his chest. "I feel like my mind is slipping away, bit by bit. *Madre de Dios*, it hurts."

Private Hook's reply was lost as the zombies plowed into the door, shaking it violently. They began hammering on it as others started pounding on the windows. Hook knew he had run out of time.

"Leave me, man. I'm dead," Gomez whispered, tipping out of his chair and sprawling onto the ground. His skin was pale and he pulled his lips back in pain as a spasm racked his body.

"Not yet, you ain't," Hook said, moving a meat rack in front of the window and locking the wheels. It wasn't much, but it might stall them a bit. He had nowhere to go, but he was going to make sure they paid for every bite they tried to take out of him.

Gomez whispered something inaudible from the floor. Private Hook looked down and saw he didn't have much time before he was going to have a ghoul in here ahead of the others. He hated to kill his friend, but in this world it was kill or be eaten.

Kneeling down, he quickly stripped Gomez of his weapons and ammo, ignoring the whimpers of pain, figuring to make them last as long as he could. Who knows, maybe he had enough to kill them all and get out of here.

Gomez whispered again. Hook heard him, but wasn't sure of what he said. Leaning down, he asked Gomez, "Say again?"

Barely audible above the banging, Gomez said, "Door." and moved his head slightly towards the far wall.

Private Hook looked in that direction and saw light coming from underneath a large rack. Hook stood up and ran over, pulling the trays away from the wall. Just as he reached for the handle, the door leading to the deli burst open, slamming into the prone Gomez and knocking him several feet in the opposite direction. Several zombies tripped into the room, crashing into the racks Hook had strategically placed to slow them down. Two of them knelt down to try a bite of Gomez, but when they got close enough, they stopped and smelled him for a minute. Hook watched in horror as they straightened up, leaving Gomez untouched. *Jesus, they know!* he thought.

As Hook turned the handle of the door, he glanced back and the last thing he saw before leaving was Private Gomez rising slowly to his feet, his milky eyes searching hungrily for his former friend.

Private Hook hurried out the door and slammed it shut behind him. Pounding from the other side hurried him away from the building. Cradling Gomez's weapons in one hand, keeping the other on his own gun, Hook began running back to the convoy.

Thorton is going to be pissed, he thought as he ran.

Major Thorton was lounging in the sun when the three men he had sent to check the houses came trotting back. They carried improvised sacks and were grinning at each other. They stopped in front of the major and showed their prizes like kids with Halloween candy.

Thorton heaved himself upright and peered into the sacks. The first one held an assortment of canned goods, from Spam to Spaghetti-O's. The next sack had a supply of ammunition, most of it for shotguns. Thorton was reminded about the nature of small towns in general. If they had any guns at all, they tended to be shotguns, which were relatively useless for zombies, or really big-bore handguns, which were good for one shot. The further east he went, the less he was finding for his men's arms, which was going to present a problem if they ever had to face a serious horde.

The third sack held about three dozen cans of various fruits and vegetables, as well as a remarkably ample supply of porno magazines. Thorton looked up at the soldier who just shrugged. Ken shook his head and waved his hand at the three, who scurried off to show their comrades and share their booty. Chances were pretty good the men had found liquor as well, but they could keep it. Thorton figured it kept the men happy enough.

Just as he was going back to his chair, the front door of the hardware store banged open, spilling two soldiers into the walkway. They rose to their feet slowly and seemed unsteady in the bright sunlight. Thorton shouted out to them.

"You two! Get over here and report!" he said loudly.

The two soldiers jumped slightly at the sound of the major's voice. Slowly swiveling their heads, they locked onto the major's position and began moving in his direction. One, Private Ellis, seemed to have injured himself and had a nasty wound on his leg. The other, Private Barnes, looked like he had something fall on his face.

Thorton cursed them for their slowness and yelled out, "I said move, you worthless pieces of dog shit! I ain't got all day!"

The two soldiers responded with their own outburst. As one, they both raised their heads, opened their mouths and groaned with enthusiasm. The sound, carried from freshly dead throats, echoed across the small town and into the surrounding countryside. It froze every living creature in their tracks for a brief second before chilling their blood to the bone. It was the calling cry of the zombies and they were on the hunt.

"Ah, shit. You dumbasses," Thorton said as he realized what had happened to the two men. Somehow they managed to get themselves infected and now they just added to the zombie army's ranks. *Nothing is going right today*, he thought to himself. *Should've just passed this stupid town by.* He walked over to the side of the road and picked up a small street sign that had been knocked over. The two former soldiers tracked his movements and moved to try and intercept him. At the trucks, soldiers spilled out with weapons at the ready, the groan of the zombies working better than a klaxon call to arms.

Thorton hefted the improvised weapon, then waited for Private Ellis to get closer. When the zombie came within range, Ken swung in a looping arc, catching the former solider under the ear and completely shearing his head off. The body of the zombie immediately fell to the ground while the head, still biting, bounced off a nearby car and came to a rest face up in the street.

Thorton didn't waste time with the second zombie. Swinging the sign in an overhead chop, he brought the weapon down onto Private Barnes skull. The edge of the sign bit deep, completely halving the hapless soldier's head. Thorton let the sign go and both it and the now completely dead zombie tumbled to the ground.

The major didn't have time to reflect. Up the street, another soldier was running at him. Thorton's first thought was *Oh shit, they're all running now?* But when he saw the man waving to get his attention, he realized two things. One, this wasn't a zombie and two, there was supposed to another soldier

Private Hook ran up to Major Thorton and bent over to catch his breath. Thorton waited impatiently with is arms crossed. When he had recovered, Private Hook was to the point.

"Sir. Gomez is dead, got infected by a little shit. Grocery store is full of the fucking things, nearly got me but I found an exit. Only got a few food items, sir." Private Hook paused to take a breath. "They're changing, sir."

Thorton tilted his head to the side. "Explain."

"Sir, we made a lot of noise getting in, but they didn't come for us until we could be cut off. If it hadn't been for the extra door in the butcher shop, I'd be dead, sir. We got trapped but good."

Major Thorton nodded, processing this bit of news. It fit with some other information he had, none of it encouraging. He shook it off and shouted his orders.

"Get their weapons and gear, then mount up. We're gone!" He strode to his vehicle and climbed aboard, just as his driver started the engine. They pulled out and moved away from the center of town.

As they passed the grocery store, Ken called a halt. Grabbing a Molotov cocktail from the back of the truck, he stalked over to the broken front door. He could see movement in the gloom and was glad he could send a few more of these bastards to hell.

Thorton threw the bomb in through the door, the flames bursting on an aisle of crackers. He could see several zombies milling about and a few actually came over to the flames to become engulfed. As he walked back to the truck, his anger was starting to mount.

He was infuriated because he lost three men to this nothing town and had very little to show for it. He was angry because he knew that what Talon had said would eventually creep through his men, undermining him and forcing him to take measures.

But worst of all, he was frightened by the implication of what had occurred in the town.

The zombies were showing signs of rudimentary intelligence. If it continued, that meant the end of every living thing on the planet.

22

Seven hours later, as the sun was winking its last under a darkening sky, Sergeant Milovich was looking over the preparations for the night. The men had travelled quickly and managed to reach the small town before nightfall. The town had been abandoned long ago and anything useful had since been rendered stolen or useless. The town actually sat in a small depression in the land, surrounded by trees. Off in the distance, Milovich could see the arching concrete arteries which once fed the nation, now just graveyards of cars and people.

He had stationed men up near the ridgeline to keep a watch for Talon. The ambush was going to be simple. As soon as the enemy reached the center of the town, they were going to cut him in half. This was going to be easy work.

Milovich was setting up his quarters in an abandoned house for the duration when Corporal Kazinski came bursting through the door.

"Sarge? Sarge?" he called.

"Right here, corporal. What is it?" Milovich's exhaustion was evident in his voice.

"Found a couple of survivors, sir, thought you might want to see 'em," Kazinski announced. He pushed forward a man of about medium height and build, with a long ponytail hanging down his back. His hands were secured behind his back and his eyes darted over Milovich's uniform and weapons before settling on the floor.

Milovich dismissed him as irrelevant and turned his attention on the other prisoners. They were two women, one blonde and the other brunette. The blonde was an attractive, buxom young woman of about thirty and the brunette was a leaner specimen, with a hard look about her. Both were bound as well, which seemed to be a good thing, since both were literally festooned with edged weapons. The blonde had a number of what appeared to be scissors attached to a wide belt which wrapped around her waist.

Milovich nodded approval and was about to order the two to be given to the men when an idea formed in his head. He let it marinate a while then smiled at the blonde, who looked back in such defiance that the sergeant nearly put a hand on his gun.

Milovich nodded to his corporal. "Good work," he said to Kazinski. "Take the man out to the edge of the town and get rid of him." The man's eyes turned wide and he opened his mouth to protest, but Kazinski's fist slammed into his head first, stunning him and bringing him to his knees. Two other soldiers grabbed him by the arms and dragged him away.

Milovich noted that neither of the two women even flinched at the violence. Excellent. He turned to the blonde and tried unsuccessfully from looking too obviously at her chest.

"As you can see, I'm in charge. Whether you live or die depends on how cooperative you both are willing to be. I need you two to be part of an operation that should be taking place in the next few days. Swear to cooperate and I can guarantee that you will leave here unmolested," the sergeant said.

"And if we don't?" the blonde spoke before her friend, nearly spitting the words at him.

"Then you will be given to the men to enjoy until they tire of you, which might mean several days, depending on your stamina," Milovich said, noting the flashes of hatred both women gave him. "What will it be?" he asked.

The two women exchanged glances and covert nods. It was obvious they figured to cooperate in order to avoid being raped to death, but they didn't know that Milovich had never kept his word in his life.

The blonde spoke. "We'll do what you want, just don't hurt us." She tried to sound defeated, but the sergeant didn't believe her for a minute. He figured she would stab him as soon as she could find the opportunity.

Sergeant Milovich smiled. This was icing on a cake that already was tasting sweet. Talon was as good as dead.

23

"Question for you."

"What?" I asked, without trying to fully wake from my rest.

"How come the young Z's are so damn fast?"

I opened my eyes and stared at the underside of the kitchen table. I had taken to napping on the bench as opposed to climbing up into the secondary sleeping area. I could sleep nearly anywhere, a throwback to my college days when I *did* pretty much sleep anywhere.

"Dunno," I replied. I slid my feet to the floor, slowly pushing myself up to a sitting position. "Maybe it has something to do with the different body chemistry," I said, scratching my head. My hair was starting to get a little shaggy without Sarah around to trim it up. I blinked and looked at Duncan, who was standing by the table.

"What do you mean?" Duncan asked, leaning back on the sink.

I looked at him closely for a second, wondering if he was serious. I glanced around and saw Tommy driving, so I knew he hadn't sent Duncan on any joke missions. Zeus the cat was up in a storage bin, his pale yellow eyes looked at me as if to say, *You'll probably regret this.*

I shrugged. "Keep in mind this is just speculation, but kids have different body chemistries than we do. Youngsters bounce back more quickly from serious illnesses than we could ever hope to. Some say that their immune systems are hyped up because they need the protection to get to adulthood, which results in different wiring. But I couldn't say for sure, because it makes no real sense. The older kids, teenagers and such, they aren't much faster than the really old ones. The brain dies and that's it. That's what the virus has to work with, just rudimentary responses to stimuli."

Duncan looked down. "What about what we saw at that apartment?"

"The doorknob turning?"

"Yeah, that."

I leaned back. "Been giving that some thought. If the zombies are actually starting to learn, then we've got to jump start our timetable and get moving to the final phase."

"That bad?" Duncan looked somewhat concerned.

"If the Z's are able to problem solve, then all our defenses won't matter for crap, because the Z's have nothing but time on their side. There is one thing I haven't seen yet, but I get the feeling it's just a matter of time." I took a swig from my water bottle.

"What's that?"

"Zombies taking shelter during the winter, or finding hidey holes to wait out the cold."

Duncan, a veteran of nearly every zombie fight I could think of, actually shuddered. "Good God," he said, as the implications hit him. "We'd have to hunt them out of every sewer, attic, basement and drainage area. And when we found them, they'd be still active.

I shook my head. "Nothing about this whole mess makes me believe in a benevolent god anymore. Want to hear the worst of it?"

"Not really."

"When was the last time you saw a lone zombie?"

Duncan thought a minute. "It's been a while, but the last one was in the parking lot back home. The one you killed. Why?"

"They are learning on more ways than one. They are laying ambushes, like we saw recently and they are attacking in groups. They seem to have learned the strength of numbers and how vulnerable they are attacking one on one."

Duncan's eyes got wide and I just nodded. "We need new tactics," he said.

I smiled and eased my way up to the front of the vehicle. Tommy was driving and he looked up as I sat down next to him.

"What's the plan, boss?" he said soberly. I figured he had heard the conversation between Duncan and myself.

"We need to stop a bit, I want to go and stretch my legs," I said, picking up a map. The road we were on was empty and there were large swaths of land on either side. Here and there were farms and barns, but I didn't feel the need to stop and see if anyone was alive. Eventually we would have to, but not on this trip.

"Where are we?" I asked. I knew we were swinging south to avoid Columbus, but as to our current location, I had not a clue.

Tommy pointed to a sign as we lumbered past. "Township Highway 160, whatever the hell that means, since a minute ago it was Carson Road and ten minutes earlier it was Township Highway 160." As we discovered, it was a running joke to try and figure out who named the stupid roads in Ohio. Currently, if the road was running East-West, it was named one thing. If running either Northwest-Southeast or Northeast-Southwest, then it was named something else. The general consensus was to just keep moving east. We wanted to eventually hit Route 50, since that would take us to the heart of DC.

"Right." Looking at the map, I indicated a stopping point. "When we get to the interstate, let's stop for a bit and have a look around."

"You got it." Tommy was another old campaigner and would be able to get us out of any trouble we happened to come across. "Hey, John?"

"Yeah?" I leaned back in the chair and closed my eyes.

"What if the zombies aren't really dead?" Tommy asked seriously.

"Explain." I hadn't travelled this course of thought before.

"What if they caught the virus and instead of truly dying, went into a deep coma, where the virus took over the brain functions. Technically, they become brain damaged due to lack of oxygen to the brain, but they are still alive, with the body responding to the virus' impulses to survive," Tommy said.

I considered it. "Not sure about that. All early reports said this virus killed people. What about the people we've seen who have been ripped in half and still coming at us? What about those with the awful wounds that don't bleed, or those with missing organs?" I didn't want to play the devil's advocate, but what Tommy was suggesting was creepy.

"Suppose the virus shuts down non-essential systems and slows down the heart rate to a beat or two a minute. There wouldn't be much blood flow and the virus could thicken the blood to prevent loss. That would explain how arms and legs could keep moving. The nervous system has shut down, save for movement impulses, making the victims immune to pain and they are decaying because the skin is not being maintained as a vital system. The bone weakness we've seen is the virus not paying attention to supporting systems, just looking out for number one.

"Basically, the virus makes the victim resemble a truly dead, back from the grave zombie, but is actually living, just not with what we consider life," Tommy concluded.

"So what you're saying is these things, which we have always believed to be dead, are actually still alive on a subnormal level?" I asked, mulling over the theory. In a way, it made sense and actually restored my faith a bit. Seeing these creatures as victims of a plague as opposed to something Hell spat forth was oddly reassuring. But one part didn't make sense.

"What about the still-living zombie heads? Remember the fight at McCard's? Those kids had a pit full of severed zombie heads, which they used to kill Kevin Pierce."

Tommy thought about that one. "Not sure, but maybe the virus goes on overload for survival when the host is truly dead, animating the leftovers for as long as possible, in the hope that another victim might be infected. For all we know, a severed zombie head will live for a while, then be truly dead."

I had to admit it was possible and made a certain amount of sense as far as reasoning goes, but for the time being, I was going to kill any zombie I came across, actually dead or not. But it was worth thinking about and gelled fairly well with the way the zombies were acting lately. I wondered if they were starting to recover, with the body actually able to fight back from some small enclave of resistant cells, which led them to increased cognitive functioning. This was going to make things really interesting and we were running out of time.

Of course, we could be wrong, they were just reanimated corpses and God hated all of us.

We pulled up onto an overpass which crossed Interstate 71. It was a big highway, four lanes separated by a grassy median. We were the only vehicle on the crossroad and I could see for miles in either direction.

I decided to get up as high as I could, so I climbed up to the top of the RV and pulled out my binoculars. To the north I could see a long line of cars stuck on the road behind an overturned semi, the unfortunate accident which held up a large exodus from Columbus. The other side of the road was full of cars travelling in the same direction, They were stopped by another series of accidents. I could see many ruts in the grass and in the surrounding fields, footprints of those who tried to escape the deathtrap of the roads. I could see the outline of the city, but I had no desire to go into that mess. We had spent a good deal of time already on the road and I was anxious to get back to my family.

As I was looking around, Nate poked his head out of the hatch. "Anything interesting?" he asked, climbing up out of the hole and sitting cross-legged on the roof. He had another pair of binoculars and unfolded a map across his lap.

"Not so far, I was just wondering where all those people went who got away from the interstate," I said, looking around.

"What do you mean?"

"I mean I see lots of cars, but no zombies."

Nate brought up his own binoculars. "Seriously?" he asked. I could understand his incredulity. Normally when we encountered a large line of cars from a major population center, there were a lot of casualties and dead people walking around. Interstates were usually fenced, keeping the zombies from wandering off.

"Seriously. I have been looking around for a while and haven't seen a single one."

"Wonder what it means."

"I've learned not to be hopeful, if you catch my drift."

"Got it. Hey, John?" Nate queried, staring into his binoculars to the northeast.

"What?" I was getting ready to head back down.

"How come you missed that blonde on the car out there?" Nate asked.

"Say what?" I looked in the direction he was and after a certain amount of scanning, I could just make out a small figure standing on the roof of a pickup truck. The hood was up and she was holding what appeared to be a towel, ready to signal anyone she saw.

"I'll be damned," I said, taking down my binoculars. "Wonder what she's doing out here?"

"Same as us, I guess," Nate said, looking at his maps and then back up at the position of the blonde. "Looks like she's on this road here, just outside this town." Nate pointed to a small junction of roads called Harrisburg.

I looked at the map and back up at the scene before me. She likely couldn't see us too well if she didn't have binoculars and to be honest, something about the scene before me was making my warning bells go off. Maybe I was being too paranoid, but I just had a heart-to-heart with Major Thorton and then this girl shows up in the middle of nowhere. I had no reason to believe in coincidences, so I had to take the paranoid route.

"Something's wrong, Nate. Look closely, tell me what's wrong with this picture." I was not sure what was bothering me, but if I could get another's eyes to think for me, that worked.

"What could be wrong?" Nate chided. "You've been on the frontier too long. You're starting to see things that aren't... really... there..." His voice trailed away as he studied the scene very carefully. I could tell something was bothering him as well, but he couldn't put his finger on it, either.

In situations like these, I found the best thing to do was to go over carefully what I could see and let my instincts take over. From where I was I could see a blonde woman and a pickup truck. The truck's hood was up and the bed was empty, the glass wasn't broken and the headlights seemed okay.

Wait a minute. I thought to myself. *Empty truck bed?* That was wrong. If the truck bed was empty, then she was running scared, but if the truck broke down, she wouldn't stay with it.

I said as much to Nate, who snorted. "You were right, before," he said.

"What are you talking about?" I asked, not understanding.

"You are better than me." Nate grinned and put down his binoculars. "So what do we do about this little trap?"

I shrugged. "See if it is what it seems to be. If not, we'll help someone out."

We both dropped down into the RV and gathered the other two men around the table. After convincing Duncan that we really didn't know what the blonde looked like and no, we didn't know if she was single, we decided on a fairly straightforward plan. We would drive the RV to the damsel in distress, leaving behind a pair of men to see if it was a trap and if so, spring it on the trappers. What could go wrong?

24

I checked the maps again, and found there was no way to get to the woman unless we backtracked and came up Harrisburg and London Road. That was the bad news. The good news was that the overland route was just about a mile, so in the time it took for the RV to circle back and hit the road the supposed ambush was on, we would be able to scout the area and see if anyone was waiting for us.

I volunteered myself to run the mile and Duncan decided Tommy needed to go with me. I laughed at Duncan's transparent attempt to have as few rivals as possible should the hapless damsel be grateful for a rescue. I took out my pack and checked the supplies, making sure I had water and food. I switched out my AR mags for M1A mags, since I was bringing the heavier weapon. I preferred the .308 when dealing with possible living adversaries, as it had a much more authoritative punch. Plus, out here in farmland, I could seriously reach out and ruin someone's day, much more so than I could with the AR.

Tommy got his gear together and we set out from the RV, running down the road a ways before we set out across the fields. The land was overgrown enough that we had to duck around some fairly large feral trees and scrub bushes. We came up to a forest and nearly had to find a way around when Tommy pointed to the East.

I slapped him on the back and we ran over to the large aluminum power line tree sticking up over the forest. Working our way beneath it, we found a clear path underneath the dormant power lines. Crews used to make sure the land underneath was well maintained and in the two years since the Upheaval, the grass and weeds had grown, but they were just knee high this late spring. We moved quickly and quietly through the brush, ever on the lookout for any Z's that might be lying in wait. Thanks to our recent encounters, we were also checking our back trail, making sure nothing was following us into the high timber.

After about a quarter mile in the woods, I could see the interstate about one hundred yards ahead of us. I motioned

Tommy into the woods and we walked as smoothly as we could through the heavy brush. More than once I had to check my compass to make sure we were headed in the right direction.

One hundred and fifty yards into the woods led us to the back yard of a largish house. It was a simple structure, two stories, with a detached garage and gravel driveway. I gave it quick glance and Tommy just shrugged his shoulders. Maybe we could investigate further when the RV showed up, but right now, it wasn't my main concern. I looked it over for occupancy, living or otherwise, but the building seemed like it was deserted.

There was another house about five hundred feet away and it was in the direction we wanted to go, so Tommy and I ran over and hunkered down behind the above-ground pool in the backyard. Peeking over the brackish green water of the pool, I looked over the small house but couldn't see if it was occupied. Behind us was another large house, but again, it wasn't a concern. Tommy pointed to the corner and I covered him as he ran to the side of the house to get a look at the front.

In less than a minute, he came back around and waved me forward. I moved up and happened to catch him wiping off his knife. At my curious glance, he pointed to the driveway where a large male zombie was lying face down with a stab wound in his neck. His body was no longer moving, but I could see his eyes darting around and his mouth opening and closing. The big sucker must have surprised Tommy or Tommy surprised it. Either way, it was a good silent kill and I nodded to Tommy in appreciation.

"You're going to think I'm crazy, but thanks to our conversation, I'm actually curious to see if the head eventually dies," I whispered.

Tommy smiled. "I was thinking the same damn thing." He pointed to the second floor window, where a female zombie was clawing at the window too weak to break it and make a lunge for us.

"Leave it. Let's get to where we can see better," I said. We moved up to a small line of trees that blocked the view of the main road. Hunkering down, I pulled out my binoculars while Tommy brought up his rifle and scanned for threats. I could see the woman and her truck and I had to say she had the necessary assets. Duncan was going to be pleased this wasn't a wasted effort. That is, if we didn't get killed for it.

I pointed to the house that was about two hundred yards ahead of us, then back to the tree line we were hiding behind. Tommy nodded and bolted for the edge of the trees which took him behind the house and out of sight of the woman. If there were ambushers, they would be keeping an eye on their bait, not on the scenery.

When Tommy reached the end of the trees, he ran directly for the house, keeping himself out of sight of the windows and doors. Once he was in place, I ran to the edge of the tree line and onto the driveway that went to the house way in the back. I moved as quickly as I could, coming to a stop in a small grove of trees. From where I was situated, I could see the front of the small house and the woman and truck on the road. I could also see the road as it crossed Interstate 71 and figured the RV was going to be along in just a few minutes.

I waved to Tommy, who ducked back around the house. Two minutes later, he came back around the house and moved swiftly to join me in the trees. I raised an eyebrow at him and he shook his head, indicating the house was empty.

I took out my binoculars and looked over the situation. If there were ambushers, they were extremely well hidden. I didn't see anything on the highway, nothing in the homes, nothing in the trees, nothing in the bushes on the other side of the road. If I had to guess, this was just a breakdown with someone who was too scared to move on.

I turned my attention back to the woman and was able to see her in greater detail. She was probably in her thirties, with sharp blue eyes and attractive features. Her blonde hair was surprisingly well maintained, but she seemed ill-dressed for survival. Her clothing was tight, showing off her ample chest and long legs. Her shoes were just hiking boots and she seemed to have a belt that had a holder for what appeared to be a variety of scissors. What she planned to do with them against a zombie I couldn't guess. Her face was lined with worry at this particular time and she kept looking back at the town as if she was hoping to see something. I wondered if she had fled something and was waiting to see if it pursued her. If so, why was she just standing there? Without an obvious ambusher, this whole setup didn't make sense.

I didn't have time to contemplate it further as I could hear the RV rumbling along. I could see the woman heard it too, as she faced the sound and waited to see what it was. I noticed she hesitated before waving her flag, making sure she had an idea of what was coming. I guess in her shoes I would feel the same, considering it could have been a biker gang or something that came over that hill.

As it was, it was a serious zombie-killing recreational vehicle, decked out in all the latest Z repellant gear. I had to admit, seeing it roll over the hill like that, it was impressive. But I had no more time to look on in wonderment and admiration, as we were here to do a job. I brought my rifle up and kept it trained on the far side of the road, while Tommy kept his gun on this side of the road. There was a house up the road to the east we hadn't checked out, but there was nothing to be done for it.

The big rig slowed to a stop and I could see Nate at the wheel. Even fifty yards away I could see Duncan's stupid grin as he got close to his mystery woman and saw she was very pretty. Nate pulled the RV to a stop past the woman's truck and angled it so it blocked the road. Anyone on the far side would not be able to see what was going on and any ambushers riding in from the east would be blocked as well. Pretty smart.

Tommy and I waited until Nate got out of the RV, followed by a fairly jumpy Duncan. We started walking to the scene, keeping our weapons ready. I could hear Nate's voice and the woman's but couldn't make out what they were saying until I got closer.

"But my friend is back there and she needs help!"

"Not my decision to make right now."

"Oh, God, please! You look like you two could handle the zombies, just pull that truck close to the building and let her jump down! Why won't you help?" The woman seemed nearly hysterical.

Nate sounded compassionate, but cynical, if that was even possible. "Like I said, it's not up to me."

The woman turned to Duncan, who clearly enjoyed the attention. "Please," she said, placing a hand on his arm. "My friend needs help. I drove out here to see if there was anyone in these homes that could help and the truck broke down. She's been with me since the beginning and I can't just leave her." I couldn't see her face, but I was willing to bet she was nearly crying. I was almost convinced myself.

Duncan nodded and the woman seemed to brighten, but slumped her shoulders when he said, "We'd love to help, but it ain't up to us."

The woman took a step back and cursed. "Well, dammit! Who the hell is in charge and why aren't they out here?"

I stopped walking and was positioned about ten feet behind her. "Turn around," I said as the woman jumped slightly at the sound of my voice. She spun about and stared at me, not sure where the hell I could have sprung from. I could see her quick inventory of my weapons, followed by a quick personal inventory of my physical features. What she saw was probably not comforting. A six foot-two, broad shouldered man in his thirties, wearing a vest full of ammo, a belt with a pistol and knife on it and holding a fully loaded battle rifle. A funny look flashed on her face, but it was gone before I could get a read on it.

I introduced myself. "Name's John Talon, these renegades are my crew. You've met Nate, the big guy over there and Duncan, the skinny fellow. Tommy Carter is the gent to the rear. Who might you be?"

The blonde tossed her hair back with a shake of her head and said, "I'm Janna Thorne. Are you going to help my friend, or not?" Her tone was belligerent, which could be excused as worry for her friend.

"We'll see," I said, motioning for Nate and Tommy to go back into the RV. Duncan went back with obvious reluctance and Nate had to pull him in just so he could shut the door. Tommy wandered over to the truck and was poking around in it.

I faced Janna. "Tell me about your friend. Where is she, what's the best route to get to her, how did you get away, etc. If I am to help and I haven't said I would, I need as much information as possible."

Janna's eyes lit up with hope at the possibility of helping her friend, a good sign that she was sincere. She spilled out her tale so quickly I was nearly lost three seconds after she started.

In a nutshell, she was working as a hairdresser in a small town when the Upheaval hit. She was able to fight her way to her parent's house, only to find they had been infected. Her little brother was killed by zombies when she was trying to get him out to safety and she spent the last couple of years on the move. She met her friend Gina out on the road and the two stayed together for obvious survival reasons. They got surprised by a large group of zombies and when she jumped from the roof to a dumpster, the dumpster tipped over and before she could right it, the zombies chased her away from her friend.

"What's with the scissors?" I asked, just out of curiosity.

Janna smiled at me. "They work as weapons. I'm used to them and they easily penetrate zombie skulls if you know what you're doing."

I had to agree. One pair of the scissors seemed to have blades over seven inches long, longer than my knife blade.

"All right," I said. "Climb aboard. We'll see what we can do for your friend." I held out an arm at the RV, which Nate had started and was waiting for us.

"Thank you," she said, clasping my hand with hers.

"Don't thank me yet," I said, taking my hand back to open the door. "Your friend is still in danger." Janna stepped inside as Tommy came up to the door.

"Truck really broken down?" I asked under my breath as he passed by.

"Battery cable came off. Might be on purpose, might be on accident. Can't tell."

"Keep your eyes open. I don't trust this at all."

"Ditto."

25

We moved slowly into town, as I told Nate to take it easy. I wanted to give the appearance of a group just looking to see if things were okay before they stopped. If we were being watched and the hairs standing up on the back of my neck told me we were, then I wanted to present as much of a humble front as possible. It was one thing to try and trap someone. It was another when the person you trapped turned into a much bigger animal than you thought..

I felt like we had a huge target on the side of the RV and were getting closer to the order to fire. Trouble was, I had no idea who might be waiting for us. I just had the feeling. In all honesty, if it was an ambush by zombies, I would probably feel better.

Janna and Duncan sat at the kitchen table and he tried to get more information from her. Zeus the cat came down from his perch to meet the new arrival and he was currently lounging on the table in front of Janna. She idly stroked his back while telling her tale. She had been travelling with two friends, as it turned out, but the guy she was with had been killed. She didn't go into any more detail. I was standing by the side window, watching the town move past.

We drove past several homes and turned onto High Street, which looked like it would take us through the center of town. We passed Harrisburg United Methodist Church and it looked worse for wear. All of the homes looked like this town had had a rough go of it, since it was so close to the interstate and all the blocked cars. When people fled their cars, where did they go? Right to Harrisburg. Who followed them? You got it.

As we passed Sycamore Street I noticed a truck sitting in the middle of the street. It seemed wildly out of place. The truck was of a military style, with a high cab and bias-ply tires. The back was canvas covered and it was just sitting there. It seemed to be a vehicle capable of hauling a lot of stuff over heavy terrain, so why anyone would leave it seemed odd to me.

"Nate," I called up front. "Stop here. I want to take a look at something."

"You got it."

The RV slowed to a stop and Tommy immediately went to the ladder to the roof. Duncan reluctantly broke away from Janna and picked up his rifle. Nate stayed at the wheel, ready to gun it and get us out of there if need be.

I went over to the door and waited and in a few seconds, Tommy thumped the roof to let me know it was clear to go out. As I went, I heard Janna talking to Duncan.

"You guys act like you've done this before..."

I didn't hear the rest as I was outside and moving around the front of the vehicle. The sun was brighter and I was wishing I had brought my sunglasses with. I moved down the center of the road, careful to make as little noise as possible. From experience, I knew that zombies might be waiting in ambush, but they would have to cross some open ground to get to me. I knew my back was being watched by Tommy and unless he was way off his game, the first shot I would hear would be his taking out a Z.

I moved over to the truck and pulled myself up to the cab. I didn't see anyone in it and a quick look through the canvas showed some supplies, but no clues as to why such a truck was here. Strange.

I was about to jump down when a map caught my eye. It was tucked into the small storage area that ran the length of the dashboard. I took it out and opened it, figuring to see just another map of Ohio. What I didn't expect was to see three areas circled. One was Harrisburg, which made a certain amount of sense. The other was a small forest preserve southwest of here and the last was a larger forest preserve called Stroud's Run State Park. There was a red question mark over the area we had stayed the other night and Route 50 was heavily penciled over. There were cross marks on several towns and some were boxed in. It made no sense at all.

I left the map and walked back to the RV, shaking my head at Tommy and Nate. As I reached the center of the road, a shot rang out from in front of me. At first I thought it was Tommy, but then in the next second I realized it couldn't be Tommy because I had been shot! The round slammed into the left side of my abdomen and there was a popping sound as the bullet hit me. Something hit my head and I stumbled backwards, dropping my rifle, and coming to a stop near the truck. My gut hurt like hell and I immediately tried to press both hands to stop whatever bleeding there might be. My head hurt and I could feel blood pouring down my face.

I heard several more shots being fired and the sound of the RV roaring to life. The last sound I heard was Tommy screaming my name as the RV pulled away. After that I didn't hear anything.

26

I opened my eyes to what I thought was some time later and stared at the weird scene in front of me. There was a long metal bar right above my face and another at a cross section. If this was the afterlife, it was already a disappointment. My head cleared a bit and I began to realize what had happened. Somebody had shot me and I was under the truck I had been investigating. I reached down to where my wound was and poked around a bit. My vest was frayed and there was a lot of busted metal that pricked my probing fingers. My side hurt like hell, but it didn't feel as bad as I thought it would. I had heard that getting shot in the gut was as bad as it could be and doomed the recipient to an agonizing death. If this was agonizing pain, I was tougher than I thought I was. I explored my head wound and found a gash near my hairline. My face was crusted with drying blood, so I was sure I looked a fright.

I could hear the sounds of gunfire, so I figured my friends were still in the fray, taking on whoever had shot me. I raised my hand and looked at my fingers, expecting to see them covered in blood. I was rather surprised they weren't.

What the hell? I started to sit up, but my side hurt again and I bumped my head on the axle of the truck. Falling back, I put my hand out and touched the stock of my M1A. I looked at it for a second and figured I must have grabbed it before I took shelter under the truck. I didn't remember doing either of those things, so it was another surprise.

I rolled over, wincing as a fresh wave of pain hit my gut and crawled out on the opposite side of the truck. Whoever had shot me was pretty lousy at assassination, since I was a fairly lively corpse. But if they were still out there, I didn't want to offer them a chance to correct their mistake.

I got to my knees and willed myself to look at the damage. I was expecting to see blood soaked clothing and a very disturbing hole in my sacred person. What I was not expecting to see was a vest pocket blown away and a very badly damaged rifle magazine. Several rounds had exploded when they had been hit, rupturing the mag and blowing out the pocket.

I thought I knew what had happened. The sniper had hastily taken his shot, since I had gotten out before the planned ambush site and the round had punched into one of the steel-sided magazines for my rifle. The steel had absorbed most of the energy of the round, but it had enough to penetrate three of my cartridges, causing them to fire and blow the mag apart at the front. One of the rounds went north and had struck me a glancing blow to the head. Two inches to the left and I'd be dead.

I was going to be sore as hell for a while for taking a hit from a rifle and having a small explosion at my liver, but there was no way around the truth. I was luckier than I had a right to be. Somewhere out there, there was a guy who couldn't walk through a doorway without bumping something. I had all of his luck, as well as mine.

I looked over my M1A for damage and it had nothing worse than a few dings in the stock and flash hider from its fall to the ground. As I wiped it off and checked the barrel for obstructions, the sound of gunfire came to me again and in a flash, I was pissed. I also clearly understood what the circles and symbols meant on the map. This was an ambush for me, sent by Thorton.

My blood went cold as I let my rage build. I closed my eyes and breathed deep, pulling in the pain from the near miss and drawing strength from it. As I opened my eyes I smiled grimly to no one. The killer was free.

The shots I was hearing came from the south, so I decided to head that way. I wanted to fight, to kill and every second of delay made me angrier. I ran back to a side street and worked my way south, with the notion that I might be able to come up behind the attackers and take them by surprise. I had no idea who was alive or how many people were still fighting. I did know one thing for sure.

I knew who was *not* going to live.

The road I limped down was called Fire Lane and it was pretty much an alley between two larger roads. But it gave me a corridor to approach the firefight unseen. I passed by the Harrisburg Community Center and I glanced at it briefly, thinking I saw something move in the shadows. But I didn't have time to care, as the firing intensified. Somebody had somebody else pinned down pretty good, but the fact that the firing kept up gave me hope that someone was still up and fighting.

Fire Lane ended at Walnut Street, where a day care center sat on the corner. Across the street I could see some houses that looked to be occupied by the dead and they were standing at the windows, looking out at the action. I still couldn't tell where the firing was coming from, but it seemed I was a lot closer. The shots were less frequent, only an occasional round being fired here and there. It sounded like the two sides had settled into a kind of a stalemate.

Crossing Walnut, I made my way around a small strip mall, aware that the firing seemed to be coming from the building right in front of me. I thought it was a grocery store, but it could have been anything. I moved further to the east to see if I could get a glimpse of the situation and when I did, I could see the RV parked next to a brick building. Moving a little more, I could see it was a post office. I smiled. Trust Nate to find the best building for defense. Old time post offices were built like bomb shelters and it would take a hell of a hit to bring it down. The brick allowed for good protection from gunfire and the steel mesh covering the windows prevented more accurate shots from finding their targets.

I could see rounds bouncing off the walls as less-than-precise firing came from the building across the street. As I looked, rifles poked out from the building next to the post office, making escape impossible. Nate and the others were pinned down, no question about it. They were going to either be killed or die of dehydration. Neither of which was an option to my liking.

I decided to take on the building next door to the Post Office, figuring it had fewer men inside. That was a pure guess, but it made sense. I needed to get across the street without being seen, so I backtracked a block and ran down Walnut to Spruce Street. I cut across Columbus and made my way through overgrown backyards, stepping around discarded children's toys and playhouses. Lonely swings squeaked a greeting as I moved quietly past. I worked my way close to a house and crawled around a swimming pool, gritting my teeth against the pain in my side. I hoped like hell I didn't have any internal bleeding or I was going to be mad.

The way looked clear and I moved silently over to the door. As luck would have it, the entrance was on the side away from the street, so I could enter without being seen by the group across the way. Hopefully, my luck would hold out a little longer.

I figured my rifle would be too much for close in work, so I slung it across my back and pulled my knife. I needed to do this quietly and try not to alert anyone I was there until it was too late. I had my SIG if I needed it, but I hoped I wouldn't.

Opening the door, I stepped inside quickly, ducking to the side and letting my eyes adjust to the interior. I was in a professional office building and that made my job easier. A large open place like a restaurant would be tough, but small offices made moving around unseen that much more expedient.

I looked quickly at a floor plan that outlined where the offices were. If I guessed right, my enemies were in the real estate offices on the far side of the building. Okay, that worked. I went to the first office and opened the door casually. I figured to act as if I belonged there and let surprise do my job for me. If I was an attacker, someone who was sneaking around would make me pay attention much more than someone who acted like they were supposed to be there.

The first office was empty, so I moved on to the next one. That one had a big conference room table right in the middle of it and I was shocked to see a slim brunette lying on it. She didn't look dead to me, so I walked over and tapped her on the back. I jumped back as she sat up suddenly, bringing her bound hands up in front of her face, a face I noted that had several bruises on it.

"Don't!" she yelled.

"Shh!" I said, holding up a hand. "I'm not here to hurt you. Who are you?" I had a suspicion I knew who she was, but I was curious to see if her story matched Janna's, the woman who led us into this trap and nearly got me killed.

"Who are *you*?" she challenged, looking at my bloody face. "If you're not one of them, what are you doing here?"

I couldn't blame her for her tone, given the evidence of her rough treatment. I had a wild notion to say I was Luke

Skywalker and I was here to rescue her, but I figured she wasn't old enough to know what in thunder I was talking about.

"Name's John. You?"

"Gina. Cut me loose and let's get out of here! They'll be back soon!" She held out her bound hands and pleaded with her eyes.

"Not yet. I need some information from you and I don't like to repeat myself. So whatever I ask you, answer quickly. Got it?" I sounded brutal, but lives were on the line as shots came from the back of the building.

Gina nodded and looked at me with big brown eyes. I had just a few questions. "How many are there? What kind of weapons do they have and why did they ambush us?' I wasn't going to get into a grudge match just because my side hurt.

"There's four of them here and six more across the street. They have black military guns, not like yours and I don't know why they want to kill you, they didn't say." The words came at a rush and she inhaled deeply when she finished. It was valuable information, no doubt and gave me what I needed to know.

"I'm going to take care of the men here, then I'm going to get the others. One last question: Did your friend Janna deliberately lead us to an ambush?" I stared hard at Gina, hoping my suspicions were false.

Gina lowered her eyes. "They killed our friend and threatened worse for me if she didn't cooperate. The men here have been telling me what they're going to do to me once they kill your friends."

I was relieved to hear that and it was strengthened my resolve to kill every one of these sons of bitches. Once upon a time I would have recoiled from wholesale murder, but that part of me was gone, replaced by a killer survivor. Mentally, I shrugged. This was what I had become.

I cut Gina's bonds and led her out to the receptionist's desk. "Stay here until I get back. I'll let you know when it's safe."

Gina nodded and before I could stop her, leaned in quickly and kissed my cheek. "Thank you," she said as she squatted down behind the desk.

I nodded and readied myself for some serious exercise. Moving through the dark hallway, I worked my way to the back rooms where shots were still being fired. As I came near the corner, a shape came around and lunged at me. I stepped back and brought up my knife, swinging my arm to deflect the outstretched arms. The heavy blade sank deep into the neck of my enemy, cutting off his air supply and dropping him quickly and quietly. As I let him fall I realized this was not a zombie, but one of the men attacking my friends. His feet drummed the floor weakly as he grabbed his ruined throat, suffocating on his own blood. He must have been on his way to keep his promise to Gina when he bumped into me.

As his thrashing slowed and came to a halt, I peeked around the corner to see if I could get an idea of where exactly the rest were. Two doors in the small hallway were open and a third leading to an inner area was open as well, giving access to what probably was a storage room. If I was really lucky, there was a wall between the two rooms allowing me to operate undetected.

I slid along the wall, trying to keep as low a profile as possible. The light from the two rooms was enough to illuminate the hallway and I could see to the other end of the building. Motivational posters lined the walls, full of crap about believing in the power of your dreams and teamwork. I wish just once they'd made one that said 'Get back to work. Staring at pretty pictures doesn't make money for the company.' At least it would be honest.

Crouching low, I approached the first open door and glanced inside. A small man was seated by the window, his rifle up and aimed at the Post Office next door. As I watched, he fired another round, muttering to himself. "Hope you get one in the gut, you fuckers. I got your man and I'm gonna get you." I looked down at my close call and bared my teeth. This one just became personal.

I darted around the corner and went full tilt across the office, slamming into the man and driving him into the widow ledge. His breath came out in a bark as I hit him and I drove an elbow into the side of his head as he bounced off the wall.

While he lay stunned, I took his rifle and threw it into the corner, quickly checking him for sidearms. When I saw he had none, I holstered my SIG. I kept my knife out, though.

The man, whose name tag read Hodges, shook his head and got painfully to his feet. The window ledge had caught him square in the chest and I was sure his head rang from my elbow strike. He looked at me with dazed eyes, then as recognition hit him, he opened his mouth to yell. I shut him up with a sharp punch to the chin, snapping his head back and knocking him over his chair. I waited for him and this time he got up slower than before. His eyes glowed with hate as he pulled his own knife and began waving it in front of himself.

"So you lived, huh? Well, I like this better. The sarge said to wait, but you got out early. Thought my gut shot would have taken you down by now." At the last word he lunged without warning, the knife blade glittering at my face. It would have taken me right in the eye had I stayed put.

I moved slightly to the right and ducked my head, letting the blade go past me and bringing up my left hand for an uppercut that snapped his teeth shut and took him to the floor once again. Hodges' eyes narrowed as he scrambled to his feet again.

I spun my knife on my hand, waiting for him to make another move. He looked at my blade and realized I was playing with him, that I could kill at my leisure. His eyes darted to the rifle on the floor. He suddenly threw the knife at me and dove for the gun. I ducked as the blade went harmlessly past me to clatter against the far wall and struck out with a viscous kick to his ribs just as he bent down to pick up the fallen weapon.

Hodges' face twisted in pain as one, probably two, ribs snapped from my kick. He hit the wall heavily and sank, holding his side as tears leaked out of his closed eyes.

"Just finish me, you shit. You'll never get us all. You and your friends are as good as dead." He was game to the end, I had to give him that. Hodges grabbed the rifle from the floor and as he swung it up to fire, I lunged forward and drove my knife deep into his chest, coming up under the sternum and severing his heart. Hodges' face twisted in fresh pain, then relaxed as death pulled his soul from him.

I drew my knife out and looked into his lifeless eyes. As I wiped off his blood, I couldn't help but wonder why I didn't feel anything about killing this man. Maybe it was because he was trying to kill me. But I felt nothing, not good, not bad, nothing.

It was almost like I was just doing a job, something that needed to be done. It was strange and I would have to reflect on it further, but I had two more men to kill.

I checked the hallway to see if anyone had heard our scuffle, but it seemed like no one had. Moving into the hall, I slid along the wall and spared a glance into the next open door. This office was bigger, with three desks and a partition. A man was seated again at the window and another was sitting in an office chair, leaning back and watching the other man fire at the building next door. His rifle was across his lap, waiting its turn to try and kill my friends.

I looked at my knife and considered my options, then sheathed it. I had no more time for theatrics and my side and head still hurt like hell. I pulled my SIG and walked right into the room, coming up behind the reclining man. I aimed at the junction of his neck and shoulder and fired, sending a round down into his chest and obliterating his heart.

As his companion died, the one at the window spun around at the shot, bringing his rifle around to try and get it into play. I didn't waste time and pumped three rounds into his chest and abdomen, killing him instantly. He slumped down under the window as blood flowed out of his wounds.

I moved back to the hallway and waited, making sure these were the last men in the building. I heard nothing and saw no one new, I wanted to send a message back to the rest of the men still firing on my friends. I could hear the shots and fortunately, I could hear return fire coming from the Post Office. I went down the hall to the furthest office and stepped inside, quickly scanning for threats. The big window on the back wall looked out over the road and across the street. I had a good view of the attacker's position and as I checked for opposition, I could see two men at an upstairs window. They were using a pretty good method of firing. One would shoot then duck, while the other would wait for return fire and then open up. I'd have to remember that one.

The good news was no one from the other position could see that the men in this building had been taken out. They'd figure it out in a bit when no one from this building fired on the Post Office. The better news was the fools in the far building were hiding behind cinder block walls. They were going to get lively in a hurry.

I opened the big window about three inches and settled down with my back to a desk. From my angle I could just make out the second floor of the opposing building. I was four feet back from the window, so it was going to be difficult to figure out where the shots were coming from. I liked their method, maybe they'd like mine. I lifted my heavy rifle and flicked off the safety, getting a sight picture with the rear peep sight.

As I was about to try my luck I got a weird surprise. Suddenly one of the men yelled something to someone behind him and then there were three men in the window. The new man kept his rifle on the Post Office, while the other two aimed their guns down the street past the building I was in. I had no clue what they were aiming at, but I wasn't going to ask this gift horse to smile.

Just as they fired, I opened up, pumping two rounds at each man. The heavy bullets thudded through them both, knocking one back and bouncing the other off the window frame, sending him tumbling to the ground below. I didn't see if he got up, as I was firing at the third man in the window. My aim was off and I hit him in the head instead of the chest where I wanted. A crimson mist spread out behind his head on the far wall as a new hole opened up in his face. He slumped down without firing a single return shot.

I kept my gun on the building, but didn't see anyone else. By this time I figured Nate and company had their guns at the ready as well, so I decided it was okay to evacuate the premises. I pulled a garbage bag out of one of the cans and quickly stripped the dead men of their ammo and weapons. We didn't need the guns, but the ammo was useful and maybe we could trade the guns for something later.

I glanced over at the Post Office and quickly jerked my head back as a bullet went screaming past my ear. I shook my head at my stupidity and decided to try another method of communication.

I worked my way back to the front of the building to retrieve Gina, but she was nowhere to be seen. Stepping out into the daylight, I looked around and saw nothing. She must have bugged out when she had the opportunity. Can't say I blamed her.

I went around the south end of the building and as I turned the corner, there was a renewed burst of firing from the Post Office. Across the street I heard a gasping scream, then a sickening thud, like someone else had dropped out the window. I guess Tommy or Duncan's patience had been rewarded. Cool.

I stayed behind cover and yelled out. "Don't shoot, you crazy bastards!" I waited for a minute, then got a reply.

"Step out and keep your hands where I can see them! Twitch and I'll blow you to hell!"

That would be Tommy. It was nice to see he was still alive. I put my hands around the corner first, then followed them. I couldn't help but grin like a damn fool when I heard, "John? Jesus H. Christ! John!"

Tommy was leaning out a window with Duncan providing backup when he saw me. Both men ducked inside and a second later came barreling out of the back door of the Post Office. I wrapped the two of them up in a bear hug, glad as all get out to see they were still alive.

Tommy grinned at me with tears in his eyes. "When I saw you go down, I didn't know what to think. Nate gunned the RV forward to try and protect you, but they were shooting from so many places we had to get away. How in Jesus did you survive?"

I shifted so they could see the pocket and blown magazine. I pointed at my skull as Duncan whistled and shook his head. "Don't do that again, man. Don't ever do that again." His own eyes were wet and he wrapped me up in another hug.

I had to admit, my own eyes were misty, as I thought about not seeing these guys again. They were as much my brothers as my own blood and meant as much to me.

Looking over the two of them, I saw they hadn't escaped injury. Tommy had a nasty burn on his neck that was going to take some tending to and Duncan had a crude bandage on his forearm.

"Let's get out of the open. There's still a couple of these fuckers to deal with," I said as I went over to the open door.

I walked in and saw Janna seated on some bags of undelivered mail. She smiled when she saw me, but I could see she was still worried for her friend. Maybe she was worried about lying to us and leading us to an ambush that nearly got me killed, but I could be wrong. I went up to the front counter, where Nate was still holding vigil against the other building. There hadn't been any firing for a while, but it took one oversight to get you killed these days.

The sunlight through the bullet-pocked window bounced off glass shards, through little rainbows of light all over the service area. The counter was heavy brick and mortar and the chipped bits of rock told how close a fight it was and how smart Nate was in choosing it as a place to make a stand.

"Hey, Nate," I said, stepping into the service area.

"Hey, John," Nate said, not taking his eyes off the enemy building. "Thought I heard a .308 talking out back. Nice work with the guys across the street."

I looked out and saw two bodies crumpled at the base of the building. "Thanks," I said, putting the garbage bag of loot on the counter. "Looks like you've been busy too."

Nate shrugged. "Could be worse. If we were up against real military, we'd all be dead. They guys weren't even close."

I figured that. It was too easy to get the drop on the guys in the other building. Military personnel would never have left their rear so unguarded. I looked over at the building. "Think we got them all?" I asked.

"Maybe." Nate was uncertain. "Only one way to find out."

"True. Well, I got a back way. Coming?" I asked, grabbing up the garbage bag.

"Sure." Nate got off the counter and headed my way. As he passed, he looked at my ruined vest and magazine, then up at me. Without warning, he wrapped a big arm around my neck and pulled me in. Holding onto me for a second, the big goof shook his head, then let go. "Thought I lost you, man," was all he could choke out.

I nodded. "Wouldn't want to leave you guys, either." I rubbed a hand across my eyes, stupid dust was everywhere. "Come on, let's finish this."

We gathered up the other three and I led the way out back along the route I had followed getting here originally. When we crossed Columbus, Tommy looked down the street and asked, "What's that?"

About twenty yards away, a small form was crumpled on the pavement. I looked closely and saw familiar brunette hair. I looked down and shook my head. "That used to be a girl called Gina." It was obvious now what had happened. Gina had seized the opportunity to run and exposed herself too long to the gunfire of the men across the way. That was what they were aiming at when I fired back at them. Unknowingly, I had avenged her death almost instantly, but it was of little consolation now.

Janna cried out and ran to the small form, dropping beside Gina's lifeless body and holding her to her chest. Duncan trotted along side, keeping his rifle ready and looking extremely grim. I raised a hand and signaled to Duncan and he nodded. We needed to be moving quickly. He and Janna were going to bring up the RV.

As we crossed the street and worked our way back along the Spruce to Walnut, I gave Nate the intelligence I had inadvertently gathered. There were ten men in the attack, we had so far accounted for eight of them. I had seen a map in the truck and from a quick reflection, I had a very good idea where the men planned on rendezvousing with their commander. That gave us an edge and me an idea. But we had to finish this first.

Running down Walnut, we came back down Fire Lane and past the day care center. I noticed the building we were looking for had an open door at the back and quickly I realized we outnumbered the guys we were chasing.

Nate and Tommy agreed to check out the building while I hung back to see if I might get lucky. I walked to the edge of the parking lot and looked around. The town seemed normal enough, but I could see zombies in the windows of many of the houses, unable to get out. These guys apparently hadn't figured out how to work the doorknobs yet.

A sound behind me caused me to look and see both Nate and Tommy emerge from the building, each carrying two additional rifles and ammo. We were well set for any more encounters.

A different sound reached my ears and I turned the other way to see the truck, the source of a lot of my misery, pull out of the side street it was parked on and roar away to the north. I lifted my rifle and though it was a long shot, I had to vent somehow. I fired six times and had the satisfaction of hearing the bullets hit the truck. If they had any effect, I didn't see it, but at least the fleeing bastards knew they had been to a fight. We had taken out eighty percent of their attacking force and had received only minor injuries in return. We had lost Gina, but since she wasn't really part of our outfit, I didn't count her in the list.

Nate and Tommy came running at the sound of firing and saw the truck lurching out of sight around the north bend.

I started walking back and waved them to come with. "Come on. We need to saddle up. I want to be waiting for those two when they get to their rendezvous point."

"You know where that is?" Nate asked, stepping in beside me.

"Yep. I saw their map before they shot me."

"Well, well. Maybe we'll get real lucky and our good friend Major Thorton will be there."

"Yeah."

27

We hit the road after burying Gina in a shallow grave. I gave Janna the choice of heading out on her own or coming with us. She decided to stay with us, probably out of a sense of self-preservation, but after overhearing her asking questions about Leport and our home, she seemed open to the idea of settling in a safe community. Duncan was thrilled, I could see and I was hoping he would be able to keep it together for the task at hand. Given what we had just been through, we were dealing with men who had no qualms about shooting anything and cared very little for life.

I was driving this time, giving the others time to treat their wounds and get some rest. I hoped we would get ahead of the ambushers, but to be sure, I was burning up a lot of gas to get there as quickly as possible.

According to the map and it was hard to tell, we could take Rt 762 to Rt 33 and then pick up Rt 50 from there. It was an odd coincidence that we would be travelling to a road we needed to get revenge we wanted. Win-win in my book.

We were on the road for four hours when we finally reached Stroud's Run. It was a very nice park with a lot of trees and a big lake. There was a National Forest directly to the East of Stroud's Run, but this was still very nice. I pulled the RV into a small road called Township Highway 213A. From the looks of things, the road was all of two hundred feet long. Whoever named the roads in Ohio sure loved their job.

The sun was setting slowly and the new growth trees were casting long shadows in the waning light. We had passed several towns on the way here and Athens was just a small jog away, home to Ohio University and about thirty thousand zombie co-eds, give or take. We had the river blocking most of them, but travelling at night with your lights on was asking for trouble, especially with those numbers. In the morning, you'd find yourself surrounded, outnumbered and up to your neck in zombie gunk. No thanks.

I parked the RV backwards near the water, keeping a safe retreat in case of serious attack. The road we wanted was directly in front of us and we could keep an eye on the approaching traffic by settling on the roof of the bait shop that was by Route 50.

With the sun sinking low, it was better to just settle in and wait. I took the first two hour shift, watching the forest become very dark, very quickly. The rest of the crew found their sleeping spots and Janna was allowed to have the "upstairs" bed to herself. She was still grieving the loss of her friend, so I was sure she appreciated the solitude.

I sat on the roof of the RV, keeping a low profile and just taking in the surrounding woods. Small rustlings could be heard from every angle and every so often, the water behind me would splash with the hunting jumps of the fish that lived there. There was s very slight breeze that stirred the cool night air, whispering through the new leaf growth. I appreciated the quiet, given the funhouse day I had and I let my mind wander back to my family, especially my son. I missed that little guy with all my heart and I promised myself I would never do something like this again. I couldn't stand the thought of him or Sarah coming to harm and once again, I prayed with all my might to whoever might be listening to keep my loved ones safe.

My musings were interrupted by the approach of the dead. Head-high glowing orbs worked their way through the trees, seeking prey and new hosts to infect. I counted fifteen zombies in the immediate vicinity and I could see more out near the road. The arrival of such a large vehicle was sure to cause some excitement in the local undead community.

I stayed put as the Z's shambled up to the RV. Hands reached out and tentatively touched the metal surface, soft to the point of being delicate. It was if they couldn't believe it was real. For myself, I stayed stock still, just watching the glowing eyes bounce among the brush. I was reminded of my conversation with Tommy, that these people might just be infected and not really dead like we had thought these last two years. Jury was out on that one, but my gut said there might be something to it.

The zombies moved around the RV, then past it, dismissing it as unimportant or scenery in their diseased minds. I watched them move, their heads turning and shifting in the wind, trying to catch a scent of prey. I had heard of them walking hundreds of miles to chase down a scent, but hadn't believed it until now.

After about an hour and a half into my shift, I began the long process of moving down the ladder. I had to move painfully slow, careful not to make a sound or any sudden movements. Zombies couldn't see too well in the dark, but their enhanced hearing allowed them to triangulate your position very quickly. And once they locked onto you, it was game on until one of you was dead for good.

Back inside, I awoke Nate and he opted to stay in front to watch the Z's. Couldn't say I blamed him. I stretched out on the kitchen bench and went to sleep.

In the morning, I awoke to breakfast on the table. Janna had arisen early and made a decent breakfast out of our stores. I gratefully accepted a cup of coffee and two granola bars. We were going to need to find some more food soon, but for now, this was nice.

After breakfast, I wanted to take a look down the road and see if there was a way to set up some kind of warning system. Duncan said he was going to try fishing and Tommy was going to clean guns. Nate was going to do maintenance on the RV, so I was on my own. It was only a few hundred feet, so how bad could it be? Besides, all the zombies seemed to have returned to their hidey-holes, as welcoming a thought as that was.

I stepped out and was surprised to see Janna come out with me. She gave me a lopsided grin and I shrugged. "Your choice. If we get into a situation, I'll back you, but don't back me because I won't know you and might kill you by mistake."

Janna's eyes got wide and I smiled. "Kidding. Come on, I want to look this bait shop over."

She smiled and stepped in beside me. I carried my AR again, as Tommy was cleaning my heavier rifle. Janna just had her little pack of scissors and a small 9mm in a holster situated in the small of her back. I wasn't surprised she knew how to shoot, since most people who survived the Upheaval had to learn or be killed. It was interesting that in the states that concealed carry was allowed, we ran into more survivors than the states that didn't. It made sense, in a way. People who were armed when the world fell apart tended to outlast those who weren't.

It was a couple of yards before Janna spoke. "I was talking to Duncan and I wanted to say I was sorry for lying to you," she said.

I shrugged. "I don't blame you. You were trying to save your friend and didn't have much choice. Although I will say had the fight gone the other way, you and your friend would not have been released."

Janna looked down and nodded. "You're probably right. But there wasn't much I could do."

"Don't think about it. You lost a friend, but we avenged her, so from here on out its pretty much a clean slate." I spoke casually, but we both knew that trust had to be earned.

"Thank you." Janna was quiet for a moment, then spoke up. "Duncan says you have a wife and son?"

I nodded as I scanned the trees ahead of us. "Sarah and Jake are back at Starved Rock, waiting for me. Jake is three and full of beans." I felt a pang as I missed my son for the millionth time.

"Duncan said this Major Thorton sent men to kill your family. Do you think they'll be okay?"

Janna was stepping into sensitive territory, but I didn't blame her. "Sarah is a very strong woman, a survivor. She's not alone, there's friends with her. There is Rebecca and Nicole, both capable and my brother Mike, Nicole's husband."

"Is Mike as good as you?" Janna asked.

I slowed to a stop and looked over the bait shop. It was about fifty feet away and looked quiet. "No, he's not," I said. "He's good enough, but not for ten men."

"Why aren't you rushing back to save your family?" Janna looked shocked that I would stay on the mission.

"Because there is someone there who is as good as I am, maybe even better. His name is Charlie James and when those men from Thorton run into him, they will wish they were anywhere but there. My family is safe." I had to believe that last statement.

Janna was about to respond when the bushes behind her burst upward as a zombie lunged out of the shrub. It had been lurking there, apparently watching us approach. It couldn't contain itself and stumbled out at us.

I couldn't get a shot with Janna in the way, so I started to move to the side. But I needn't have bothered, considering what happened next. Janna ducked down and rolled to the side, drawing a pair of her scissors in one smooth motion. The zombie followed her motion and got skewered under the chin for its trouble. Janna used her other hand to draw another pair and shifting her grip so quickly I missed the maneuver, plunged the long blades into the temple of the Z.

She withdrew both blades at the same time and wiped them off on a bit of the zombie's clothing. Sheathing them without even looking at her pouch, she glanced over at me and gave me a shrug. The attack took all of six seconds from start to finish and during the entire time, Janna kept a sober face, killing the zombie with as much emotion as taking out the trash.

"Nicely done," I said appreciatively and Janna preened a little at the praise. "There's a kerosene spray bottle on the back of the RV to clean your weapons with later."

"Thanks. Shall we look over the shop?"

"Certainly. Ladies first."

"Ah, chivalry. Sarah must love you for it."

"More like beats it into me."

"I see. I like her already."

We crossed the distance and looked over the bait shop. Things looked normal from the outside, so I carefully approached the front door. The building was built like an old southern sharecropper's house, with a sloping metal roof and wide porch. Big refrigerators occupied one half of the porch, advertising live bait in faded letters. I didn't feel the need to open any of them.

I looked into the window of the shop, but didn't see anything moving around. Taking that as a good sign, I opened the screen door and pushed the heavier door open with the barrel of my rifle.

As soon as the door opened a small shape flew out of the store and barreled into me, knocking my rifle out of my hands and driving me backwards. I fell off the porch and twisted, shoving my attacker away from me, trying to give me some room. Janna screamed from the porch, but I didn't have time to worry about her, as the thing that attacked me was getting up.

I jumped to my feet and reached for my SIG, only to find the holster empty. Cursing, I faced my enemy and got a shock when it spoke.

"God works in mysterious ways. We missed you at Harrisburg and we worried the whole way here how we was going to explain to Thorton how you got away. But here you is, all gift wrapped and ready." The speaker was a short man, maybe five feet five if he was lucky. But what he lacked in height he more than made up for in sheer muscle. The fabric of his uniform was stretched tight over large biceps and his legs filled his fatigue pants. I really could have used my SIG right now, since I figured this was probably going to hurt to do it the hard way.

He grinned an evil little grin at me and readied himself for a charge. "I'm gonna kill you with my bare hands and you know somethin'? I'm gonna enjoy it." He looked over at Janna who was being held hostage by another man who had her by the throat and was holding her gun to her head.

I placed a hand on my knife but pistol shot sent a bullet near my ear as Janna screamed again. I felt my rage rising and thought *The hard way it is. You're going to earn this.*

A glance down the road showed the truck we were seeking and it wasn't hard to figure out they had arrived early this morning. It was just our bad luck that we came tumbling into their sleeping place.

Kazinski, as his name patch said, spread his arms wide in a rush to try and take me down. I knew I couldn't let him get hold of me, because that would have been the end. I had to keep him out of reach and wear him down while I figured out how to beat him.

He barreled forward and at the last second, I pivoted left and planted a fist on the back of his neck, sending him crashing to the ground. In the second before he got up, I spared a glance at Janna, who surprised the hell out of me by smiling slightly and giving me a wink. The other man, a sergeant, glowered at me, as he obviously was hoping his friend would be beating my brains in by now.

The man jumped to his feet, surprisingly agile for his bulk and came at me again. This time he lunged to the right, expecting me to pivot like I had done earlier. But now I went down to one knee on the opposite side and struck out with my left foot, connecting with Kazinski's left knee and knocking him over again. I didn't wait for him to get up, I jumped over to where he was and slammed two punches into his kidneys. I hit him with nearly everything I had, making sure he felt it.

I didn't stick around for his response, I jumped off of him as quickly as I had gotten on. I backed up a few feet and couldn't resist taunting him. "Crude and slow. Your attack was no better than a clumsy zombie."

Kazinksi snarled as he got to his feet and a hand reached to his injured back. His little piggy eyes measured me, as my punches probably had a lot more power than he expected. Twice his rushes had failed and I figured him to try something different.

He moved in close, weaving from side to side and bringing his big hands up to try and grab. I waited for an opening and punched hard and fast through his hands, mashing his lip and popping his head back. If I had expected that to take him down, I was seriously mistaken. He recovered and punched hard twice, the second blow getting past my arm and striking me in the head. He followed up with a hard left to the ribs and managed to back me up a few paces.

I stepped back with him following, tough blows raining on my shoulders and arms. I was deflecting his worst efforts, keeping him from striking a serious punch, but I was getting annoyed with the way things were going. I let a jab slip past my head and I struck from underneath, popping him hard on the chin. When his head came back, I slammed my fist forward, planting the edge of my hand right between his eyes. The punch knocked him far enough off balance that I struck out with my left hand into his solar plexus, toppling him over into the grass. The soldier clambered to his feet, shaking the fog out his eyes and glaring bloody murder at me.

Kazinski, trying for a killing blow, pulled his right hand back for a roundhouse that would have leveled me if I had stood still for it. But I took the opening and jabbed him in the face, causing his nose to bleed profusely. I followed it with a second jab to his eye, cutting him and causing blood to flow into his vision.

The pretend soldier stumbled back, trying to wipe the blood out of his eyes. I pressed my advantage, knowing I would not get another chance. I pounded his head and gut, punching with everything I had. The blows rocked him back and forth, with blood flying from his wounded face.

Suddenly rushing like a wounded bear, the soldier spread his arms wide to wrap me up to take me down for the final time. I timed the punch that came from my knees and you could hear the crack echo through the trees as my fist broke his jaw and flipped him onto his back. The battle lust was on me at that point and I grabbed him by his greasy hair. Holding his head I snapped short punches to his face, pulping his lips and swelling his eyes.

When at last his big arms slumped down and my opponent was unconscious, I dropped his head on the ground like a busted pumpkin. My hands were swollen and bruised and my head felt like a river with the rushing in my ears. My arms stung and my wounded side was numb. But I stood over my defeated enemy, wanting him to get up, wishing he would so I could continue to smash and destroy.

When he didn't I whirled around to see what I could do about his buddy, although I fully expected to be shot for winning the fight. I was not prepared for what I saw on the porch.

Sergeant Milovich was on his knees, with his hands over his head. Janna was standing behind him with her gun to the back of his head. He looked like he was covered in blood and when I looked closer, I saw the handles of a pair of Janna's scissors sticking out from his shoulder. Apparently, our little orphan was quite capable of taking care of herself.

Janna grinned at me and I tried to smile back, but it actually hurt to do so. I didn't want to know what my face was going to look like in the morning.

Janna's face got serious quickly and I heard the rushing of feet behind me. In a flash, I drew my knife and struck blindly behind me.

Luck guided my blade, as it pierced Kazinski's left eye and buried itself to the hilt in his face. Four inches of steel sheathed themselves in his brain and killed him instantly. His body crumpled to the grass, his face wearing a shocked expression into the afterlife.

Janna's pistol barked once and I turned to see the sarge fall on his back, a smoking hole in his forehead. In his left hand he held the scissors Janna had stabbed him with. I guess he had pulled them out and tried to gain the upper hand. One more point for her.

As I dragged the bodies out of the way, Janna went into the bait shop. After a few minutes, she re-emerged with a few bottles of water and soda, as well as some packaged crackers. The soda and crackers had expired, but recently, so I gratefully accepted them. Sitting on the porch, I gingerly explored my bruised hands, testing to see if any bones had been broken. That little shit could take a punch.

"It's not as bad as you think," Janna offered, trying to be kind.

"Any fight I walk away from is a good one," I said.

"You do pretty well. That piece of shit is like a lot of guys I've known in my life. All muscle and no regard."

"Well, he's got one last job for us, then he can rest in piece."

"What's that?" Janna asked, curious.

"He and his friend are going to deliver a message to Thorton."

"Nice."

I rummaged around the bait shop until I found what I was looking for. Fortunately, the shop had some marine supplies for boaters and it wasn't long before I had a good length of nylon rope. As I was dragging the bodies to the main road, Janna was guarding the rear, having picked up my rifle. After the way she handled herself today, I had no trouble with her backing me up. She even found my SIG, which had landed only a few feet from my fight with Kazinski. That would have helped.

I dragged the bodies to the main road and situating myself under a street lamp, tossed the rope over. Tying the bodies up was quick and in short order I had them trussed and hanging like deer in the garage.

Admiring my handiwork, I started walking back to the RV. Janna fell in beside me and asked, "What do you think Thorton will do when he sees those bodies?"

I thought a minute. "A sane man would cut his losses and head home. But I don't think Thorton's ego will let that happen."

"So what next?" Janna wondered.

"We do what we've set out to do. The road we wanted is here and DC is just a state or two away."

"What about me?" Janna seemed concerned.

"After the way you handled yourself today, you're free to do what you want. If you want to go, I won't stop you. If you want to come along and be part of the crew and help us save our country, I'd say you earned your place today." I wasn't just blowing smoke. Janna had done well, stayed cool and got the job done. Couldn't ask for a better partner.

We walked in silence to the RV and I watched with amusement as Tommy and Duncan covered us with rifles. They must have heard the shots and wondered what had gone on. I'd tell them in a while, but they'd see the message to Thorton soon enough. I hoped he understood it as thoroughly as I meant it.

We were playing for keeps.

THE END

Coming Soon

WHITE FLAG OF THE DEAD BOOK 4

UNITED STATES OF THE DEAD

Check out www.severedpress.com for more zombie mayhem.

THE LIVING END
James Robert Smith

**One Hundred and
Fifty Million Zombies.**

Sixty Million Dogs.

**All of them hungry for
warm human flesh.**

**The dead have risen, killing
anyone they find. The living
know what's caused it-a
vicious contagion. But too
late to stop it. For now, what
remains of society are busy
shutting down nuclear
reactors and securing chemical plants to prevent runaway
reactions in both. There's little time for anything else.**

**Failed comic book artist Rick Nuttman and his family have
joined thousands of other desperate people in trying to find a
haven from the madness.**

**Perhaps refuge can be found in the village of Sparta or maybe
there is salvation in The City of Ruth, a community raised from
the ashes of Carolina.**

**In the low country below the hills, a monster named Danger
Man changes everything.**

**While watching over it all, the mysterious figure of BC, moving
his gigantic canine pack westward, into lands where survivors
think they are safe**

**And always, the mindless hordes neither living nor dead,
waiting only to destroy.**

There will be a reckoning.

Available at www.severedpress.com, Amazon and most online bookstores

ZOMBIE PULP

Tim Curran
Dead men tell tales.
From the corpse factories
of World War I
where graveyard rats
sharpen their teeth on
human bones to the wind-
blown cemeteries of the
prairie where resurrection
comes at an unspeakable
price...from the compound
of a twisted messianic cult
leader and his army of
zombies to a post-
apocalyptic wasteland
where all that stands
between the living and the
evil dead is sacrifice in the
form of a lottery.

Dead men do tell tales. And these are their stories.
Zombie Pulp is a collection of 9 short stories and 2 never before
published novellas from the twisted undead mind of
Tim Curran..

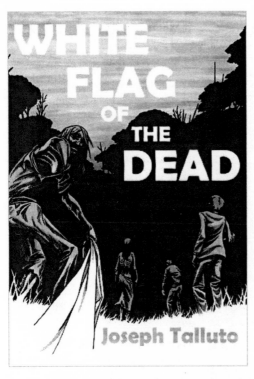

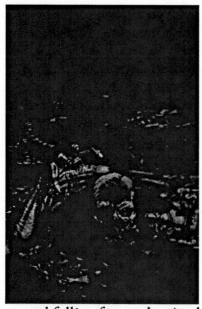

ZOMBIE ZOOLOGY
Unnatural History:

Severed Press has assembled a truly original anthology of never before published stories of living dead beasts. Inside you will find tales of prehistoric creatures rising from the Bog, a survivalist taking on a troop of rotting baboons, a NASA experiment going Ape, A hunter going a Moose too far and many more undead creatures from Hell. The crawling, buzzing, flying abominations of mother nature have risen and they are hungry.

"Clever and engaging a reanimated rarity"
FANGORIA

"I loved this very unique anthology and highly recommend it"
Monster Librarian

Available at www.severedpress.com, Amazon and most online bookstores

The Official Zombie Handbook: Sean T Page

Since pre-history, the living dead have been among us, with documented outbreaks from ancient Babylon and Rome right up to the present day. But what if we were to suffer a zombie apocalypse in the UK today? Through meticulous research and field work, The Official Zombie Handbook (UK) is the only guide you need to make it through a major zombie outbreak in the UK, including: -Full analysis of the latest scientific information available on the zombie virus, the living dead creatures it creates and most importantly, how to take them down - UK style. Everything you need to implement a complete 90 Day Zombie Survival Plan for you and your family including home fortification, foraging for supplies and even surviving a ghoul siege. Detailed case studies and guidelines on how to battle the living dead, which weapons to use, where to hide out and how to survive in a country dominated by millions of bloodthirsty zombies. Packed with invaluable information, the genesis of this handbook was the realisation that our country is sleep walking towards a catastrophe - that is the day when an outbreak of zombies will reach critical mass and turn our green and pleasant land into a grey and shambling wasteland. Remember, don't become a cheap meat snack for the zombies!

Available at www.severedpress.com, Amazon and most online bookstores

BIOHAZARD

Tim Curran

The day after tomorrow: Nuclear fallout. Mutations. Deadly pandemics. Corpse wagons. Body pits. Empty cities. The human race trembling on the edge of extinction. Only the desperate survive. One of them is Rick Nash. But there is a price for survival: communion with a ravenous evil born from the furnace of radioactive waste. It demands sacrifice. Only it can keep Nash one step ahead of the nightmare that stalks him-a sentient, seething plague-entity that stalks its chosen prey: the last of the human race. To accept it is a living death. To defy it, a hell beyond imagining

"kick back and enjoy some the most violent and genuinely scary apocalyptic horror written by one of the finest dark fiction authors plying his trade today" HORRORWORLD

Available at www.severedpress.com, Amazon and most online bookstores

CPSIA information can be obtained at www.ICGtesting.com
Printed in the USA
242427LV00004B/9/P